Lock Down Publications and Ca$h
Presents

PRODUCTS OF THE STREETS 3

Treasures of War

Written By
Demonde "Money" Anderson

First Edition 2025

Printed in the United States of America

Lock Down Publications
P.O. Box 944
Stockbridge, GA 30281
www.lockdownpublications.com

Like our page on Facebook: Lock Down Publications
www.facebook.com/lockdownpublications.ldp

Stay Connected with Us!

Text **LOCKDOWN** to 22828 to stay up-to-date with new releases, sneak peaks, contests and more…

Like our page on Facebook:
Lock Down Publications

Join Lock Down Publications/The New Era Reading Group

Visit our website:
www.lockdownpublications.com

Follow us on Instagram:
Lock Down Publications

Email Us: We want to hear from you!

Chapter 1

News vans and camera crews lined the sides of San Jancinto street in downtown Houston, Texas, while news reporters chatted boisterously over one another to report the news from today's live events and the extreme, yet unfortunate, events that led up to the most streamed, watched and televised re-trial criminal court cases the State of Texas has ever seen.

Leaders of activist groups crowded the streets with throngs of their loyalists and supporters in their journeying fight for 'Equality' in what they consider a 'White America'. Due to their outstanding connections and lengthy reach, they were able to win over the leading Judge's sympathy in all who then agreed to a fully televised, no-holds-barred battle against the Federal Bureau of Investigations versus Mackentosh Miller Sr.

Despite the adamant cries and desperate pleas from the higher ups, the decision was made to allow a full viewing of the high-profile case. After weeks of back and forth between the prosecutors and defense attorneys, accusations and exposures to the exploitation used by the Bureau, the sudden deaths of key witnesses, and the sudden reluctance of anonymous witnesses to testify, the case was a fiasco and a media circus for all to see. The Federal Bureau had never looked so bad in the eyes of the public with the verdict landing only days after the final deliberations. The jury had found the defendant, Mackentosh Miller Sr., not guilty of all charges passed against him except for one: federal tax evasion related to a natural resource investment he made through a wealthy oil tycoon he'd met through mutual friends.

Mr. Mackmillions pleaded guilty to the infraction and was charged a huge fine by the Internal Revenue Service. The fine covered all profits from the investment dating back to the date it was filed. Mr. Mackmillions happily paid off those fines and, with the help of some paperwork, his finances were cleared and the transaction was concluded. Mackentosh Miller Sr. was now a free man. However, he was issued a stern warning from federal authorities to tread carefully, as he would be under careful watch from various government agencies.

***

"Let's get one thing straight before we move any further, Young Mack, I don't trust you!" Rob stated while grinding his teeth together in anger.

"That's good because I don't trust yo' ass either. In fact, nigga, fuck you and fuck yo' feelings!" Young Mack turned around in the passenger seat of the stolen Nissan Pathfinder to look Rob in the eyes and let him know it was real.

Both men made it perfectly clear that neither fucked with the other not by a long shot. Young Mack was still unaware of why Rob held ill feelings towards him, but he was done handling him with care. If he wanted to be mad, fuck 'em is what Young Mack thought. Once upon a time, they ran in a tight three-man circle, pulling capers orchestrated by Young Mack's pop from the inside of a federal maximum security prison. Eating from the same plate back then, Rob had sworn to Young Mack to put loyalty before everything, but clearly Rob went about by a different set of rules.

"So if we don't trust each other, what the fuck are we sitting out here together for?" Rob yelled, clearly annoyed by their situation.

Young Mack laughed while doing his best to keep his anger in check. "To be honest, you're here because the only other option would've been to knock yo' cup over, but being that you once had my loyalty, I feel I owe you a chance to get outta yo' weak ass feelings and handle shit like a grown ass man should. With that being said, just know that you, yo' bitch and them two logs are being heavily watched and if my men so much as think you or anyone of them are outta pocket, yo' clock stops fuck, bitch."

Rob was furious. Murderous thoughts of smoking Young Mack dominated his mental, but he wasn't a fool to try anything. Nawl. That would be too transparent. Plus, Young Mack rolled heavy with hittas from their streets that held murderous reps, and the new Mexican cats looked like they killed shit just to pass time. His thoughts were indeed murderous, but not suicidal.

"K-Dawg, you and Ash will come in from the back while me, Hogg and dumbass here approach from the front, understood?" K-Dawg was busy watching Rob through the rear view mirror, but nodded to let Young Mack know that he'd heard his order. Ash cocked his M-90, then strapped his vest into place, ready for the take.

"Gianna I know shit might sound weird right now because it does to me too, but you gotta trust that no harm shall come to you unless you warrant it." Young Mack watched her dark eyes as he spoke. "For this operation to go as planned we're gonna need you to get to that front door and admit their signature knock. Hell . . . they want you just as bad as they want me but I'll be there to protect you every step of the way." Young Mack knew that his words would affect Rob and knock him off point, but he didn't answer to him, and said what he said how he saw fit.

"Okay, I'm game." Gianna agreed.

"What da fuck is you doing! My bitch ain't 'bout to play bait in this shit, nigga, is you crazy?" Rob jumped in.

"Okay, Billy badass, how about you go over there and knock while we watch 'em blow yo' shit loose," K-Dawg spoke up. He was tired of hearing Rob's mouth.

"Do I look like Willie foo-foo to you, nigga?" Rob ice-grilled K-Dawg from the back seat.

"Damn, straight, now what's next?" K-Dawg challenged.

"Fuck that. Y'all kill that noise and let's get in here and take everything these niggas got. Y'all know it's a drought out here." Young Mack cut into their power struggle.

"Yo, if something happens to mine, nigga, I'm killing the fuck out on everything!" Rob submitted, then grabbed his heat from Gianna.

"Sprung ass nigga 'bout to make my stomach flip," K-Dawg said before checking his weapon.

"Yeah, thanks for the tip," Hogg spoke from behind Rob in the third row seat.

"A'ight, let's get to it," Young Mack said before sliding the Jason mask over his face, followed by the other men. Gianna was the only one without one.

Young Mack was the first to reach the stash house owned by Gurdo. He took up one side of the front door while Rob took up the other with Hogg on his heels. He waited a full minute to be sure that K-Dawg and Ash were securely in position before waving Gianna over from the corner.

Gianna approached the front door, wearing a cut off t-shirt that showcased the pink diamond piercing in her belly button and a pair of mean boy shorts that left little to the imagination. Her sex appeal was outta this world. She smiled at the fellas before rapping on the door.

"Yo, who the fuck is that!" one of Gurdo's men asked as he listened to their signature knock resonating at the front door.

"Julio, check the door!" the same guy yelled out from the kitchen where he was keeping a watchful eye on the naked women preparing their packages for Gurdo's deliveries.

"Fuck, man. I'm getting my shit licked. Why can't you get it!"

"Because it's right there next to you, dumbass! Plus, I'm watching these bitches with our shit!"

"Ahhh, fuck, ma, watch out," Julio nudged the Latina dick-sucking bitch away from him while standing and putting his dick back into his pants. He grabbed his favorite .45 S & W, and made sure it was ready to pop off if the time presented itself. Looking through the peep hole, he couldn't believe his eyes.

"Damn, who the fuck are you?" he asked once he swung the door opened, amazed by the sight of the cutie standing on their door steps with all the sexy ass tattoos.

Young Mack didn't hesitate before he slammed the butt of his AR-15 in the obviously stunned youngster's face, knocking him out cold. He then set his sights on the guy standing in the kitchen before sending three rapid shots that took him down before he could even raise his weapon.

The sound of the shots ringing out brought some more of Gurdo's men rushing towards the action as doors opened with fire being sent in their direction. Young Mack lounged behind a couch while the women screamed and scrambled for cover. Young Mack flinched and put a few rounds into the dead body of one of the naked women, who was blown behind the couch with half of her face missing.

Rob barged in through the front door, raining fire to cover Young Mack. Hogg delivered death shots to two men once they set their sights on Rob. Gunfire erupted at the back of the house as Rob and Young Mack struggled to their feet.

Young Mack, Rob and Hogg made their way up the stairs and stopped suddenly before shots exploded into the wall, barely missing them as they approached the second floor.

Rob quickly took the female shooter out behind them as Young Mack and Hogg continued further up the stairs.

Young Mack surveyed the second floor hallway as they made it up the last steps. Nothing seemed outta place or alarming. So, they stayed the course.

None of the upstairs rooms had doors on them and they carefully split the hallway with their backs to each other.

"Seems clear up here," Hogg stated as he eyed the empty rooms.

"Yeah, but stay on point just in case we missed someone and let's search this bitch from top to bottom," Young Mack replied.

Ash and K-Dawg made their way from the back of the house and into the kitchen with their minds on murdering anything still moving that wasn't one of them. The sight of all the coke and one dead gunman excited K-Dawg. Ash felt a bit sick from the sight of the dead women, but he swallowed the spicy acidic fluid back down his throat as he moved ahead of K-Dawg.

"Whoa!" Rob shouted as Ash gripped his trigger, ready to exterminate his ass.

"Damn, boy, you damn near made me knock yo' shit," Ash lowered his weapon, but K-Dawg kept Rob in his crosshairs.

"Where is Young?" K-Dawg growled, not trusting Rob one bit. "Upstairs," Rob replied through clenched teeth.

"Well, let's get to it then."

"You first," Rob snickered.

K-Dawg lowered his AR-15 and quickly drew a .9mm with a long clip and shot Rob point-blank in the vest. Rob dropped his heat and rolled on the ground in agony. K-Dawg picked up his weapon and strapped it around his shoulder while staring at Rob with hatred.

"I don't know why Young feels he owes yo' punk ass shit, but you just lost all chances with me. Buck me again and I'ma send you to my father in hell, bitch ass nigga. "K-Dawg kicked Rob in the chest where he'd shot him before stepping over him.

"We all good up here," Young Mack smiled as K-Dawg stepped into the room and saw all the stacks of bills from different denominations spread across the bed.

"I see," K-Dawg smiled at their success but it was short-lived once Ash and Rob made their way inside with Rob holding Ash's shoulder.

"Fuck happened to you?" Hogg asked almost in laughter now that he noticed Rob's weapon flung over K-Dawg's shoulder.

"We need to get the fuck away from here. That was a lot of shots and I'm sure twelve is on the way," Rob said before turning on his heels, leaving the others to do the packing.

Chapter 2

Daniel couldn't believe their bad luck as he thought back on what the accountant reported to him about a certain account. Two weeks had passed since he dropped the package off to some of their young wolves and yet none of the other traps had received their share of it. On top of that, they hadn't paid their end of the package. Nothing pissed him off more than late money other than no money at all. Late money usually meant shorter packages with taller price tags, while no money usually meant broken bones and possible toe tags. Daniel was beyond furious.

He'd made attempt after attempt to call all of their phones and even went as far as checking their social media pages which brought about the gut feeling that something bigger was at play and it was far much greater than mu'fuckas skipping out on them. It just wasn't like his people to go without answering his direct calls, even though they never did like he told them and fell back with all the social media capping. With everything the way it was, he knew he had to make the call he was dreading to make.

"'Sup, Mexican?" He heard Gurdo's cheerful voice come through after the second ring.

"Problem in the slums," Daniel exhaled, blowing out his frustrations.

"Speak on it."

"Remember the spot I convinced you to invest in?"

"Uh-huh'," Gurdo mumbled, tryna keep his attention on what Daniel was saying which was hard as hell because his wife was running circles around him in the sandy beach of their New Seabury, Massachusetts mansion in a skimpy Gucci bikini.

"Well, that account hasn't opened and neither have any of the others from last round. Plus, I'm not getting answers from them," Daniel explained as he and two of his security men loaded up into his armored Benz wagon.

"Wait . . . do you think it's . . . "

"I hope not because that would certainly mean we're back at war," Daniel cut Gurdo short because he'd done his best to make sure that their operations were low-key and off the grid from their enemies.

"Check it out and get back with me before you green-light anything," Gurdo ordered.

"Yeah-yeah, most definitely," Daniel replied before their call ended.

Thirty minutes later, Daniel and his men were pulling up outside of the house they'd visited only two weeks prior, and now everything seemed different. No one was hanging around outside on the front porch and all the windows were boarded. His mind ran rapid with possibilities as he climbed the steps to get to the front door where he then noticed a white paper posted on the door from the owner; it was a number, and Daniel decided to give him a call as he made it back inside of his vehicle.

"Yes, hello!" A strong Arabian accent resonated through his phone.

"Ye-yeah, hello," Daniel stammered from the high pitch in the man's voice.

"Who dis?"

"Umm-you don't know me but I'm calling about one of your properties over on Tangiers Road, the one with the boarded window."

"Awww-yes, nothing going on with that one, police investigate that one . . ."

"Wait . . . police investigation?" Daniel knew something was off but not once did he think of the police kicking the door in.

"Murder of young men and women with lots of weapons found . . ." Daniel needed to hear nothing more from the man. He ended their call immediately.

"So you know how to do your homework even better than I gave you credit for, huh?" Daniel said to himself before ordering his driver to take him home while thinking of a celebration he could not wait to attend.

***

"What's the point of hitting all their places and killing low-level workers?" Stephanie Valdez asked as she handed Young Mack a glass of straight vodka. She was dressed in a white and gold Versace bikini with the matching silk robe that she dared not tie up. Stephanie was a stunning woman and Young Mack always enjoyed her company. To him there was nothing like being in the presence of a sexy older woman, especially one as complete as Stephanie. She was wise beyond the street life. She was definitely easy to talk to, and she and her brothers were his connection to the best coke Mexico had to offer. He and his crew had never touched anything as close to what the Colombians put out as what they got from the Valdez family.

They also shared a common enemy. An enemy that used to be Young Mack's connect, a connect whose fiancé (now wife) Young Mack had been sleeping with way before and after his time with her. Gurdo's attempt on Young Mack and his family's lives set the tone, and he was prepared to stop at nothing to quench his thirst for Gurdo's life and the life of his right-hand man.

"The point is that nothing is off limits after what he tried to do to me and mine and until we actually find out where they're hiding, everything in connection with them must cease to exist." Young Mack's reply wasn't what she was looking to hear, but she thought better than to call him out on his way of thinking. It could bruise his ego, and that was something that she wasn't willing to chance especially while enjoying his presence alone with her.

"Your hands are so dirty," she stated while taking his right hand in hers. "So much blood cover these palms now."

Young Mack wasn't a virgin to her touches, and her flirting was a norm, but he'd never allowed for things to go past that. His relationship with Aeriella was blossoming and turning out to be everything that he wished it to be. Nevertheless, he couldn't help that he was attracted to Stephanie in ways that he shouldn't be. The sexy vixen hunted him every time they were around each other. She was indeed beautiful and had a body that most chicks, both young and older, envied.

Stephanie looked him in his eyes as she moved his opened palm to her lips, then kissed the center of his hand. She smiled when she felt no resistance from him, then licked her wet tongue from his palm to his index finger before taking it in her mouth and sucking it down past the knuckle. His dick jumped inside of his Dior shorts and he had visions of her sucking his dick off just as she was sucking his finger. He wasn't sure if it was the vodka or her finally being able to break his resistance, but her persistence definitely turned him on. "Let me *wash* your hands for you, papi." Stephanie moaned as she pushed his hand down her bikini bottom and felt his fingers touching her wet lips. He spread her lips with two fingers and felt her river flowing excessively.

"Damn, you're soaking wet," Young Mack said as he moved two fingers into her velvety tunnel.

"This is what you do to me even when you're not around. Please take me the way I always dream you will. I-ahhh-I

14

need you so baaaadd," she moaned louder as his ministration increased speed. She opened her legs wider to give him better access to her center.

"You're making it harder for me to resist this pussy, Steph, you're making it so hard," Young Mack admitted as he expertly manipulated her clit with his thumb.

"Yes-you should st-stop holding back! Ahhh-shiiiit-I'm coming!"

"That's it, ma, let it all out," Young Mack aroused her to an earth-shattering climax and she drenched his hand and her thighs.

"That was the fastest I've ever came in my life," Stephanie giggled before tasting herself on his fingers.

"That's cool, but next time I'm charging you." Young Mack smiled.

"Don't threaten me with a good time, papi. Money is never a problem." He laughed at the seriousness in her voice. It was the first time he'd allowed himself to touch her in this capacity. He knew he would have to watch himself because he was certainly slipping and was sure she would be right there to catch him with opened legs.

"Go clean yourself, ma, we need to talk because I see that you don't approve of the way I'm handling things and I need to pick that clever brain of yours." He spoke as he stood at the kitchen sink, washing his hands.

"Yes, papi." She blew him a kiss before removing every article of 'barely there' clothing and sashaying her way outside to the crystal clear-blue water of her meter pool, then jumped in.

"Come on in so we can, you know, talk!" Stephanie smiled seductively as she watched him thinking about whether to join her or not.

Fuck it, he thought, then got down to his Dior briefs before hopping into the pool, splashing her in the process.

Their play fighting and splashing around turned into a heated scene once he allowed her to wrap her legs around his waist. She wasted no time tasting his lips and sucking on his tongue. He even kissed her back for a moment until his phone broke his trance.

It chimed over and over while pulling him away from the seasoned seductress. His mind was so caught up on going after his enemies and Stephanie expertly seducing him, he nearly forgot he had to be in a certain place at a certain time and Aeriella's messages kicked him in his ass and got him moving, guilt-stricken and all.

Chapter 3

Mr. Mackmillions looked up to the sky and said a silent prayer, thankful for his new-found freedom. He had weathered the heaviest of storms in his tempestuous life as the king of Houston's underworld and even as an inmate in the federal max prisons he'd been assigned to for fifteen years. Now he sat triumphantly and eager to gain back the life and status that had been maliciously snatched away from him.

He looked over to his right and smiled at his sleeping queen and how peaceful she seemed. Staring at her as she slept caused him to imagine the years of pain and downpour brought upon her life because of his downfall. Anger pierced his calm heart like an arrow shot from a hunter's bow, and as sure as he was that his face betrayed his heart, he was even more sure that the yellowish-red eyes that stared at him through the rear view mirror of his polished Rolls Royce truck saw it and felt it too. Max, a goon of all goons, stared intensively at his boss, his best and only friend, gauging his rage and emotions and with a simple nod. Mackmillions let him know that hell hath no fury for the back stabbers that allowed for his demise and done nothing. To him they were just as guilty as the ones who transgressed against him and were now six feet deep under the earth.

Twenty minutes passed after dropping his wife, Sylvia, off at their presidential suite at The Post Oak Hotel in uptown Houston, and now he and Max were parked in the back of a secluded old meat packaging warehouse. Being there now brought back so many old memories that a slight chuckle left his throat. Looking up into the rear view mirror, Max's eyes were still trained on him.

"Remember when we first visited this place, Max?"

"Could neva fo'get," Max replied with a devilish grin. Mackmillions thought back on a time some twenty years ago.

It was deathly dark outside on a cold winter night and Mackmillions was doing his best to keep his hands warm as he and his most trusted killer, Max, stalked the activities going on yards to the north of them. The warehouse was brightly lit, and men worked diligently to complete the tasks that were handed down through their bosses.

The McAllen brothers were a force to be reckoned with in those days. With endless amounts of cocaine and heroin and some of the city's top politicians in their pockets, nothing could penetrate their iron-clad operations. The brothers triumphantly big-chested their way through Houston's underworld effortlessly. That was until they pissed the wrong man's grass and he sought after their heads to be mounted on his private mantle.

Not sooner than the money could hit Mackmillions' untraceable overseas account, he and Max meticulously found ways to exterminate the two brothers and take down their entire operation. Days turned to weeks and weeks turned to months before Mackmillions felt it was time to execute.

"Max, gun!" Mackmillions whispered through the frostbite of the record low temperature.

Doing as he was told, Max skillfully assembled the modified Israeli 5.56mm. The suppressor, shell catcher and explosive tracer rounds made the semi-automatic sniper rifle the perfect dealer of death, and Mackmillions loved his gun.

"Once I knock these two off their pedestal, Max, I want you to go ahead and release the gas, got it?" Mackmillions stated as he found his spot lying in the grass behind the scope of his Israeli power rifle.

"Got it," Max responded while removing the trigger mechanism from his beaver fur coat pocket.

THEW! THEW! THEW! THEW!

Max smiled as he watched through field binoculars as both men's heads exploded from the silent whispers of Mackmillions' pin-point accuracy. He then quickly released the toxic gas that was infused with hazardous bio-chemicals that, once inhaled, would swiftly deteriorate the lungs, cutting off all oxygen to the brain and killing the targets within seconds.

"Deadly night," Mackmillions stated after snapping back from his reverie.

"Worse fa da clean up."

"It's what we get paid to do, Max." Mackmillions smiled. Looking out the window, he silently observed all the vehicles in attendance for the very important, yet super exclusive, meeting that was set and arranged by none other than himself. After being able to put his case behind him, he thought it be best to make his first move his best move, and what would be a better move than to meet with the Realm, or so to speak.

"Seems like the stage is all set," Mackmillions stated after a short silence. Max just nodded.

"I think it's about time we assembled a small crew of workers that could, you know, work so we could just kick back and enjoy some of life without all the worries of what tomorrow may bring." Again, Max nodded.

Mackmillions picked up his cellphone and dialed a number he remembered for over fifteen years and got an answer on the second ring.

"Speak on it, Mack," the voice answered.

"Good evening, Governor, is everyone in place and on time as scheduled?" Mackmillions already knew the answer to that question but wanted to be an asshole about it.

"Of course we are, everyone's here. Wait! What th—" Panicked coughing and extreme pandemonium broke out in the background and could be heard through the vehicle's sound system moments before there was absolute quietness. After two full minutes, Mackmillions pressed the button for the warehouse's exhausts to come to life to clear the facility of any remaining gas. Max had already taken the liberty to kill all of the drivers and leftover guards outside of the warehouse once they arrived, so there was no problem as they calmly pulled away from the scene.

"Nice meeting!" Mackmillions laughed once Max hit the highway, leaving behind what was sure to darken the days for Houston's political world for a long time. Nothing, absolutely nothing, would give him a sense of security and humbleness on a level so many bosses and made men sought after, besides extracting his revenge on the ones who betrayed him and deemed themselves disloyal.

Death to the new realm and bright new beginnings to a new old realm, Mackmillions thought to himself as he watched the world move outside the back passenger window.

"What's the plan?" Max asked soberly after long minutes in complete silence.

"To disable the machinery of greed and connect back to the origin."

"Possible war." Max thought carefully about how to choose his next words when speaking to his longtime friend and mentor. "We lack manpower."

"Do you see how everyone of those suckers have lasted so long in a game that's known to wipe people like us out? It's because I gave them the blueprint and because of that alone we have the strength of a thousand men. I taught them how to be who they are and no one can fight what they can't see, but I see them, Max, I know them all. They can't hide from me." Max knew that he was right and realized that no one spoke wisdom as well as Mack. The fact that he understood how to utilize the wisdom that he had proved to

Max that there was no one more deadlier than his longtime friend. The thought alone brought a smile outta him.

"After the wedding I think it's time for a long vacation, what do you say?" Mackmillions knew that Max now understood their advantages in the so-called possible war.

"Islands are beautiful, almost as beautiful as death."

"Surely you share my same heart," Mackmillions laughed as he thought of all the deadly plans for the remaining members of old, in different parts of the world.

***

"Has he called yet?" Sylvia asked her daughter-in-law as she was being fitted into her pearl and diamond combination necklace designed by Cartier. The necklace in itself was worth more than a quarter million dollars and had her feeling like a true queen again. As a young scarlet, being married to a street legend and city icon for so many years set her above the rest. Together, she and Mackentosh "Mr. Mackmillions" Miller enjoyed the stronghold he had on the game. Operations ranging from human trafficking to prostitution, drugs and firearms, even extortion and racketeering, and of course if you were paying the big dollar signs, murder for hire, even fit the bill. He'd gotten away with it all; that was until someone dropped the dime on him and sent everything down the drain, including his precious Sylvia.

Sylvia fell into a deep state of mental depression and anxiety after losing her husband to the system. For years her symptoms progressed until it drove her to over-the-counter drugs to prescription meds, to hard drugs like PCP, crack cocaine, and she even experimented with heroin. While Mackmillions rotted in prison, Sylvia rotted away in the streets. There was only one true blessing in their lives, and that was the genetic makeup in their son's DNA. Mackentosh "Young Mack" Miller II.

Just thinking about the dreaded past after so much of a good life was enough to make her wanna ball up into a corner and cry her eyes out. But, that was the drug-addicted weaker version of herself, and she was now stronger than she'd ever been in her entire life. The things she went through while at her lowest are the exact things that make her a stronger person. That and her knights in shining armor . . . and she was indeed grateful for them and their unconditional love.

"No, he hasn't, not even a text yet," Aeriella said as she looked from her vanity mirror to her iPhone. "Something is not right about this."

"Don't even allow your mind to go there, chile. He'll be here, you better believe that much for sure." Sylvia assured her as she checked herself over in the floor-to-ceiling mirror just as music began to play.

"Well, that's our cue!" Sylvia said as her face lit up with joyful pride being in this moment.

"I guess it is, so how do I look?" Aeriella stood next to her mother-in-law, checking herself out in the mirror.

"Lovely as always." Sylvia smiled at her through the mirror.

"I can't believe he's gonna be late for the wedding." Aeriella' s mood was crushed and it showed in her posture with her drooped shoulders and pouty face.

"Chile, it's not like it's y'all's wedding, so stop all the worrying and pick this tail up so I can go marry my husband again." Sylvia smiled joyously as she tapped Aeriella on her backside, then moved towards the door.

"Okay then, let's get you going," Aeriella stated with a start as her mood lightened up a bit due to Sylvia's joyful radiance.

Sylvia led the way through the double doors, pacing herself, with the fine music announcing her approach. "Huh," she flinched, caught off guard by the hand that took her arm.

"Didn't think I would miss this, did you?" Sylvia just smiled and stared up at her handsome son before rising to her tip toes and kissing him on his cheek. She couldn't catch the water that escaped her eyes but Young Mack was smooth with his Armani silk handkerchief and did the honors.

"I love you," she mouthed the words as they skillfully moved forward towards the altar.

"Love you too," he returned the gesture before looking up ahead at the strapping older version of himself.

Mackmillions was dapper in his silk white three-piece Armani tuxedo and platinum iced-out jewelry. He also sported a red silk handkerchief folded and tucked inside of his breast pocket. His mind ran rapidly through the lustrous years of riches and fame they shared as king and queen of Houston's underworld. He also thought about the many restless nights and years he spent worried sick about her while living in federal max. This moment in time could not be defined in words as he gracefully watched the love of his life being escorted down the aisle by the soul of their essences.

"I believe this belongs to you," Young Mack smiled and shook hands with his father before they shared a tight hug, once they reached the altar. "And this belongs to you," he kissed his mother on both cheeks before connecting his parents' hands.

Sylvia swallowed her emotions as best as she could once she stood face to face with her true king. There was nothing stronger in her world than his presence and his love; the effect it had on her womanly nature was mind-blowing.

"You look lovely, baby," Mr. Mackmillions whispered in her ear, causing her panties to dampen.

"Mmmm, so do you." She sheepishly smiled, feeling the moisture threaten to cascade down her thighs.

The church of at least two hundred people quieted as the Justice of Peace recited verses from the Gospel about husbands honoring their wives and wives honoring their husbands. Young Mack sat lost in his own world imagining the things he wanted to do to Aeriella as he rubbed his hand inside of her thighs through her dress. Shocked by his hands touching her there and remembering that she was still mad at him for not answering her calls or returning her texts, she casually removed his hand and placed it on his own thigh. Hell . . . she couldn't believe he'd shown up late to his own parents' wedding or re-wedding, whatever one would choose to call it. She even noticed that his cologne had a strong sweet smell mixed into it, clearly indicating that he'd been in the presence of another woman. Eyeing her closely, he could see the anger in her posture, but like always, he refused to allow her to stay mad at him. "Whatever it is baby, I'm sorry," he whispered but chose to keep his hands to himself.

"Not as sorry as you will be if you don't hush up." Young Mack was shocked by what be heard because Aeriella's lips hadn't moved in the slightest bit. He looked back over his shoulder and smiled with a slight nod at Aeriella's mother and father before turning back around to face the altar just in time to see his parents exchange rings. A movement to his left quickly caught his attention where he turned to see K-Dawg standing next to him. K-Dawg bent down and whispered into his ear that their crew had reported spotting suspicious looking cars driving the area of the church. He told K-Dawg to go out and check things out and handle things with care as he didn't wanna disturb his parents and the wedding goers. K-Dawg did as he was told and for the rest of the ceremony everything went off without a glitch.

Mackentosh "Mr. Mackmillions" Miller had once again made Sylvia his wife even though the couple had never gotten divorced. The reception following the ceremony was a blast for everyone, especially for the bride and groom who murdered the dance floor all night long, laughing and having a great time.

"So, where's the honeymoon going to be?" Young Mack asked his parents once they were outside of the comforts of the Post Oak Hotel in uptown Houston waiting on valets with their tickets.

"We were real big on Hawaii," Sylvia gushed, then kissed her husband on his lips.

"Yeah, Hawaii and all the other greatest touring destinations around the globe." Mackmillions smiled as he secured his wife in his arms just as their stretched Rolls Royce Cullinan pulled to a stop in front of them. The happy couple quickly got inside. "Son!" Young Mack turned to his father. "Whatever that situation was earlier, finish it before we make it back." Young Mack wasn't at all shook that his father was aware of the shit normal people would have never been aware of because his men were discreet in how they handled things in public. All he could do was nod his understanding to his father. "I have big plans for you and that crew of yours. Plans beyond your richest dreams, but like you I have to get my shit in order before any of what I have planned for the future can blossom. Be quick but be smarter than them. Don't slip because slippers count." They finished the last bit in unison and Mackmillions smiled before saluting his son, reclining as the chauffeur shut the overly expensive door, then rounded the truck and took them away.

Young Mack sighed as he climbed into the back seat next to Aeriella in the blacked out Chevy Suburban that Stephanie Valdez had designed for them to travel in. It was customized with Rolls Royce features including a mini bar and foot massagers built into the Polar Bear fur-cushioned floors. The first five minutes of their ride was silent and Young Mack couldn't take her not talking to him but he knew she needed her space in order to get past whatever was bothering her at the moment. She could feel his eyes boring into her as she stared outside into the night. She was deep in her own head with feelings about the way he'd been acting lately. Trip after trip in and out of Mexico like he was one of their drug cartel leaders, and not once had he ever invited her along on any of those trips. Yeah, she was in her head for real because there was definitely another woman at play. She couldn't pretend like she wasn't happy to see him when he swooped in outta nowhere and captured his mother's arm to escort her down the aisle to marry his father. But, hers were the tears he didn't catch with his smoothness and silk designer scarf and as the night went on, she remembered why she was mad at him in the first place.

"Are you fucking her?" her voice was just above a whisper but he heard her clearly as if she'd yelled them through a loud speaker.

"Who are you referring to, love?" he asked but didn't mean to avoid answering her question first.

"We're grown, Mackentosh Miller, so there is no need to play games because you know exactly who I am referring to." She turned and burned him with her gaze. "First, you go a whole ass day without answering my calls or your mother's, knowing what we were all preparing for." She caught the tear that threatened to escape her eye.

"Then you show up late to your own parents' wedding and to make matters worse you smelt just like . . . like her. I thought maybe I was being a little paranoid, but that was until I kept seeing her watching us, like we literally kept locking eyes all night."

"You're giving her too much of your attention," Young Mack replied before taking his turn to look outside at the world passing by their window.

"Shitting me if I am. Every time I locked eyes with her or caught her staring throughout the night she wasn't looking at anything but you. She followed us around the reception smiling at me every time I noticed her watching you. Now I'm asking you to man up and tell me, are you fucking her?"

"Oh shit, bae, get down!" Young Mack yelled, using his body to push her down and shield her from the automatic gunfire that erupted on her side of the vehicle.

"What's the problem, what's wrong?" Aeriella yelled from underneath him in near panic mode after seconds passed and nothing happened.

"Of course, she bullet-proofed the car, look." Young Mack sighed in relief as he stared at the Mexican hitmen that rode right next to them with their windows down and weapons hanging out.

Aeriella scooted from beneath him and followed his eyes until she too was looking at the Mexican crew and their weapons and mean mugs on their faces, but nothing prepared them for the loud explosion that propelled them into the air while moving down the highway at eighty miles per hour. The explosion sent the truck soaring over the concrete wall of the highway, snapping trees and branches as the SUV slammed into a heavily wooded area below.

Young Mack flashed in and out of consciousness due to him hitting his head hard against the bullet-proofed window. He could see images of Aeriella's body twisted upside down but he couldn't see her face which was below the seat resting on the floor board. He tried moving but his body wasn't responding accordingly. He looked towards his driver and noticed movement and when he tried to call out, nothing came from his mouth. Then he felt a throbbing sensation in his rib cage, bringing back to life old wounds. Soon, before his vision slipped into darkness, he saw the driver looking over the seat as he spoke into a cellphone that was pressed against his ear. Young Mack could not make out the things that he was saying before his vision faded away, but something, or should he say someone, stood out to him in his last image of their attack.

"Daniel!" Young Mack heard himself yell as he sat up in bed before becoming immediately light headed and feeling nauseated.

"Rest up, sweetheart, I am here and you're safe with me as always." He heard her voice before his eyes settled in on her angelic face in the dimly lit room. He could see the concern in the features of her face as his sight once again became blurry. "We'll get them back. You just rest up." Those were the last words he heard before sleep took him.

Chapter 4

K-Dawg and the rest of the crew sat in the waiting area of Memorial Herman Hospital vexed by last night's events. Outside of the early alert about the car circling around outside of the ceremony, everything went smoothly. K-Dawg was the most heated because he never got to lay eyes on the suspicious vehicle, being that it never came back once he stepped outside and now here they were. No one felt the presence of the threat and it almost cost Young Mack and Aeriella their lives. The mood in the room was congested with guilt and everyone felt as if they played a role in missing what was never supposed to be missed. Luckily for them, Stephanie wasn't about to allow Young Mack to slip from her sight without proper protection. An armored vehicle clearly saved their lives.

"Fuck did we let this happen?" Deuce mumbled what everyone else was feeling but no one chose to speak the obvious. "Tree and Sham should be on his front and back at all times from here on out."

"No one anticipated this, not even myself," Stephanie pointed out as she picked up on the extreme guilt that was consuming them all because of their relaxed security on such a major event. She knew that they weren't experienced on protecting someone with Young Mack's new found status but they were his friends and would surely give their lives for him. They just needed a little bit of training. "You guys need to pull yourselves together. He is not dead and I was there when he awoke for the short period of time. There are no broken bones, just a lot of bruises and swelling in small places." Of course she had to examine him from scalp to toe once the nurses finished cleaning his wounds. The constant urge to sexually assault him ran rapid through her mind but she thought better of it. She smiled inside at her own crazed thinking.

"We'll be allowed to visit just as soon as he wakes back up. So, everyone, please just chill out," Stephanie stated.

"Oh, this is chillin'. Don't get shit twisted because I'm fried the fuck out and everyone knows how shit goes when I'm like this!" K-Dawg fumed as he continued to pace the floor. He was dressed in a crisp Gucci trap suit while sporting a diamond-encrusted AP on his wrist and a fist full of diamonds on both hands. Plus, a pair of iced out Cuban link chains set his neck off in a rainbow of colors. Of course he had the top buttons of his trap suit unclasped almost to his toned stomach to show off his infinity of tattoos.

"Yeah and I second that!" Hogg made his feelings clear.

"Y'all know somebody gotta die over this, lots of smoked bodies!" Rolla said, adjusting his Cartier wood-framed glasses. Like K-Dawg, he too was dressed in a Gucci jogger set with diamond jewelry all over. He even showcased thirty thousand dollars' worth of flawless honeycomb set diamonds in his mouth.

Ashton sat as quiet as a trained assassin. Not once did he say anything to anyone; he didn't even acknowledge that the other crew members were there. He only had two things on his mind and he was clearing one of them at the moment by making sure Young Mack and Aeriella were okay. Secondly, his sister was heavily on his mind.

For the most part, he loved his crew and Young Mack as the brothers he never had, growing up with only a twin sister, and he would do anything for them. On the other hand, he loved his sister with his whole heart and could not see himself standing idle and allowing any harm to befall her.

She was his twin, his own flesh and blood, and nothing was stronger than that. Silently, he worried about her more now than ever before. He knew an act of this magnitude and so brazen could only mean one thing: the war had been awakened from months of tranquilized sleep. A war between his people and her husband's organization, and he had to find a for sure way to protect her if no one else did.

"Family of Aeriella Garcia and Mackentosh Miller II!" Everybody stilled at the sound of the soft feminine voice.

"Yeah, I am his brother," K-Dawg lied.

"Well, I'm sure you know that both patients have been through a traumatizing event last night, which is the bad news. But, thank God, everything with your loved ones is okay and neither patient required any surgeries and have both awakened with stable vitals and sane minds," the gorgeous older woman in the white coat with deep dimples stated with a very disarming smile.

"Can we see 'em now?" K-Dawg requested.

"Absolutely, but first I am going to need one of you handsome young men to accompany me while I get your brother's fiancée because she's demanding that we take her to him or she is going to sue our hospital!" The doctor laughed. "Throwing her lawyer credentials around and everything, chile, please come take this woman next door to see her man."

"Wait a minute, did you say next door, like, in the next room over?" Deuce laughed at the comedy in that picture.

"Yes! I do think it's beautiful for young black couples to be so far in love like those two clearly are, but anyways, come on so y'all can get to y'all's loved ones," the doctor said before turning to escort them down the hall to Young Mack and Aeriella's rooms.

"What it is, gangsta?" Deuce was all smiles once he laid eyes on his homie.

"Damn, I didn't think all of y'all were out there," Young Mack laughed as he shook up with everyone but wondered where K-Dawg was. Stephanie made sure to squeeze him tight before planting a kiss on his neck, careful not to leave any lip prints.

Young Mack smiled at the sexy way her ass cheeks connected and disconnected as she stepped away from him. He could feel his dick begin to brick just from the sight alone. His eyes traveled with her until they stopped on the movement at the door where K-Dawg stood there behind the wheelchair that Aeriella sat in. Water threatened to escape his eyes, seeing her in that wheelchair, but the smile that graced her face quickly corked his dam.

"'Sup, hunter?" K-Dawg wrapped his brother from another up in a strong embrace.

"Blessed beyond measures, that's for damn sure," Young Mack stated as they shook hands with their signature blood handshake.

"Well, I'm glad that y'all know he's okay and of course I am fine, thanks for asking, but he and I have something important to discuss in private please." Aeriella struggled to stand before K-Dawg helped her to climb beside Young Mack in his hospital bed.

"We got you, sis. Bro, do know that it's imperative that we talk at the earliest," K-Dawg stated as he and everyone else filed outta the hospital room.

"I'll be at you in a minute," Young Mack promised.

"Good, now I'm about to go and sign y'all outta here," K-Dawg said, then slapped the lights out and left the couple with the glow from the television.

"How are you feeling?" Young Mack spoke first before kissing her lips.

"I'm good, just a little shaken and banged up, but I'm glad to be double jointed." Aeriella laughed, thinking about the way the doctor described how the paramedics found her unconscious body.

"That makes two of us because you be really putting them moves on a nigga." Young Mack kissed her lips again, smiling hard.

"Okay, now that we're past that part I need to know if I should be concerned about the relationship you have with Steph?"

"You . . ."

"Wait! Before you answer that, just know that I watched her kiss you on your neck just now and how your ass was cheesing with no protest. I don't need you to confirm if she is into you or not. What I need to know is: are you into her the same way?" Aeriella questioned openly. "Are you fucking her?"

"To be truthful about everything, no, I haven't fucked her and I haven't planned on it either, but I would be a lying scum bucket if I said I wasn't attracted to her sexually and have been since I first met her."

"I'm cool with you being attracted to her, hell, it's hard not to be."

"What do you mean by that?" Young Mack asked, intrigued.

"I mean, shit, I am attracted to her my damn self. I've experienced being intimate with women before in college and you have seen all of my friends from those days and we're still close even until this day." Her revelation surprised the shit outta him and aroused him at the same time. She felt his hardness press against her thigh. "Don't be getting no funny ideas," she smiled while squeezing him in her hand, already imagining what he was thinking. She was happy that her man hadn't fallen between the older seductress' legs like a weaker man certainly would have.

"No ideas, just planning." He laughed just as K-Dawg walked in behind the young attractive nurse who tended to the couple since they entered the hospital.

"Can't say I saw that coming." Young Mack shook his head.

"What-what did I miss?" the gorgeous young nurse asked, showing off her pierced dimples without the jewelry in both cheeks.

"Oh, he's talking about the part where you and I—" K-Dawg bent down to whisper something in her ear.

"Ooookay, in that case here's my number." The nurse smiled while turning a bright shade of red.

"Y'all ready to go?" K-Dawg asked while accepting the nurse's number before throwing his arm over her shoulder possessively.

Young Mack and Aeriella shook their heads in amazement as they helped each other outta bed.

***

Mr. Mackmillions stared at his beautiful wife as she happily played around with some of the local Jamaican kids out on the rich white sanded beach. The island's tranquility was forever young, and Mackmillions could never grow away from its wonders. Every single time he visited the island felt like his first time.

"Didn't know you were into kidnapping Federal Agents," he heard the voice before he tore his eyes away from his queen to look the man over.

Cedrick Chandler, a former special agent for the Federal Bureau of Investigations. A man who hadn't seen a normal day since the last and the first time he laid eyes on the street legend. His life changed drastically after meeting Mackmillions, whom his director had him following after being released on bond during the appeal of his federal charges which dated back over fifteen years. Chandler, by intuition, had soon become suspicious of the Director's unhealthy infatuation with the subject of Mackentosh Miller. After being warned by Mackmillions of their seeded deceptions, he began to keep close tabs on the Director. Shortly thereafter, he discovered the Director himself tampering with evidence at the scene of a mass shooting where tens of people were killed. After confronting him, nothing would have prepared him for the shots fired into his body by his then partner, Agent Alex Drexler, with his own service weapon. Chandler barely got away with his life. Now, nearly a year later, he was awakened outta his sleep by three burly Jamaican men with long bleached dreads, gold teeth and assault rifles, then escorted across the globe to the place he now stood looking at the only familiar face on the entire island so far.

"Did you enjoy your flight?" Mackmillions ignored the ex-special agent's comment while looking at a dreaded version of the man he once highly regarded through tinted Cartier shades.

"Couldn't have been better," Chandler stated while placing both hands inside of his linen Polo shorts.

"Why am I here?" Chandler asked after a moment too long of silence between them.

"How eager are you to get revenge on those that wronged you and left you for dead?"

"I'd have to say, pretty damn eager but not at the cost of my soul." Chandler probably sounded strong and honorable to himself but Mackmillions knew way more than what he thought he did.

"I'd say your soul is slowly drifting away in the form of that poison you've grown pretty close to."

"What do you mean?"

"No need to try and hide what I already know, Cedrick." Mack tore his attention away from his wife again to face the young man before him. "I've kept a pretty close watch over you since you were planted here to take the fall for taking my life in the game your supervisors were playing, unbeknownst to you, that is."

"You think they were using me to try and kill you?" Chandler stood puzzled but not surprised by this revelation.

35

"I don't think I know but that's neither here nor there. You have been soaked and wrung out to dry and I am willing to give you a chance to not only seek revenge but to gain your life and status back as one of the best agents the bureau has ever seen." Mackmillions explained before turning back to see Max escorting Sylvia back over to their umbrella-covered seats.

"And just how are you gonna do that?" Chandler asked, curious to the matter at hand. He reminded himself about the great deal of troubles the man went through to have a meeting with him there outside of the States.

"See that cabbie over behind the drink stand?" Mackmillions pointed out without looking.

"You mean the young boy on the scooter?" Chandler raised his eyebrows at the rundown piece of machinery.

"He'll take you to where your first answer lies," Mackmillions concluded as his queen reached their seats.

"And what if I decline all of this?"

"You won't. See you in a week. I'm on my honeymoon." Mack smiled before kissing his wife. Chandler locked eyes with Max and knew the meeting was over for now. He remembered the hard man and wanted no parts of him on an island with nothing to defend himself with. Hand to hand, he wasn't even sure of himself anymore.

"Congratulations," Chandler stated as he moved along the beach until he reached the young Jamaican businessman. The boy didn't speak a word to him; he just nodded and motioned for him to hop on, which he did. Wasn't like he had much of a choice, being that he was stuck on an island with no way home. He had no money, no phone, no identification or passport; and most importantly, he had no place to lay his head. Not to mention he had no way to appease his addiction.

The moped ride through the crowded island streets wasn't bad, being that the driver saw no problem with taking shortcuts through sodded alleyways and sidewalks when the street traffic was jammed up. Chandler held on for dear life as the boy maneuvered the hard running machine. He enjoyed the rural views of all what this side of Jamaica had to offer its locals and tourists alike. Their way of life was seemingly a lot different from what he was accustomed to in America.

The sound of the small straining horn of the moped taxi caught his attention and brought him outta his zone. They were now stopped in front of the luxurious S Hotel, a popular place on the island. He wasn't sure where they were on the island but what he was absolutely sure of was that this hotel meant definite comfort for him.

After dismounting the small moped taxi, the boy escorted him in to the receptionist desk in the hotel's lobby where he spoke confidently in his native dialect to a very pretty woman behind the receptionist desk. Her eyes searched Chandler quizzically. Even without a smile or words, he could tell she wanted to examine his package and experience what his sex game was like. Call it the intuition of a one-time top federal agent. He smiled and held up the key card his young guide had given him. He was sure that she understood his invitation and if not, fuck it if he was missing something; it was just pussy.

He stepped inside of the elevator. For the first time since being away from home and away from his foiled packages, he began to itch uncomfortably and immediately wondered where he would get his next fix. Mackmillions had to know he'd need it since he knew so much already. The elevator sounded. Once he reached the ninth floor, the doors opened to yet another beautiful young native who smiled when she saw him standing there with his hands in his pockets. She was dressed in what he guessed to be island-casual attire and sporting long, blonde dreadlocks. Her eyes were honey-colored, and her lips were full and plump, typical of many women he'd seen on the island since arriving in Montego Bay. Her silk button-down dress shirt clung to her toned upper body, clearly revealing her dark-colored areolas and spiked nipples, which were large. It was amazing how effortlessly this sexy siren aroused him without even the slightest touch.

"Follow me." He was surprised yet again at how clearly she spoke English, though her accent was still evident. He had to bite his lip at the sight of her luscious backside. Her body moved with the fluid grace of someone dancing in one of Rihanna's raunchy music videos. It was hard for him to hide his erection as they made their way through the hallway and entered a room, which he guessed would be where he'd be staying while on the island.

"Remove your clothes and meet me in the shower." Shocked was an understatement for how he felt about what happened next.

The sexy young woman quickly stepped into his face and took his lips into her own. The shock quickly wore off, and soon he was kissing her back, their tongues dancing in a lustful rhythm. It felt like they had been locked in their embrace for half an hour before she pulled back and looked into his eyes. "The receptionist downstairs, my cousin, will be joining us shortly, so we have to hurry," she breathlessly explained as she rushed to get undressed.

"Say less," Chandler said, hurrying to strip off his clothes.

"Here, take these," the pretty island girl reached out her hand.

"I'm good on those. I got enough energy, sweetheart, plus I'm not as old as I look." He spoke with pride while making his erection jump with excitement.

"Mr. Mack's orders. He said it will help you with what you don't have, whatever that is." Instantly, he understood that Mackmillions was trying to help him cope with not having his *juice*, as he liked to call it.

He took the pills and thanked her before tossing them into his dry mouth; then, as if by magic, she produced a glass of what he assumed was water. He drank it to wash down the meds and took in its toxicity and immediately knew that it wasn't water or vodka he'd just consumed. She saw the look in his eyes and smiled mischievously.

"The drink was from me, to help you fuck my brains out." He disliked the thought of her drugging him, but the look in her eyes told him of her attentions.

"What was in it?" his face involuntarily frowned up. "Organic roots from my grandmother's herbal garden, though it is not narcotic. It's all natural. My special blend heightens male enhancement and strengthens male stamina."

"Sounds like you're some kind of doctor."

"Ummm . . . showing is proving," she stated as she dropped to her knees and engulfed his entire length. Slowly, she popped him out of her mouth and examined the thick veins protruding from his hardness and the dark shade of purple in its head. She immediately knew that her concoction worked yet again. "Perfect," she mumbled before taking him back into the wetness of her throat.

***

Daniel couldn't believe their luck as they moved through the hallways of the Memorial Herman Hospital's Intensive Care floor. Even though the receptionist wasn't eager to help them with the information that they needed, he quickly persuaded her with a nice big stack of crispy hundred dollar bills. She then searched the roster for a silent minute, only to inform them that no one had been brought in from a car explosion in over three months. The news shocked and angered him to his core, especially because he was sure that their targets saw his face and that would definitely open the deep wounds of war that had been closed for a time.

"Fuck!" He exhaled harshly as he and two of his men left the hospital and entered his truck.

"Don't worry, bossman, we'll get 'em," one of his workers said as they rode the city streets.

"It's either we do or the lucky fucks will be our downfall, imagine that," Daniel stated just before his phone chimed. "Yeah, talk to me."

"I guess you missed, being that you haven't called me to confirm your success like you normally do," he heard Gurdo's faith in him fading as he spoke.

"The car they were traveling in was bullet-proofed but the grenades blew the truck over the highway and the lucky fucks landed in a bunch of trees. I'm telling you this fucker has some kind of angels protecting him!" Daniel tried explaining but he knew Gurdo didn't care about anything but completing the mission.

"At the rate you're moving, we better hope that the angels and Mother Mary are with us in the end." His words confirmed what Daniel already felt. His right-hand whom he considered a brother from another mother, and the new boss of their familia, was losing faith in his abilities to get shit done.

"Allow me to take the gloves off and we'll see who really needs those angels and Mother Mary as you say," Daniel challenged his brother in crime.

"Take 'em off, but you better not let any of this shit make it out of this room." Daniel swore to his duties before their call ended.

Chapter 5

"So, where to, Ms. Pretty?" K-Dawg smiled, showcasing twenty of his perfectly diamonded out teeth.

"I'm with you for the night and I believe it's only right that you choose unless you're afraid of lil' ol' me." Sade had her game face on. She was tired of spending countless hours of mandatory overtime at her correctional facility job downtown, then clocking into her job at the hospital without the pleasure of getting any sleep in between. The shit she went through at both jobs was pressure, but it cost to have the designer and luxurious staples she'd grown accustomed to trying to keep up with her high-maintenance girlfriends. Tonight she was trying to capture herself a baller, a big fish, and she planned to do it by any means necessary.

"You talk a good game but I'ma let you off easy tonight because you know not what you're getting yourself into." K-Dawg chuckled as he sized her up in her tight work scrubs. Her pussy print was so puffy and evident he wondered if she kept it shaved and was anxious to find out for himself.

"I can definitely walk it like I talk it, but you better last more than a minute in this wet ass pussy that's for sure." K-Dawg, marveled, bit into his bottom lip as he watched her rub her middle finger between her thick nether lips.

"It's like that, huh?" K-Dawg said as he checked his rear view mirror for any sign of authority as he was ready to get shit poppin' right there in the lot, but that view changed everything because just like that the drama popped off. "Oh, shittt!" he mumbled while ducking just in time for the first rounds that came exploding through the driver side window to miss him as he smashed his foot down hard on the gas. Hundreds or tiny pieces of debris from the glass window showered him but his nurse friend wasn't so lucky as the first three rounds of fire caught her in the neck and face, killing her instantly.

"Damn!" K-Dawg shouted as he swerved his Mercedes onto the shoulder of the road, doing seventy miles an hour. Cars honked their horns, and people shouted indecent threats towards him as he fled past them with the tinted out Mercedes truck on his tail.

Driving with the little nurse lady slumped in the passenger made him a bit nervous because the police could pop out and give chase, then he would definitely be a goner with his weapon in the car. He reached as best as he could, while keeping his eyes on the road, but couldn't quite get a firm grip on the carbon-replica Draco he had modified and built to his liking.

Growing tired of the public attention to the chase, Daniel ordered his driver to fish-tail the speeding Sedan, and he sped up in order to carry out his order, but K-Dawg saw it coming and he quickly slammed on the brakes and made a right turn, desperate to make it to the residential side of Third Ward.

Moments after K-Dawg executed his turn, he turned it up a notch on the back streets. He tried for his weapon again but was once again unsuccessful, so he grabbed his phone from the charger and voice-dialed Deuce's cellphone. "Talk quick, lil' bro I'm on the dice."

"Where are you, kid? I got some hot shit on my ass right now and I need you!"

"What's goin' on?" Deuce stood up on high alert.

"I'm speeding down Alabama with a truck full of niggas on my ass."

"On God, you gotta lead that ass straight to the Bricks, we out here waiting!" Deuce spoke into his phone, sounding almost as panicked as K-Dawg on the other end.

K-Dawg could hear Deuce shouting out for some pick up shooters and offering cash on hand for any bodies they drop from the other side. "I'm flying past DTA as we speak, kid, and these hoes ain't letting up, bro. Get ready!"

"Nigga, we already see you, just get to Burkett and slam on the brakes hard!" Deuce shouted.

He didn't have to be told twice what to do, and he knew what to expect. When the time came, he slammed on his brakes while activating the emergency brakes all at once, then anticipated the hard collision but it never came. Breathing heavy and sweating through the cold air conditioner inside of the Mercedes, K-Dawg slowly opened his eyes one at a time. He knew he wasn't dead because he was staring in the eyes of death as his nurse friend's body rested towards the driver side of the vehicle with half of her face mangled from the high-caliber bullets that tore through her.

He tore his stare away from her and looked through the windshield and saw Deuce and six shooters all standing in the middle of the street with their weapons trained on something behind him.

After eyeing his saviors, he checked his rear view mirror and saw that the Mercedes SUV had stopped more than a hundred yards back.

Daniel was more than sure of the ambush they were being led into after they entered the neighborhood. Why else would a man trying to save his own ass drive through his own hood instead of taking his chances with the superior motor on the highway. "Pussy!" Daniel spat before ordering his driver to reverse back the way they came.

"Stomp shit lil' niggas!" Deuce shouted as they watched the vehicle back away. He reached into his pocket and handed each armed shooter two grand apiece.

"You know we steppin' on shit this way fo' shit sho!" one of the youngsters stated before watching the body fall out of the Mercedes they'd just saved. "Damn," he gasped.

"Damn," Deuce seconded as he recognized the girl as the one K-Dawg had been macking on at the hospital not long ago. "That shit was close! Pussies almost knocked my cup over!" K-Dawg shook his head in disbelief.

"Too bad lil' momma can't say the same." Deuce pointed out. "Yeah, that's fucked up, but it ain't on shit. What's done is done and we can't bring her lil' fine ass back."

"What are you gone do with her because surely we ain't 'bout to leave her out here like that?" Deuce asked.

"Which one of y'all tryna make ten racks to get rid of the car and the body?" K-Dawg went into his pocket and produced the money.

"It's done," Rico said and snatched the bread from K-Dawg's fist.

"Deuce, I need a ride." K-Dawg cocked the action on his Draco-Carbon.

***

Gurdo paced the floor of his master bedroom as he impatiently waited for his wife to come outta the bathroom. The slow passing time and anticipation was kicking his ass as he walked a mile in the same space. She had been in there for five minutes and it felt like forever to him. Curiosity was getting the best of him and it was causing him to worry, but just when he thought he couldn't take it any longer, the bathroom door opened and there she stood. The look in her eyes told a story of their own as both excitement and worry battled for a dominant position. Gurdo did his best to conceal his feelings as he calmed himself and waited to hear what his heart so desired. There was nothing more that could make him the happiest man on earth than the news his wife could possibly deliver any second.

"Well?" he nervously spoke up after a moment too long of her silence.

"Positive," Ambrea smiled weakly, not yet sure whether to be happy or worried by this new revelation.

"Positive!" Gurdo shouted, unable to contain his excitement any longer, causing her to flinch a little before a smile grew larger on her face. "This is the best news a husband can get!" he gushed.

"Easy for you to say. You won't have to go through all the changes to your body, not to mention being the one that has to push it out."

"It? You mean him." Gurdo laughed, ready to be the father to his son just like his father was to him and Daniel growing up.

"Seriously, bae, this is great news and you should call your family to deliver the news while I call mine." Gurdo was smiling harder than she'd ever witnessed him smile before. The news really excited him beyond anything she had ever seen.

Gurdo, unbeknownst to his wife, not only saw their child as his first born, but it also meant something else that was extremely important to him. Boy or girl, Gurdo would now have an heir to his throne and it would permanently remove his father and make him jefe (boss) in their organization. The child was truly a blessing from God Himself in Gurdo's eyes.

Unbeknownst to Gurdo, his wife had something heavy weighing on her mind as well about their unborn child. The ideas swarming around inside of her head would not have such a joyous and praiseworthy outcome as that of his. Her heart raced rapidly with thoughts of her and Young Mack resonating in her mind. Thoughts of their restless uninhibited sex and lovemaking. It troubled her because she wished that the passion she felt coming from her husband could be coming from him instead. She missed him and all that they had and silently wished it would have never come crashing down. She picked up her phone and searched her contacts, only to come up empty. She didn't even know what she'd say to him if she did still have his number, a clear indication of the time and how much had changed in such a short period. Maybe she would sit silently and hold the phone while listening to him ask who the caller was over and over again, then somehow figure out it was her. Then she'd be able to gauge him after realizing it was her, and after all that had happened between her husband and him. She even thought of hitting him up on social media, but instantly went against that idea because it would be way too public. Then an idea hit her like a ton of feathers. She quickly found the most trusted number she could have stored in her phone right up there with her mother's number. She listened intently as the line rang while actively listening to her husband talk to his family in the doorway of their master bedroom.

"Sup, sis?" she heard her twin's voice and felt an immediate relief.

"Where are you right now?" she whispered, feeling all sorts of emotions behind calling him.

"Out, but why are you whispering?" he asked, mimicking her on the other end of their call

"Don't do me like that. I need you to meet me at my place asap. It's a family emergency."

"Say less, I'm on my way now," he replied before ending their call.

Thank God, Ambrea thought once her call with her brother ended.

"Who was that?" Her husband's voice startled her a bit, causing her to jump. "And why are you so jumpy?" He eyed her suspiciously.

"That was my brother, and hell, you scared me. I thought you were in the hallway talking to your family, then out of nowhere, you're right behind me." Ambrea rebounded from her fear of being exposed, even though she was overreacting.

"Cool! Did you give him the news?" Gurdo asked, eager for all their loved ones to know they were expecting. "Not yet. I didn't want to tell him over the phone, so I invited him over. I thought it was a good idea since I haven't seen him in weeks. I'm going to go help Emily prepare a small late dinner for us three."

"Might as well make it for four; Daniel is on his way here as well."

Her nervousness returned at the mention of Daniel's name. At one point in their lives, the two of them had been thick as thieves, but that had all changed, like most things in life. It hadn't been long enough for things to return to the way they were before, so they still weren't in a good place. She didn't like being around him, just as Gurdo didn't like being around her brother, with the two of them on different sides of the war. It was safe to say they were all tolerating each other for the sake of love—her and Gurdo's love and marriage depended on it.

"I'll be sure to keep that in mind," she said as she moved to walk past her husband.

"Are you okay, love?" Gurdo asked as his suspicions returned.

"I'm fine for now but I feel for you and Daniel's asses . . . once my hormones start raging, the mood swings kick in, and my feet get all swollen."

"Hey, hey, hey! I ain't ducking a thing when it comes to this pregnancy, so there will be no fear in me throughout the whole thing. I'll be here for you every step of the way. I love you."

His assuring words softened her to the core, but now that Young Mack was back in her life, her husband's words made her hunger to hear them from him even more. "I love you too," she said, kissing his lips tenderly before leaving the bedroom.

"Yes!" she heard her husband's excitement as she descended the stairs headed for the kitchen, and all she could do was shake her head in silence.

***

"This is Special Agent Chandler," the sex goddess, who told him her name was Queeny, introduced him to her equally beautiful cousin. Both stood at the perfect height of five feet six inches tall and had radiantly beautiful chocolate skin. Queeny's breasts were smaller, but her huge gumdrop nipples and large areolas made up for what she lacked.

"Agent, this is my cousin Rastanya."

Rastanya was the spitting image of the wild party girl turned fashion icon, Riri, but with darker skin and a figure sculpted from every man's fantasy. Both women had flat six-packed stomachs that dropped down into nearly invisible waistlines and both had hips for days. His dick thumped up against his stomach as he observed the two sexy vixens.

"Nice to meet you, Special Agent Chandler," Rastanya purred as she stepped out of her red lace panties with the help of her sex-crazed cousin. Chandler had his hand filled with his dick as he watched Queeny kiss along Rastanya's thick-toned thighs until she was licking and slurping loudly from her cousin's womanly juices.

"Ooooh, she knows just how I like it," Rastanya moaned as she rubbed her protruding clit and opened her pussy lips as Queeny ate her out.

"You two stop playing games and get over here," he demanded while pumping himself. He could still feel the remnants of Queeny on himself.

"Queeny, you heard the man," Rastanya said but showed no effort to stop her from licking her to orgasm. She was close.

"Ummmm hmmmm, I'm coming, cousin, suck me there, suck me! Ahhh-shiiittt!" Rastanya screamed as her climax rocked her, and her juices squirted into her cousin's hand. Queeny sat back on her haunches and caught the waterfall, slowly sucking up her honey.

That was all Chandler could take before he scrambled off the bed and positioned himself between Rastanya's spread legs, swallowing the rush of her secretions. Queeny crawled between his legs and took him back down her throat again, impressed by the size of his package. He was surprised she could handle him whole, not many past conquests could.

"Damn, I need some of this pussy," he muttered, then stood and roughly flipped Rastanya over the king-sized bed, entering her from behind.

"Ahhhhh, shittt, this pussy good and tight!" he groaned, stroking her long and deep. Her pussy gushed and creaked with each thrust, her moans echoing with his powerful dicking.

Queeny sat on the floor beneath their writhing bodies, licking her tongue along his pole as it pumped in and out of Rastanya's super wet twat. She eagerly returned to sucking on Rastanya's clit once familiar vibrations from her cousin's thighs signaled her approaching climax.

"Fuck me harder! Please—Ahhhh, shittt! Fuck me hard with your big dick, motherfucker!" Chandler pounded her as hard as his body allowed, feeling their juices splashing between them. But he still hadn't come yet.

"Queeny, get that ass up here next to your cousin so I can see what both of these asses can do," he instructed, and she obeyed.

He quickly rubbed his wet dick between Rastanya's swollen pussy lips, spreading her juices across her dark, chocolate globes before shoving the mushroom head of his ten-and-a-half-inch cock into her rear canal.

"Holy shit, that's a lot, oh my god!" Rastanya exclaimed, attempting to scoot away from his forceful advance.

"Oh no, get that ass back here!" Chandler growled, gripping her waist tightly.

"It's too much! Arrrgh! Slower, slower!" she yelled as he sawed in and out of her wet asshole, struggling to insert his entire length.

"Give it all to me, she can handle it yet, agent, give it to me!" Queeny declared, twerking her juicy ass cheeks together.

"I'll finish you off later," he said, slapping Rastanya's ass before moving over and slamming into Queeny's wet pussy from behind. Their sex was a chaotic rhythm, their strokes sounding like two people fighting, as Queeny threw her pussy back to meet his every forward thrust.

"Fuck this pussy like you hate it, arrrrgh!" Queeny yelled as he fucked her like a crown-holding stud.

"Damn, it almost feels better than before, ummmm shit, but I gotta get this ass. You two motherfuckers got these fat asses and I gotta get me some," he said, pulling out of Queeny's dripping wet clutches before slamming a forceful stroke deep into her asshole.

"Arrrrgh-damn—it is a lot!" Queeny yelled, drawing a chuckle from Rastanya who was sprawled on her stomach, fingering herself to orgasm from both holes.

"One of yall gonna take this dick like a big girl!" Chandler barked as he pounded into Queeny's ass. He enjoyed the sight of his dick disappearing into her tight asshole and stretching her insides with each pullback before slamming back in.

"Yeeeees! Yesss! Good dick, good good dick!" Queeny cheered him on as he neared his climax.

"Fuck, I'm about to come!" He sped up his thrusts, erupting deep within her anal cavity before collapsing on her back, still stuffed inside of her.

"That was fun, yeah, now it's time to kill." Rastanya's voice shifted from friendly sex kitten to cold and deadly.

"Yes, we must shower now, for we have work to do." Queeny agreed, her voice no less serious.

"Let me guess, am I supposed to work alongside you two?" Chandler laughed, but his smile vanished as he realized their chilling seriousness.

"Fun is over for now, but don't worry, I have more love potion for us later." Queeny smiled before catching up with her cousin for their shower.

This shit's almost too good to be true, he thought to himself as he too entered the walk-in shower with the two sexy Jamaican assassins.

Chapter 6

The acrid smell emanating from the warehouse made Young Mack hate leaving the comforts of Stephanie's villa. He had been laid up with Aeriella when Stephanie showed up after a long night out on the town, dressed in a vintage Donatella Versace dress with the stomach and back blown out. She told him they had important business to tend to that could not wait. He was out of bed and dressed within minutes and now, half an hour later, was entering the secluded steel factory-like structure behind Stephanie.

The lights inside the warehouse were bright, and Young Mack immediately noticed all the naked women hustling about, along with speedo-clad men doing their jobs for the drug cartel family. Young Mack's eyes opened wide in awe at so much cocaine being stored and handled in one place in its various forms of preparation. There had to be at least sixty men and twice as many women milling about the large warehouse.

"Come, we must go to the back," Stephanie grabbed his hand to keep him close as they moved through the packaging and distribution center. She wasn't trying to allow him the chance to get lost in the pool of beautiful Latina women of all shapes and sizes; she was also letting it be known that he was with her, and their workers knew not to play with what was hers. "Come, this way."

"Why are the lights off?" Young Mack started but was silenced by her lips attacking his. Her hand made quick work of his Gucci belt. Truth was, she had him worked up from the moment she stepped inside the guest bedroom he occupied at her home with his fiancée and saw him in his designer briefs with his package clearly present before her eyes. Her panties soaked as she delivered her message and stayed that way until this very moment.

"What are you doing, ma?" His words fell upon deaf ears as she was determined to get a taste of him. Reaching inside his underwear, she smiled at the revelation of his rock-hard penis and immediately knew that he was just as turned on as she was.

"I'm really-hhhorny-right now-ummm! I want to please-ooou," Stephanie managed to get out between taking him in her mouth, going deeper and deeper until she had him housed deep inside her throat.

"Damn," Young Mack relaxed himself in her clutches and could not believe that he'd been missing out on such great head for so long.

Stephanie gagged from his now drilling thrust into her throat, but she never complained and took the dick like a big girl. She loved sucking cock, but to be sucking him was bringing her close to orgasm without him even touching her. Loving the sensations of his penetrations, she began to hum her favorite song while applying pressure to her sensitive clit, hoping to explode with him at the same time. Almost hitting her targeted goal, she came just seconds before his heavy stream of seeds rushed down her throat. It was so much that she had to swallow twice, not wanting to let any get away from her; she was indeed hooked. At the last moment, she pulled back a bit to catch some on her tongue in order to savor his flavor before making a show of swallowing it down like the true freak she was.

"That was fire, Steph, but I know you didn't bring me here just for that, did you?" Young Mack asked as he righted himself with a pleased yet concerning look on his face.

"Unfortunately not. We must go and meet with my brothers now." After filling her mouth with spearmint gum, she explained some of what was going on as they made their way around the warehouse. Most of it didn't even register once she mentioned capturing some of Gurdo's men and a shipment of his goods. He couldn't wait to get his hands on their captives to find their boss's whereabouts.

Once they made it to the back of the warehouse, he hastened his steps to get to where the action was already underway. Miguel was clobbering one of Gurdo's men over the head with a metal baseball bat over and over again, as if he couldn't get enough of the gruesome act. "Stupid pussy!" he heard Miguel shout once his assault was finished.

"I don't think it was nice of you boys to start the party without me before company starts leaving," Young Mack shook both Valdez men's hands while observing the bloodied scene before him. Obviously, Miguel hadn't been in the mood for bullshit tonight because he saw that that was his second victim so far.

"They seem not to want to talk," Jalamon summed up the situation at hand.

"Someone always talks!" Miguel shouted, more to their captive than to them.

"My question is, how the hell did we get so lucky?" Young Mack wondered as he thought about the small trap houses they ran across here and there back in the States as he walked along the line of men, all staring bravely back into his eyes.

"That would be a question for Steph, my friend," Jalamon confessed as he slowly shadowed behind him.

"I'll be sure to ask her, but first, I'd like to talk to this one right here."

"You know him?" That was Miguel, still holding the bloodied metal death instrument over his shoulder like a true major leaguer.

"I couldn't possibly know him, but outta all of them, he has to be the only one who's bilingual," Young Mack gave his observation.

Miguel quickly ordered his men to unbind the man Young Mack selected and drag him inside of the warehouse where they normally tortured their prisoners. The workers immediately followed their boss's orders and were careful enough to add a knot or two to their victim's pain from the harshness of their handling.

"Wait, don't sit him down yet!" Young Mack ordered, hoping the men understood him. Once they halted, he knew then that they did. "Knife," he requested, and Jalamon fulfilled his request with his trusted machete that he kept sheathed inside his blue jeans while working around the warehouse.

Young Mack accepted the big blade before moving to the old woven-seated chair, then cutting the bottom out of the center, just like he'd seen in one of his favorite movies.

"Strip him," Young Mack ordered, but the men first looked to their bosses for confirmation before they moved to follow any further orders passed down from Young Mack. One thing was known about the Valdez family and their henchmen throughout Mexico: they weren't the largest or strongest of the many powerful families, but one thing was for damn sure and no one would ever contest—they were top three amongst the most ruthless when it came to murder, extortion, and war tactics. It was only right that he respected their workers seeking their permission before following his orders because to them, he was an outsider, just another business associate of their bosses. After a slight head nod in approval from Stephanie, the workers moved hastily to strip their captive against his useless struggling and fighting. Once stripped down to nothing, they then bound him to the chair Young Mack had cut the bottom out of.

Young Mack moved close to Stephanie and noticed how amazing she always smelled and smiled. Even with the light hint of sweat mixed well with her perfume, it made him wonder if her pussy smelled the same as the rest of her. Thoughts of his talk with his fiancée played inside of his mind and caused his dick to stir, but he quickly suppressed the instant sensational urges and put his mind on the business at hand. He smoothly reached down beside her feet and grabbed the thick rope that rested against the gritty surface of the warehouse floor.

"You know how to use this?" he whispered in her ear, careful to allow their skins to touch.

"Of course, James Bond!" Stephanie smiled at his reference to the torture scene depicted in the famous movie.

"Let's see what we can make happen as a team then," he smiled before gently kissing her cheek then tying a thick knot at the head of the rope.

"Do you understand and speak English?" Young Mack asked their captive loud enough for everyone to hear. The man simply smiled and shook his head in a blatant attempt at being defiant. Stephanie didn't wait to be told to strike; she struck without hesitation for the disrespect. The knot caroused through the air twice before lurching in an upward swing, making direct contact with their prisoner's hanging testicles.

The shrilling cry that nearly burst everyone in close proximity's eardrums sounded more like an injured woman than that of a pained man. All the men present grabbed at their jewels as they watched the man wheeze heavily before losing consciousness. Both Valdez men looked at each other in approval before turning their eyes back to the action.

"Wake yo' bitch ass up!" Young Mack demanded while repeatedly slapping the man across the face. His eyes twitched uncontrollably for a minute before they shot open, and the recognition of pain re-registered with his brain.

"You crazy bitch! You crazy bitch, I'll fucking kill you! Ahhh—fuck you motherfuckers!" The man yelled in Spanish but moved no one in the room. As far as Young Mack was concerned, the dude would meet death too soon to make good on any threats, and he was sure that everyone else present felt the same way.

"Do you speak English?" Young Mack asked, devoid of any emotion for the guy. Again, the man ignored him as he stared at Stephanie.

"Fuck it, hit his ass again," Stephanie said.

"Please no—no—no! Don't let her do that again!" The sweat-drenched naked man screamed in protest in plain English.

"So you do speak English," Young Mack moved in front of the guy to block his vision of Stephanie, who still held the knotted rope in her hands. His pear-shaped eyes were releasing tears effortlessly and were a dark shade of red, telling a story of pain that Young Mack didn't care to sympathize with.

"Where can I find Gurdo?" The man blinked his eyes as if his brain was a computer processing those words.

"I don't know," he finally sighed, as if his life was now over. In that moment, he began to silently pray for his wife and eight kids back home.

"Hit him again," Young Mack moved out of the way, and Stephanie obeyed his order. This time the guy only emitted a hard grunt before his eyes shut to blackness. Young Mack and the others observed the slight drip of blood running from underneath the captured man's seat. They felt no compassion; he was the enemy, and they were determined to find and kill his leaders.

"We need some water," Young Mack stated, and Miguel gave the order for one of his men to retrieve it.

"Can I offer you advice?" Stephanie's words drifted softly into his ear from just over his shoulder. She was so close he could nearly taste the spearmint emanating from her mouth. Once again, her sensuousness was getting to him, and he had a sudden urge to kiss her, but he fought it off because he didn't need her brothers thinking that he'd gotten soft and broken weak to their powerful sister.

"Always, ma'am. What's on your mind?"

"Us as bosses here in Mexico, we have our men trained to withstand torture. You had the right idea to choose the bilingual guy because it's safe to say that he is definitely a carrier for their organization. A runner."

Young Mack then saw her vision. Maybe he didn't know where to find Gurdo himself, but one thing they were willing to gamble on was the fact that he would definitely know where to find Gurdo's drugs and pipelines.

Young Mack kissed Stephanie's cheek before moving past her and picking up their victim's clothes. After retrieving what he was after, he smiled and silently thanked Stephanie Valdez. Shortly after, the barrel of water was rolled into the warehouse where they all stood looking on at their unconscious hostage. Young Mack dumped a bucket of water over the guy's head, and he sprang awake in his seat as far as his binds would allow, gasping for air.

"Drugs, amigo. I need drugs, lots and lots of drugs," Young Mack said while squatting to face the man. His eyes traveled from Young Mack to the three leaders of the Valdez family, then back to the only black guy he'd ever seen call any shots in their homeland. To say he was confused would be an understatement. Young Mack turned to see what the guy was looking at, then smiled. "I need Gurdo's drugs, not theirs, and I know you know where I should begin looking."

"No can do, no . . . no . . . no! I'll be a very dead man if I do!" The bound man fussed and fought against his binds.

Young Mack removed the item he'd searched the man's clothes for and held it up to his face. The fighting and cursing stopped immediately and turned into deep sobs as if he already knew what time it was.

"We'll start youngest to oldest and save your wife for last unless you give me what I want. Give me Gurdo's tunnels and save your family. Save yourself by a show of good faith, but I must tell you how that all of your men will die here tonight. You can't help them." Young Mack saw the gleam of hope light up the man's eyes, but it quickly faded once he mentioned that all others will be killed.

"My son, Trejo, is amongst those men, sir. If I help you, we must come to an agreement."

"I'm listening," Young Mack replied.

"Me and my family go free, no harm more than what has been done." Young Mack stared into his tear-soaked face.

"Done. But I can offer you nothing more. Your son will be our guide, so direct him well. Or his death will be on your hands."

***

"So how long are we supposed to sit on the sidelines and let shit go?" Deuce asked after he put fire to yet another blunt of kush, their third one in less than an hour.

"As long as Young needs us to. Hell, you know I'm stuck on go, fa sho!" K-Dawg stated as he gave the news channel his full attention. They were covering a story about a rapper out in Memphis getting gunned down earlier that day. "Fuck, they wigged Dolph!"

"No shit?" Rolla sat forward now, taking his attention off of his Instagram account to take in the breaking news.

Suddenly everyone's attention was snatched away from the television as the doorbell sounded throughout the eight-bedroom, eight-bathroom, seven-thousand-square-foot pad. Deuce checked the guard station cameras and saw that all was normal on that end, yet they all sat puzzled by the surprise visitor. Deuce then checked the cameras at the front door of their home and quickly noticed the small feminine figure standing there in tights and a hoodie.

"One of y'all get the door for whatever thot somebody forgot they invited over," Deuce said as he walked back into the large living area.

"I know I ain't invited no hoes over," Rolla replied and sat back on the white Italian leather sofa. He was high as fuck and wasn't about to leave his spot.

"Me either," Hogg added.

"Well, I know it wasn't me," Deuce spoke. Then they all looked to K-Dawg who was still very much lost in the breaking news coverage of the known Memphis rapper that he personally followed on Instagram.

"What?" he grunted after Deuce kicked his foot to get his attention.

"D . . . Did you invite one of your P.O.s over?" Deuce asked accusingly.

"No, why?" K-Dawg asked curiously, but the resounding of the doorbell answered his question. "I'll get it."

"We know," Deuce chuckled then took his spot on the sofa. K-Dawg's mouth dropped open when he saw Gianna's face through the stained glass door. He smoothly removed a small Beretta 9mm from his back pocket as he made his way to the door.

"What are you doing here and where's your Chihuahua?" K-Dawg asked after he opened the door for her.

"I'm here because I wanna go after Daniel, and I know of a few locations. As far as my guy, he's more like a Rottweiler, dick all big and shit," Gigi chuckled as she looked him up and down.

He was huge when it came to her small frame, but she silently wondered just how big the killer's dick was.

"If you tryna kill up some shit, I'm with it, but yeah, this dick here makes even a Rottweiler think he's a Chihuahua," he laughed as he grabbed his dick print for her to see that he wasn't bullshitting. Her eyes bulged and she shook her head as she took in the sight before her.

"You are too damn silly," she playfully punched his arm. "Hey, you the one brought up lil' homie's package. Remember that shit next time," he said as he stepped aside and allowed her entry into their home.

"Oh, I'll remember it alright," Gianna smirked as she brushed past purposely making contact with his groin.

"You won't walk straight for two days," K-Dawg whispered in her ear before they made it inside the living area with the others. Gianna shook her head but had to admit to herself that he was indeed turning her on. She was glad that she wore the hoodie as it concealed her hardened nipples.

"Yo, fellas, Gigi popped in with some leads on that action Deuce was speaking on earlier," K-Dawg informed the others before he took a seat while taking in her thick thighs and protruding hips. Her waist was small, and he knew from previous run-ins with her and her crew that her ass was super fat. Staring at her as she talked with the fellas made him wonder for the first time how good the tattooed beauty was in bed. His dick bricked up just thinking about all the things he'd love to do to her.

"Why haven't you and your crew taken action already if you have the intel?" Deuce questioned her because he was certainly curious to know her true motive for coming to them as if their crews were buddy-buddy or some shit.

"We didn't wanna chance fucking it up because we would surely be outnumbered and outgunned. The only thing working in our favor is the element of surprise."

"What do y'all think about all of this shit?" Deuce asked his crime brothers.

"How did you even get this address and how did you get past security?" Hogg addressed the elephant in the room.

"I have my ways," Gigi stated before raising her hoodie to reveal her firm, tattooed, and pierced breasts.

"Damn!" Rolla blew out a whistle.

"Second that," Hogg stated and slapped high fives with Rolla.

"Be that as it may, we still need to holla at Young about all this," Deuce spoke as a true team captain, bypassing temptation.

Gianna tossed him her phone, and he caught it with a slight frown on his face. But once he saw that her screen displayed an ongoing call, he looked at her suspiciously before putting the phone on speaker.

"Speak on it," Deuce spoke to the person on the other end. "What's up, brozay?"

Young Mack's voice put them all in awe. "What's the hood with all this phantom shit, kid?" Deuce sounded offended that Young Mack didn't send them a heads up about Gigi.

"Stop being a drama king, Deuce." K-Dawg snatched the phone away from him.

"Dawg here. What's up, big homie?"

"My nigga," Young Mack said, then paused before continuing. "Look, I need y'all to check up on what Gianna's brother just put her up on, but be very careful and don't play no muthafuckin' games. Crush everything until we get our hands on the head honcho."

"We will do, big dawg," K-Dawg agreed.

"Loyalty, loyalty," Young Mack concluded.

"Loyalty, loyalty," the crew said in unison before the call ended.

***

Chandler couldn't believe his luck as he moved ahead of the two beautiful and sexy beasts that Mr. Mackmillions had set him up with. He was stepping in style, though he tried his best to keep it smooth. He still wanted to fit the profile of an associate of Mr. Mackmillions. His three-piece Tom Ford was put together nicely, and the Tom Ford Aviators over his eyes were tinted to match his coffee-colored Tom Ford leather loafers. The girls opted for Armani cologne, saying it was something about the expensive smell that made them horny. He laughed at their bluntness and how serious they were all at the same time.

His mind drifted back to the crazed sex sessions they experienced on the plane ride back into the United States. He hardly got any sleep without waking up to a mouth or wet pussy covering his dick. He smiled, thinking about how he'd just joined the mile-high club on a private jet Mr. Mackmillions paid to charter.

The sound of the elevator doors sliding open brought him back from his reverie. He stepped in and allowed the girls in after him. He quickly pressed the button for the doors to close, then pressed the button for their desired floor. Every wall in the compact elevator car reflected an image from its mirror, and Chandler couldn't help but stare at the girls on the ride up. Both of their faces were set in stone, but their beauty still dominated with their feminine features. He smiled as Queen popped her pink gum in the thick of the quietness on the elevator. Rastanya slowly turned and chastised her cousin in their native island tongue. Even though he didn't understand her, he could tell she meant business.

Moments later, the elevator stopped with a ding as the doors separated. This time, the trio switched formations. Queeny took the lead, Chandler followed close behind, and Rastanya brought up the rear. There was a receptionist desk right outside the elevators. Queeny stepped forward and, without making her presence known to the young blonde woman who was deep in conversation, hung up the phone as she reached over the desk.

Chandler smiled internally as the bottom halves of Queeny's juicy ass cheeks went on display. He heard the women exchange a few words, but couldn't make them out. His attention was snatched away by the sound of a very familiar voice coming from somewhere close. The voice was then followed by a second voice that he didn't recognize. Immense anger and hatred took over his heart as the face behind the voice rounded the corner, heading straight towards them.

As if sensing his uneasiness, Rastanya hooked their arms together and swiftly pulled him in the opposite direction in a hurried attempt to avoid detection by anyone who could identify the former special agent.

"Don't fuck this up," she spoke through clenched teeth as they rounded the corner behind Queeny, who looked graceful in her peach-colored Chanel skirt and top. Her silky tresses flowed as she stopped. Chandler looked her in the eyes and nodded silently.

"Hello, you must be Mr. Blackman," a jovial, professor-looking older white man greeted him as he stepped into the office door that Queeny politely held open for them.

"Yes, nice to meet you, Mr. Botingale," Chandler smiled while accepting the man's hand. Then, pulling him into a backwards embrace, he snapped his neck.

"Quick, Queeny, take his legs!" Rastanya ordered. The women moved the dead Mr. Botingale into the restroom in his office.

Chandler made haste with the sound device as he turned the dial on the dead man's safe. In less than five minutes, he had the safe wide open and was passing the confidential files to the girls. "Piece of cake," he thought to himself just before a light knock startled the trio. The door handle moved and in stepped the young blonde receptionist.

"Sorry to disturb you, Mr.—" The blonde stopped dead in her tracks when she noticed him still kneeling down in front of the office safe with its door wide open. "Wh—" She never got a chance to object. Without hesitation, Queeny swung a sharp left and chopped the woman in the throat. Rastanya followed with a powerful kick to the woman's right knee, which caved in gruesomely at a backward angle. Queeny then sprung into the air, clasped both legs around the woman's neck, and swung backwards, taking the woman down with a loud grunt. She then twisted hard with her hips and legs, snapping the woman's neck with a loud pop.

"We must move now!" Rastanya voiced. But they all knew they had to wipe the office clean before doing so, to get rid of any trace of them ever being there.

Chapter 7

Ashton sighed heavily once he parked his new 2021 Corvette Stingray convertible in the driveway of his sister's crib. Coming here always made him feel uneasy because he could never accept his sister's husband as a brother, not with all the trouble he'd caused for Young Mack and his family. He was aware that bodies had fallen on both sides, but he could never go against his closest friend, so accepting his sister's husband would never happen. He could never get used to being so close to the enemy, and it was the reason why he didn't frequent their home, no matter how close he and his twin sister were with each other. That, and it made him feel the burn of betrayal deep inside himself because he knew and always would know where the enemy laid his head, but to protect his sister, he could never divulge that information. He felt a great deal of pride in honoring his sworn secrecy to keep his sister safe.

Safe as he kept her, it never made him feel that same security while being so in reach of the sworn enemy of his best friend. Hell, he was even aware of their inevitable war being about his sister in the first place. He never overlooked her role in the whole of things.

Snapping from his own thoughts, he shook his head as he picked up his phone and sent her a text letting her know he was outside. Minutes later, his eyes trained in on a lone figure standing in the doorway of the massive ten-bedroom, ten-bathroom estate his sister had picked out for herself and her husband.

"Here we go," Ash let out a deep, dark cloud of exotic smoke before stepping out of his white-on-white Stingray that was customized, sitting on twenty-four-inch Forgies.

"Nice wheels," Gurdo said as Ashton made his way up to the front door.

"Surely can't compare to nothing in your garage," Ashton said, shooting him a fake smile.

"It's still nice though. By the way, it's good to see you. How's your friend?" Gurdo's voice took on a different tone when he asked the last question.

"Don't know right now because I haven't talked to him in a few weeks," Ashton lied.

"Yeah, I bet." Gurdo then chuckled as he watched his wife's twin brother walk past him and into their home. Even with their distaste so evident for each other, they tolerated one another for the sake of pleasing Ambrea.

"Same shit he says when he asks about you," Ashton pointed out as he grilled Gurdo once he stopped in the home's incredible foyer.

"Loyalty goes a long way in life, Ash."

"Easy for you to say when you don't have to look into the eyes of your best friend and act as if you don't know where the guy who tried to kill him and his mom along with his fiancée, lays his head." Ashton hated the queasy feeling he got being around Gurdo. He felt as if a sword was being sawed in and out of his stomach.

"Damn, I'm almost impressed with you. You are far from the shy little game-crazy boy I met years ago, and I am almost honored that you know how to keep your mouth shut," Gurdo snickered.

"But we both know why you won't disclose certain information, don't we?" Ashton followed Gurdo's eyes and met with his smiling sister as she descended the stairs down to them.

"Hi, twin. I'm glad you could spare the time to kick it with me for a spell."

"You already know I'll always come when you need me," Ashton pulled his sister in for a tight embrace. He could feel how tight she hugged him back and was surprised to feel a tremble in her arms.

"Well, I guess I'll leave the two of you to it then," Gurdo said, doing his damnedest to not show his hatred for his wife's brother.

"Thanks, baby. I really gotta talk to him about something that may rock his world, and I'm sure he won't want you to see him crying," Ambrea joked as she playfully punched her twin brother in his arm. Ashton just smiled and hugged her again. Unbeknownst to Gurdo, he already knew the news his sister supposedly had for him and the issue she needed his help with.

"Of course, love. I have to meet with Daniel in half an hour anyway. I might as well let him know that I'm on the way over while you have time to speak with your brother." Unbeknownst to her, Gurdo switched his plan to meet up with Daniel elsewhere instead of there at their home.

"I love you," Ambrea moved out of her brother's arms and into those of her husband's. She whispered her congrats, and it brought about a sincere smile to his face before he took the opportunity to kiss his beautiful wife before leaving their presence.

"You need to call him," Ashton broke the deep silence once he and his sister were tucked away in one of the home's many bedrooms.

"How can I after all that's happened?" She recognized the sting of the decision to come clean to Gurdo about the affair she had been having with Young Mack for years. She was also aware of the attempt on his life and the threat her husband caused to the lives of his loved ones. Everything came to the open after she witnessed Young Mack infiltrate their old home in a murderous rage and nearly killed them.

After all that had happened, she just didn't know how to open a conversation with him, knowing how betrayed he must've felt.

"Somehow, some way, you gotta let him in on what's going on with you. Just think about it for a second. You're pregnant, and let's just say that the baby is Gurdo's seed, okay, cool. Life goes on as normal, no problem. But if it turns out Young is the father, how do you think your husband will view that child?" Ashton gave it to her straight, no chaser.

"My niece or nephew deserves a life of peace and love, not hatred and war. Because I have a real good feeling that your husband would probably use this child as a poker chip against him."

"Damn, I don't need to be stressed out this early. I know it can't be good for the baby," Ambrea sighed as she reached out for her brother to embrace her.

"We ain't stressing at all, we just got some hard decisions to make, and soon," Ashton said as he wrapped his sister up in his arms and massaged her scalp.

"I love it when you do that," she giggled.

"Don't I know it, you always have," he smiled, knowing he had brought a bit of peace to his sister's world.

"Can you talk to him for me?"

"Huh?"

"Young Mack. You do know that you could talk to him for me and kinda explain everything and get a meeting set up between us, if all goes well with your talk."

"I'm not sure if that's the best way. It should be you that talks to him," Ash appealed.

"Well, I'm glad that you've never known how to turn me down, twin, because I don't know what I'd do without your help," she smiled, knowing he would never resist her.

"I'll get straight on it once I leave here," he gave in. "I love you."

"I love you too. Now I gotta get out of here if I'm going to catch him before he takes flight back into the states."

"Back into the States?" Ambrea questioned.

"Yeah, my niece or nephew will have a boss for a father either way," Ash smiled.

"He's really doing good for himself, isn't he?"

"He really is, and he's making it good for all of us to eat just as well," Ashton replied before starting his Vette from his key fob as they stood in the front door.

"Damn, that's a pretty ass car," his sister told him.

"Thanks to Young and the rest of the crew, it's just a little plaything for the time being," he laughed after kissing her cheek then jumping in behind the wheel of his vert.

"Thank you for this," Ambrea sincerely stated.

"You're more than welcome. I love you."

"I love you more."

Ashton pulled away from his sister's crib on a mission to get to Young Mack and give him the news that would possibly change his life and everyone's around him. He expertly held the wheel with his left hand while he removed his phone from his pocket with his right. After glancing at the screen, he saw the missed calls from a few women he frequented, but he quickly chose to bypass them in search of Young Mack's direct line. The phone rang four times before the automated voicemail picked up. He left him an urgent message telling him to get up with him as soon as possible.

His phone buzzed, and his car's Bluetooth took over just as he reached a red light before he was to hop on Interstate 10. He knew it was Young Mack calling back by the sound of Money Bagg Yo blaring as his ringtone. He briefly glanced down to accept the call, and that's when everything changed in his world.

BOOM!

The impact from the crash knocked Ash out cold, so he never felt himself being dragged from the wreckage and laid inside the heavy-duty diesel van that sped away from the scene like a blur in the night.

***

Gurdo sat demonically still, angered to the max after receiving the news about a huge shipment of his pure kilos being hijacked before the haul could even leave Mexico. He was beyond pissed that his drugs were missing and none of his crew of transporters had been found. He and Daniel both knew it could only be those damn Valdez clowns and Young Mack biting them in the ass again like some blood-sucking arachnids. The mere thought of such a great loss to foes he deemed so much lesser than him really did piss him off something serious.

That was the reason he was so happy to know that his disloyal-ass wife would be calling her twin brother over to join them. His mind immediately began to plot out of anger and hatred, so he phoned Daniel, who was more than eager to kidnap Ashton. Now, sitting inside one of their many small warehouses, Gurdo stared deathly at one of their nemesis' close friends. He didn't give a damn what his ties to his wife were.

"Wake him up," Gurdo spoke, barely above a whisper in the dead silence of the warehouse. Two men were present, and neither hesitated to grab Ashton. He couldn't wait to get his hands on their enemy, but he knew better than to jump the gun and waited for his boss's order. With that given, he stepped before Ashton and delivered a monstrous blow across his face. The sound and impact of the blow woke Ash immediately. His vision was blurred for a moment, but the dim light in the darkened warehouse aided his eyes to gain focus.

"Wh-what the fu-fuck!" Ashton stumbled with his words. The pain he was in forced a tear from his eye.

"Where is my coke?" Ashton wasn't sure if he was dreaming or just hearing him wrong, but he shook his head all the same, not having a clue about what he was talking about.

71

"What coke, I don't deal coke," Ashton replied.

Gurdo had a feeling it would go this way, so he took the time to gather Ashton's phone. But it pissed him off that the screen was broken, and he hadn't looked it over after his men gave it to him. "Fuck," he thought to himself before tossing the phone hard against the floor.

He jumped to his feet in anger and moved until he was standing behind Ashton. The sound of metal clinking alerted Ash and caused him to become even more nervous than he already was. "Gee, man, I don't know what you're talking about," he stammered.

"We'll see about that," was all Gurdo said before piercing Ash's right hand with a big metal hook. The screams coming from Ashton were deafening, and Daniel looked on in glee. He absolutely hated Young Mack and his entire crew of low-lifes; they were at the top of Daniel's shit list. Though proven to be very evasive when he was on their asses, he was even more eager to body every last one of them, and the Valdezes they'd deal with them last.

"I am going to ask you one more time, where is my coke?" Gurdo yelled, with spittle flying from his lips.

"I-I don't knoooow!" Ash cried out as sweat drenched his body. The pain he was in made him crave a kush-filled blunt and the comforts of his home.

The piercing of his left hand made him wish he could take a bullet to the dome. He screamed out until his voice went hoarse, and his stomach knotted up, giving him the sudden urge to throw up. And that's exactly what he did.

Knowing the drill all too well, Daniel moved and untied his wrists. Then he brought out the floor clamps that were molded into the thick concrete floor: metal chains with identical hooks at the ends, just like the devices Gurdo used on Ashton's hands.

"I find it amazing that your pussy-ass homeboy is still a fucking thorn in my damn side," Gurdo ranted, beyond the point of being persuaded. "Time after time, this scumbag has escaped death by the hands of my men, as if he's being protected by some guardian angel. Well, I'm about to show him that their asses aren't that guarded, and that I am the angel of death." The thoughts of all that coke and the lives of his most trusted runners laid in the balance, pushing him further past any point of reason.

"You know what though? I do believe that you don't know where to find my coke and my men . . ." Gurdo paused a minute to remove his black Tom Ford turtleneck. "But, you' re gonna tell me exactly where I can find and kill your bitch ass homeboy!" Gurdo shouted as he forcefully sent one of the floor mounted hooks through the tough leather and bone of Ashton's foot.

"Fuuuuuuck!" Ashton yelled before nearly passing out from all the pain.

Daniel slapped the shit out of him yet again to make sure he remained conscious for the moment. He hadn't expected for his best friend and boss to be putting in the actual work himself. He had grown so used to keeping him away from the killing field, but the gruesome display of heartlessness before him showed him that his homie still had it in him.

"Location!" Gurdo asked in a fit of rage.

Ashton remained speechless, as he huffed and puffed, sobbing loudly through all the pain he was feeling. He now felt dizzy and light-headed from the rapid blood loss, but it didn't stop him from operating on a righteous wavelength.

"Fuck you, Gurdo! You're gonna kill me regardless. I can already feel my death right now, and I haven't done a fuckin' thing but remain loyal to my crew and my sister. I know I ain't making it out of here, so fuck it, bitch boy, one and rock me because I choose loyalty, pussy!" Tears rushed from Ashton's eyes, soaking his face more than his sweat already had. He had never felt he would die in a fucking warehouse, chained to the floor and ceiling rafters. But, fuck it, if it had to be this way, then he knew he'd rather go out in glory than bitch up and turn pussy on the ones he loved most.

"Fuck me! Ain't that a bitch, no fuel for you, pussy!" Gurdo growled as he stabbed the remaining hook into Ashton's other foot, then spitting on him. "Up!" Gurdo shouted his order in Spanish, and his men obeyed.

Suddenly, the plangent buzz of a chainsaw could be heard coming to life. Moments later, Ashton's cries became deafening once again as his body was being pulled to the limits by the hooks grotesquely protruding from his swollen hands towards the ceiling. The tremendous amount of pain caused him to fall momentarily unconscious. A very sudden sleep that was short-lived. He was forcefully awakened by the bulldozing tugs on his flesh as it ripped at his abdomen by the chainsaw Daniel eagerly swiped across his body. Ashton watched with his own widened eyes as all of his innards spilled to the ground in full grotesque view of all who stood below him. He sighed his last breath, proud of the choice he made to die with dignity and as a real nigga. He just hoped that Young Mack would save his sister before she too became another pawn in Gurdo's wicked game of 'Capture the King'.

***

"You really think that he's in there?" K-Dawg asked as they watched the warehouse through the thick tall weeds from across the street.

"That's Daniel's Benz truck," Gianna pointed out after recognizing the bullet-proofed G-wagon.

"Yeah, that's the one that was following you for shit sure. Either way, I'll be satisfied if we get one or both of their bitch asses here tonight," Deuce stated as he checked for a round in the chamber of his MP5K sub-machine gun. He had two extra sixty-round drums attached to his waist so he was definitely ready to bring it to their enemies one way or another.

"Fuck it, let's move." K-Dawg motioned for Rolla and Hogg to move towards the warehouse at a steady pace.

The piercing sound of someone screaming slowed their approach a bit, but still, they moved on. Once they made it to the grounds of the warehouse, two guards rounded the corner and Gigi dropped them both with her silenced Sigma .40cal handguns. She also carried a selection of throwing knives but there was no way for her to reach them without allowing the guards time to alert any others that may be around the corner.

"Good shit, ma!" K-Dawg whispered with a wink and Gianna nodded, accepting his approval.

They continued around the corner from which the guards had come with Gianna leading and K-Dawg on her heels. The others fell in line one behind the other with Rolla bringing up the rear. The undeniable sounds of a gas-powered chainsaw could be heard as the crew neared the side entrance of the warehouse. Gianna soon paused and suggested they split into groups to avoid all being detected at once. She also felt that it would stop anyone from escaping without first coming through them. K-Dawg motioned that he'd stick with Gigi and that the three of them should take up the other side.

They all agreed and were once again on the move. Gianna could definitely smell the unforgettable smell of death as she continued forward with one handgun leading the way and the other stationed beneath it. K-Dawg was amazed at her agility and wondered where she'd gained her killer instinct. Gigi paused again as they neared an opening still surrounded by a sea of crates and boxes on both sides of them. Once she had a clear visual of the warehouse's main floor, the scene made her eyes mist over and bulge in disbelief. The slackening of her body alerted K-Dawg, and he immediately knew something bad had happened. Moving up behind her, he could clearly see over her head and onto the main floor of the warehouse. She tried pushing her body back into his body to remind him to keep his emotions in check, but as she looked back over her shoulder, she could see the pain and hurt in his eyes.

She silently shared his pain and knew that this would be very sad news to the others as well once they entered the warehouse. With everything that she knew he was feeling, she needed him to focus further into the area and see what she saw, so she signaled for him to scan the area, and he complied. Once his eyes locked on the figures they so sought after, the beast in him could no longer be contained. He kneeled using his right knee for balance as he trained his sights on Gurdo's temple as he stood conversing with his men as if Ashton, his wife's twin brother, wasn't hanging there lifeless.

A commotion sounded on the far side of the warehouse and got the men's attention. The startled jerking reflex on Gurdo's behalf saved his life. The thunderous roaring rounds from K-Dawg's golden Draco pistol erupted throughout the warehouse seconds later. The noisy three-round burst rattled the reinforced wall just inches beside the place where Gurdo once stood, then all hell broke loose.

Gunfire echoed from both sides, and bodies dropped while the rest of Gurdo's men moved close to protect him. Daniel dove for cover and luckily found his men fighting for position just yards away with the intruders. He upped his .45 handgun and sent round after round into the back of one of their attackers with a sinister grin on his face. A shot to the back of the head finished the struggle for good, and Daniel shouted for his worker to follow him. They quickly made a dash into a storage room that housed an exit door. After making it outside, his truck pulled up within yards of them, and they made a quick dash once again but not without some raging heat being sent in their direction. Daniel slightly paused as Roseman went down after taking a few rounds in the back courtesy of Gianna's marksmanship. Their eyes locked intensely for only a brief second before more shots threatened to take his life, pushing him forward and into the safe confines of his luxury tank of a vehicle.

Gianna, K-Dawg, and Deuce continued to send shots at the fleeing vehicle but it was of no use. Daniel and Gurdo had escaped, snaking their way through their grasps only inches away from certain death. The secludedness of the warehouse made it safe to say that there would be no police presence in the near future for them to flee from, so the trio made their way back inside after each putting some hot shit inside of every downed victim of their attack outside to ensure that death was final for them all. They were so focused on the task at hand that they never spotted the dark set of eyes watching their every move.

After making it back inside the warehouse, they all stopped in fear before rushing towards Rolla as he solemnly rocked back and forth with Hogg's lifeless body in his arms. Blood soaked his clothes, but he was numb to it all. After being knocked unconscious and slightly coming to as Hogg was being gunned down, he just wasn't feeling anything at the moment.

"Rolla, are you hit?" Deuce asked as he searched the young hitta's body for gunshot wounds.

"Somebody snuck up from behind and hit me over the head," Rolla sniffed before continuing, "I came to just as Brody was getting slammed in the back with shots as he tussled with one of the Mexican mufuckas over his weapon. Had to be the mufucka that snuck up on me from behind."

"Damn, we just lost two in one night. Young gone flip!" Deuce couldn't stand seeing his little homie stretched out leaking his brain. He put a hand under Rolla's armpit, and K-Dawg followed suit from the other side as they lifted him to his feet.

Rolla softly laid Hogg's limp body to the earth before looking up to see the sadistic way they'd killed poor Ashton. He shook his head while silently saying a prayer for their fallen homies.

"Killed his own wife's twin brother," Deuce spoke what they all thought in their minds. He had a habit of always doing that. "We gotta find something for their bodies because we ain't leaving them here like this," K-Dawg stated.

"I'll help you guys," Gigi offered then moved to lower Ash's body to the ground while the others searched the warehouse.

"Yo! Y'all come in here and look at what I found!" Rolla yelled out in excitement. He was in a small office once they all reached him and saw what had him so hyped at a time like this. "That gotta be like a milli in cash," Rolla eyeballed the loot.

"And the same in gold bars," K-Dawg concluded.

After taking care of their fallen and getting them secured inside the utility van, K-Dawg and Rolla made a trip back to get their new-found wealth. They couldn't believe their eyes once they made it back outside the warehouse.

"Damn, lil' man, I thought that you'd be better at watching y'all's asses than this," Rob stated cockily as he held Gianna roughly around her neck with his two tree-sized goons keeping their weapons trained on them. K-Dawg's eyes traveled to the ground where Deuce's body lay motionlessly still.

"He ain't dead, I kinda cut 'im for gee," Rob chuckled.

"What are you doing?" K-Dawg asked.

"I'm coming to take my bitch back home. I left the doggy door open while I was out," Rob mugged the hell outta Gigi.

"Oh, and I'ma need those bags there too," he added.

"Don't-" Rob punched Gigi in her ribs to shut her up. "Don't go against me, Gianna, I'd hate to have to kill you over some bullshit! Okay, now fellas, drop those bags." K-Dawg and Rolla did as they were told, and Rob's men retrieved the goods then sat them inside the trunk of Rob's Bentley.

"Thanks for my lick back," Rob stated with a crooked smile.

"What li-" K-Dawg was cut short by the violent blow to the chest that sent him to the ground in pain.

"That lick, mufucka!" Rob laughed as he pulled Gigi inside his whip. The brothers both kept their weapons locked in on Rolla as they climbed in and sped away, leaving a cloud of dust and debris in their wake.

"Disloyal ass pussy!" Rolla yelled and kicked dirt as they got away.

"Rolla!" K-Dawg yelled, and Rolla rushed to his side. "I'ma kill that pussy mufucka!" K-Dawg said, showcasing his vest.

Chapter 8

Cedrick Chandler stood out on the open balcony overlooking the beautifully vast Pacific Ocean on a hot day in the Hawaiian Islands' heat. The tranquility this view produced was a sure indication to him that God was really real, because nothing or no one other than the Almighty Himself could have created something so beautiful. Chandler was taking advantage of the peace and quiet, just looking back on his life and the events that led up to now. He started life out on the rougher side of things, growing up in Newark, New Jersey. He was just like every other black kid growing up in a house with four siblings and only a mother to provide for them. Times were hard back then, he told himself as he remembered having to run around all semester long with only one pair of kicks, and he'd be lucky to get the name-brand pair. Having one parent to provide and his mother already getting all the government assistance allowed for her household, the kids had to take turns getting the name-brand stuff.

Chandler laughed at those times because he could still hear their childish banter while capping on each other when it was their turn to receive the name-brand gear.

"Those ain't even that fresh," he could remember hearing one of his older sister's words as she hated on his fresh Bo Jackson sneakers.

"Nor is your hair, but punks ain't paying any attention because they too busy jocking my Bo Jackson's," he could hear his own words vividly and smiled back on the times.

He did good in school, actually, he'd done great for himself.

Growing up in the streets after junior high school would take a toll on any young soul, and Cedrick Chandler was no different. From ditching crack cocaine to boosting car audio systems, he had his hands in it. Anything from running muscle for the local numbers guy to bodying enemies from rival hoods, he was knee-deep into it all. After finishing up high school, he had a bright idea. He figured out how he could remain knee-deep in the streets without always having to look back over his shoulder for the laws. It was an easy decision for him, and he made it effortlessly. He joined the biggest gang in America, the police force. He kept his nose in the streets while doing his job the way he saw fit. Hell, he was licensed to do as he pleased so long as he first got approval from the higher-ups who saw no problem with a black man sliming another black man.

Chandler sighed as he thought about all the dirt he'd been a part of and wondered if the wrong done to him was God paying him back for all the havoc he wreaked in the lives of many others before he turned his life around and became a good cop, helping others over hurting them. A rage began to stir deep inside of him, and he began to squeeze the glass partition that separated him from the open air at sixteen floors up. Instantly, his face softened once he felt a pair of hands rub up his back then down before wrapping around his waist. Rastanya was outta bed and had begun to make breakfast for the three of them, which was different because normally they'd be too tired from their animal sex to physically stand and operate in the kitchen, so they'd almost always ordered room service.

He turned around to face the dark-skinned West Indies beauty who was the darker of the two. He silently stared into her hazel-green eyes, and the sight nearly pierced his soul, same as any other time he was ever in close quarters with her. He slowly leaned in and kissed her lips while running his hands through the opening of her silk robe to tease her succulent nipples. Ever since he'd been with the girls doing Mackmillion's wishes, he had not had a major urge to indulge in his favorite pastime, heroin.

Rastanya felt lucky to be in the arms of such a sensual and strong man. Being in the line of work her and her cousin, Queenie, were in, men tended to be a lot worse off than that of the man whose arms she felt so comfortable in.

"You try ta take me breath away, nah?" Rastanya's accent normally always came out when she got excited sexually, and he loved it.

"I don't wanna take it away. I want to give you breath to live and to hold on to for when the time comes that we will have to separate, you'll never be able to forget me," he said.

"Deep," Rastanya blushed at his sincerity.

"That goes for the both of you. You girls deserve someone that understands you like I do." He squeezed her body close to his and cupped her juicy ass cheeks as he again stuffed his tongue down her throat.

"Whew! Bedroom, now!" she ordered, and he made his way inside, removing the pair of Burberry linen shorts and briefs he had on.

His dick was already bricked by the time they made it to the master bedroom of their suite where Queeny was still sleeping soundly without a thread of a piece of fabric on her voluptuous body. Seeing her laying there in the king-sized bed with her ass protruding so sexually made his dick jump up and slap his stomach in arousal. Rastanya purred in his ear as she snaked her hands around his waist and took hold of his thick meat before sliding both hands back and forth over his length repeatedly while he never took his eyes off of her cousin's sleeping form.

After his dick accumulated enough pre-come fluids and moans could be heard escaping his throat, Rastanya came around and kissed his lips before kissing her way down to his raging hardness. Not one to play many games, she went straight to work deep-throating as much of him as she possibly could. It didn't take long for him to develop a rhythm while humping faster, filling and unfilling her throat. She was definitely a beast, just like Queeny when it came to the head game. They had to be equally talented. The euphoric feeling was too much for him, and he neared his peak mighty quickly and soon decided to deposit his first load down her throat.

"I'm coming, ma! Swallow that shit for me!" Chandler moaned in absolute pleasure as his joy rushed from deep within him and into her mouth. "Damn, ma, get up and bend yo sexy ass over. I gotta beat this shit before you burn breakfast," he ordered, and she obliged.

Still hard, he sunk deep into the furthest depths of her tunnel with a forceful first stroke. Her pussy was so wet that her juices were splashing out every time he slammed into her from the back. "Pussy so tight and wet!"

"Yesssss-sssss, fuck me just like that! Don't you stop, ya hear me! Don't you stop!"

"Fuckkkk!" Chandler growled as he stroked deep and forceful with the sound of their skin slapping together when his hips met her meaty ass cheeks. His excitement heightened once he saw that Queeny had awakened from the sounds of their sex session. She was all thirty-twos as she watched on as he fucked the shit outta her cousin. Seeing the both of them going at it live caused her pussy to pulse and her clit throbbed, and in a second, she had begun to rub her shaved pussy.

"Break her in back door," Queeny stated while exposing her pink inside with her forefinger and middle finger.

"Yes, do it! I'm ready, do it! You still owe me for it last time!" Rastanya felt empty when he pulled out and used the head of his dick to lube her up back there. Her juices were so thick that he soon had her lubed up and slowly eased his way into her tight hole inch by inch until he had over half of his muscle inside of her.

"Ohhhh, shit, don't you dare stop now," Rastanya growled through the pain mixed with something way more pleasurable than she'd ever experienced.

"I gotta get it all in there, ma, relax a bit for me and hold tight," he stated before he began to drill her. "Aww-shit, so damn tight!"

"Ahhhh-shittt-he's killing me! Queeny, it hurt so good!"

Rastanya screamed as her climax exploded and caused her body to shake and tremble.

"She's hooked now, ohhh God, I'm coming too-shhhhit! Fuck her harder!" Queeny demanded as she slapped her super-wet pussy and manipulated her clit, coming so hard her eyes rolled to the back of her head.

"Yes! Yes! Yes-uhh hmmm, I'm coming again so fast-ssshit!"

Rastanya's screams mixed with Chandler's grunts and moans as he released a hefty load of semen deep inside of her rectum.

"Ummmmm! A tri-max, I like that," Queeny giggled while sucking her own juices from her fingers.

"You're right, I'm hooked," Rastanya blurted out between breaths.

"I told you," they both laughed as they got up on wobbly legs and headed into the master shower.

"Damn," Cedrick Chandler said to himself as he thought about how lucky he was to have those two at his side. His life had been spun in a whole three-sixty in the blink of an eye, and now he wasn't even sure if he missed his old life anymore. He hadn't had this much intimate excitement since he was running wild in the crooked streets of New Jersey.

His thoughts were soon interrupted by the constant vibrations of his phone. He hadn't even realized that he'd set the ringer to vibrate, then he thought maybe one of the girls did it so as to not allow it to wake them from their much-needed rest. He then wondered how many calls he'd missed so far.

"Long time no hear from," he stated once he identified the caller then took the call.

"Conversing should be held to a minimum for us, Cedrick. There's just too much at stake here," Mackmillions replied.

"Say less, so what's on your mind?"

"Just wanted to check up on you and the girls. How's everything going with y'all?"

"Ah, shit, everything's fine on this end."

"They wearing your ass out, aren't they?" Mackmillions interrupted him, laughing.

"Damn, jeez! These lil' women are demons," Chandler whispered with a chuckle. "But I'm much grateful for that unique distraction though. You know I haven't had the urge to . . . you know . . ." he trailed off.

"You're more than welcome, but remember that all that you're doing is to win your life back from the ones that destroyed it," Mackmillions assured. "And you'll be well compensated, no worries there either."

"Yeah, I get it," Chandler replied.

"Good, now take care," Mackmillions said.

"Your bath is ready," Chandler heard Rastanya say. Mackmillions caught her voice from his end of the line, laughing before hanging up.

Rastanya smiled, and Chandler loved the dimples in both of her cheeks. It was hard not to notice them even with her business-first attitude. She always kept a serious look on besides in bed where she allowed him to dominate her.

He smiled once he entered the bathroom and saw Queeny smiling seductively while sitting on the edge of the huge fountain tub awaiting his presence.

"Queeny, no funny business, we have work to do," Rastanya's mode had changed as she stood there in the door of the bathroom with her phone clutched in her hands.

"Come, I must wash you quickly, we're needed," Queeny waved him over to her as she too climbed down and into the hot bath along with him.

***

Young Mack stood in astonishment as he watched kilo after kilo of coke being removed from the underground passage. Gurdo and his cartel family had hidden out in the middle of dry desert land close to the Texas border wall. He'd never seen this much coke in his young life, and the huge profit margins were obvious. Finding the drugs was bittersweet for Young Mack and the Valdez family as well. Yes, the drugs meant wealth, but they still couldn't get their hands on the infamous kingpin.

"You look happy," Stephanie Valdez stated as she approached him in the wide-open desert.

"A win is a win, I guess." Young Mack wasn't sure how he truly felt with all that was going on in his life. He also couldn't understand how he'd missed Ashton's call, and the message only made him overthink things now that Ashton wasn't answering any of his calls. He brushed it off as nothing and continued to take care of the business at hand until he could get settled and search for answers.

"You really do want his head as much as we do, don't you?" Stephanie could feel his hatred for their rival.

"If not more. He crossed the line when he almost killed my mother and fiancée, and for that, he has to go. He can no longer be a threat to me, my family, or you and yours if he's dead." Young Mack couldn't wait to get his hands on Gurdo and Daniel. Thinking about that reminded him that he needed to check on the fellas as soon as possible.

"Patience, sweetheart. We might not have to look so hard now with this," Stephanie turned and watched as her brothers directed their men on handling the cocaine.

Stephanie backed up until she could feel her body pressing against Young Mack, who gently wrapped his arms around her. He couldn't imagine the things going through her strong mind. He had always thought her to be as clever as a fox and a hunting feline combined in one. She was powerful yet sensual, wealthy yet alone, and Young Mack couldn't understand why such a dynamic woman her age wasn't married with children. Maybe it was the lifestyle. He made a mental note to ask more about her life and past the next time they were alone.

The ride back to the Valdezes' warehouse was bumpy, but Young Mack kept his eyes peeled through the vast darkness of the night.

Ping! Ping! Thew! Thew! Thew!

"Stop the truck! Men, get in position! We have shooters on our asses! Hurry! Hurry!" Stephanie shouted orders to her men in Spanish, also broadcasting over the high-frequency radios she and her brothers communicated on.

Young Mack could see the hail of tracer rounds being sent their way as men approached quickly on ATVs and dirt bikes, firing away. Stephanie knew this could possibly happen and was glad she chose to use their armored cargo trucks for this mission.

"Kill every one of those bitches!" Stephanie yelled viciously in her native tongue as she produced an M4 carbine with an M203 grenade launcher. "Please don't leave this truck, this shouldn't take us long!" Stephanie pleaded with Young Mack.

"Hell no! If I'm staying here, then so are you, but if not, you better strap me up because I'm coming with you!"

"My men and I know these deserts, and we don't need help to see in the dark. I promise this won't take long. Don't leave this truck. It's double-paneled with the lightest Kevlar material ever made, so you're safe here. There's a weapon beneath your seat – strap up and hold tight!" And with that, Stephanie disappeared into the tumultuous darkness of the night.

Young Mack quickly moved from the bench-like seat and squatted to retrieve the weapon from underneath it. He nodded his head in approval of the balanced weight of the weapon once he unstrapped it and brought it before his eyes. It was an H&K G35 custom with a fifty-round drum magazine.

"I wish a motherfucker would!" Young Mack whistled and got the attention of the driver.

"What?" the Mexican man asked, hoping he hadn't missed an order while keeping his eyes focused on the action outside of the vehicle.

"Just thinking out loud! Where the fuck is the night vision gear!" Young Mack yelled out over the rapid gunfire.

"Here!" the driver yelled back and tossed him a pair of night vision glasses the Valdez family always supplied their drivers with.

Young Mack strapped himself up with the night vision glasses and looked out into the night. He could see Stephanie and her men strategically lined up side by side in a kneeling and standing pattern. Two of her men were down, but the heavy fire they were once under had dwindled to about two relentless shooters who seemed to be backing further and further away with each second.

"Let's go! Move out! Grab our men!" Stephanie shouted once their opposition ceased firing. She knew they were retreating and would soon return with reinforcements. They couldn't be there when that happened.

"Are you okay?" she asked Young Mack once they were all back inside the vehicle and moving again.

"I should be the one asking you that question," he smiled at her bravery.

"But I asked you, and I'm serious. Are you okay?" Stephanie insisted, clear concern lacing her voice.

Young Mack held back his words for a moment before moving in and capturing her lips. He soon found her tongue with his own. "Wooow, you're soaking my panties. I love when you handle me like that!"

"Tonight we finish what you've always started," Young Mack stated, knowing he couldn't go another night without having her in his bed.

"Can't wait," Stephanie smiled before pecking him on the lips.

***

K-Dawg, Rolla, and Deuce made silent prayers for their fallen soldiers as their bodies lay on the cold stainless tables in the back of Pruitt and Pruitt's funeral home. Young Mack couldn't find any words to describe the pain he felt from losing two of his closest homies. It was the first time they'd lost anyone since forming as a team, and damn did it hurt like a motherfucker. It nearly took an entire hour before anyone said anything as they silently mourned their friends.

"We gotta make them pay!" Deuce stated, echoing what everyone else was thinking.

"Most definitely! And I'm straight punishing that fuck nigga Rob and his two tall bitches!" K-Dawg said.

Rolla was still too emotional to speak, but a deep hatred had formed in his heart over the past twenty-four hours. He had an urge to kill, but not just to kill – he had an urge to kill some shit in the most gruesome and grimmest fashion ever. Ashton and Hogg were amongst the youngest of their crew, and now they were both gone. It only left him, the youngest, feeling betrayed and robbed of his comrades.

Young Mack sat silently as he observed Ashton's bruised and mangled body. He thought about all they'd been through coming up together. He then thought about all the pain and harm Ashton experienced before his death and knew that he died protecting him and everything he'd built for them. Ambrea snuck into his mind as he thought about delivering the news to their mother as well as helping with all the arrangements. The mere thought of it all caused a tear to escape his eye, and he didn't bother wiping it away – it had earned its way into the world.

"Set up a meeting with all of our people. I want everyone who's anyone on deck for this one because we're about to change the game on this fuck nigga Gurdo. I got a surprise for the team and will be there before the sun sets." Young Mack ended their FaceTime with a heavy heart and a burning desire to avenge his friends' deaths. "Siri, call Gator!"

Chapter 9

The Law Offices of Gama and Berdstein sat in the center of the highly populated Hawaiian capital, Honolulu. This mainstream law firm worked for all of Hawaii's upper echelon and served as a base for the best and up-and-coming lawyers and paraprofessionals, with clients ranging all over the island. Cedric Chandler was surprised by the ambience of the building for such a thriving and prestigious place of business.

Stepping out of the Uber, he checked his attire in the window before passing the driver a crisp hundred-dollar bill. He turned, silently taking in the whole scene around him. Like everywhere else in the famous tourist destination, the streets were vibrant and buzzing with people. Looking first to his left, he saw at a short distance that the girls had already arrived, parked in a rented M3 BMW. He winked in their direction before striding into the prestigious law firm.

"Hi, welcome to Gama and Berdstein. How may I be of assistance to you this afternoon?" A young, beautiful woman with a dark tan spoke as he approached the front desk in the lobby.

"Afternoon, gorgeous," Cedric spoke as he eyed the honey-eyed beauty. "I'm here to speak with Ms. Berdstein."

"Do you have an appointment, sir?" she asked while staring back into his eyes.

"Yes, check the itinerary for a Mr. Childs," he smiled.

"Ah, yes, Mr. Childs. I see here that your appointment is set for one-thirty p.m. Okay, Ms. Berdstein should be back from her lunch break in about ten minutes, sir."

Cedric casually checked the time on his expensive IWC wristwatch then smiled at the beautiful woman seated behind the desk before moving to the comfortable cushioned chairs in the lobby's waiting area. The two almost never took their eyes away from each other, and he was sure he could bed her under different circumstances. Being brought up in law enforcement had taught him the patience of a monk, so ten minutes was nothing to him and definitely not a long wait for his targets.

He passed the time reading through Kiplinger's magazine on finances. Carefully setting it down, he spotted a short, petite blonde woman dressed in a form-fitting pinstriped business suit enter the lobby, followed by a well-dressed, muscular guy. The blonde woman spoke quietly with the young beauty he'd taken the liberty of learning was named Shayell. They were both in laughter. Seconds later, both women looked over at him with radiant smiles bright enough to shake any normal man's equilibrium. But Cedric Chandler was far from normal, having seen his share of beautiful women clothed and unclothed. He generously returned their smiles with one of his own and quickly resumed the role of Mr. Maurice Childs.

"Hi, nice to meet you, Mr. Childs," Brenda Berdstein spoke once they met up in the middle of the lobby and shook hands.

"Likewise, Ms. Berdstein, but call me Maurice," he smiled, taking in her aging beauty. From afar, he could already tell she was a beautiful woman, not one equal to Shayell, but one of a woman older in age but close in clarity.

"Has anyone ever told you that you could pass for a famous actor? And, please call me Brenda," she caught his attempt at flirting with him and smiled her best smile, conscious of the fact that she had yet to release his hand.

"I've been told that a time or two but not enough to actually believe it to be true. Who knows, maybe after we discuss our business, you could bill me for the time it takes you to make me a believer," he replied.

"Make you a believer I shall, but who knows, maybe you'll be the one billing me," Brenda Berdstein replied with a sensual peep at the print that was totally evident in his tailored Armani slacks.

Before long, they were fucking like they'd known each other for a long time.

"Ahhhh! Yes, that's it, you big dick hunk, fuck the hell outta me! Oooooh-fuck me like you're mad at me!" Cedrick had her skirt pushed above her waist with one of her legs bent up on the desk while he stood behind her, pounding her through several cosmic climaxes.

"You love this black dick, don't you!" he asked before slapping her reddening ass cheeks one at a time. Brenda couldn't verbally respond as yet another orgasm rocked her to the core.

"Say it, bitch! Tell me you love this black dick," he now demanded while thrusting harder into her ocean, picturing her sexy assistant, Shayell, as he slammed her upper body down onto the desk.

"I love th-this bl-black diiiiick! Oh my god, you're killing my pussy!" Cedrick smiled at the irony of her last statement as he gripped the back of her neck with his left hand while pointing the business end of his silenced Sig.45 at the back of her head and squeezed the trigger twice.

Her body slumped in his hand, and he released her neck, which caused her head to hit the desk with a heavy thump. He removed himself from her essence, then tucked his condom-clad dick back into his expensive slacks before readjusting his designer belt. He wasn't sweating the fact that he hadn't yet come before relieving Berdstein of her life. He was sure that the girls would certainly finish him off later. Queeny and Rastanya silently entered the dead lawyer's office, both holding silenced handguns that matched the one he sat next to Brenda's leaking head on top of her desk. Both women smiled at the sight of the dead woman before taking in their accomplice's appearance.

"You were not supposed to fuck your target," Queeny shook her head in disbelief. Cedrick remained silent as he removed the USB chip from his inside breast pocket.

"At least he fucked the white bitch to death," Rastanya added, taking in the comical scene.

"Yeah, and we should have fucked Gama and that beefy-ass bodyguard to death too, right?" Queeny asked sarcastically, her face showing her distaste.

"It did cross my mind to at least make them eat our pussies at gunpoint," Rastanya replied, drawing a good laugh from Cedrick. She was normally the most serious of the two, and it was nice to see her humorous side.

***

Castro.

It wasn't even the fact that he ultimately made the caustic decision to betray a very close friend and good business associate that ate at his conscience. The fact that he knew it was the wrong decision to cast a stone in a war that wasn't his battle is what made him distrust himself for the first time ever. He was a firm believer that money wasn't the root of all evil. He was sure that humanity's greed over the monetary notes is what sparked ninety-nine percent of the evil associated with acquiring it. Yet, he fell into evil's constrictive grips when all that was promised from the fall of Mackentosh 'Mackmillions' Miller was dropped into his clutches before the thought to cross him ever entered into his mind. Yeah, that's certainly what got him.

"Yes," his deep baritone voice came alive as he answered.

"Have you been paying attention to all that's been happening on this side of the world?" the voice on the other end of the call spoke. The squeakiness of the voice immediately let him know who the caller was.

"Yes and no," Castro replied nonchalantly.

"What do you mean yes and no? You gotta be kidding me, right? Because this son of a bitch is on a silent but boisterous rampage, and you mean to tell me you're not bothered by this?"

"I never said I wasn't, Dick."

"I can't believe your attitude right now. What the hell are we gonna do now?" Dickerson was Castro's main man, brought up through an honest career in the United States Government, a Harvard graduate in law and criminal justice, born into a respectable family.

***

Mackmillions checked his phone as it vibrated on the nightstand inside the luxurious suite out in The United Arab Emirates. A smile spread across his face as he scanned the information taken from the dead lawyers of the last remaining three Realm members of the old.

"Hell hath no fury," he said aloud before placing his phone back on the nightstand. He felt his wife Sylvia stir a bit while pushing her naked backside into him invitingly. Instantly, his arousal grew with his hardening dick, and he wasted no time sliding into her garden.

Somewhere deep in the frozen mountain sides of the Southwest Peninsula, in Alaska, a phone rang, disturbing the wonderful solace of one of the most important and influential beings of the underworld and the leading secretary of the House of Representatives. Amir Castro-Pella, nothing short of the modern-day American gangster, had calculated moves early in his sixty-four years of living, gaining him worldwide fame and fortune in both the political world and in the belly of the streets in nearly twenty of the largest states and cities in America. Born a Houston, Texas

95

native, Castro, as he loved being referred to, had definitely made his mark on the world. It wasn't until later in his life, some decade and a half ago, that he stumbled over his own footing – something he'd never done in all of his life. Aiding in the highly publicized demise of one of the most notorious kingpins known to have blue-blooded American parents and the youngest of four children, Castro took a liking to the man. From the moment they first met at a party of mutual friends, he took him under his wing. But years later, after discovering the dark side of Jonathan Dickerson's life, Castro was disgusted and started to use him in every way possible, either with or against Dickerson's will. Just thinking about the sickening shit Dickerson and his buddies were into brought an acrid taste to Castro's mouth.

"I'm not yet sure what we can do, Dick. There is no way for us to link him to anything, and we're definitely not going down the muddy road again with this one because, as you can see, he certainly doesn't lay down too well. We definitely can't link ourselves to the deceased because that would bring about our own demises, which would also deliver our lives and the well-being of our families directly to him," Castro sighed from the revelation of the hard facts behind their situation with Mr. Mackmillions.

"Again, sir, what shall we do?" Dickerson's panicked voice was shaken, and Castro couldn't really blame him. Hell, they were both in over their legal limits with this situation.

"Give me some time to come up with a plan of action. As bad as things already are, we may end up having to make a deal with the devil himself."

"Hell, I'd be willing to kiss his red-hot ass for that matter if I had to," Dickerson said.

"Yeah, I know," Castro ended their call in deep thought. He already knew Mackmillions had obtained accurate information on both of them and their families. It made him want to shoot himself before the devil finally delivered his wrath, but he wasn't at all cowardly like Dickerson. He was a powerful man and had acknowledged that even he had overplayed his hand.

"What's it gonna take, Mack?" Castro thought to himself before making a much-needed phone call.

***

"So, you think it's cool to be out there sliding with the opps?" Gianna was so tired of Rob whining and complaining about her teaming up with Young Mack's crew to slide on Daniel and his boss's operation. She knew that Rob was missing the point of how deadly Daniel and his men were. If he knew better, they would be out searching for any leads to find Daniel and erase him for good. She knew exactly how dangerous and rich those motherfuckers were and thought it best that they try to get rid of them before they had all of them pushing up flowers. In her eyes, Daniel and his crew were the opps, not Young Mack and his men.

"You obviously don't get it," she sighed, frustrated that he surely wasn't about to let it rest.

"Don't get it? Fuck you mean I don't get it. Them niggas are all my enemies, and you're out there killing shit with 'em like shit righteous." Rob was heated. He couldn't for the life of him understand how this bitch thought she was in the right.

"Listen, Rob-baby, I love you, and all I admit to that, but you are not about to keep handling me like I'm some average bitch you're fucking," Gianna stood from the couch and made her way into the kitchen.

"Whatchu mean average bitch I'm fucking!" Rob yelled and followed her into the kitchen. "Bitch, you're the only one I'm fucking, for now anyway. Plus, I don't do average pussy." Rob slammed the refrigerator closed in her face.

Gianna's nostrils flared as she stared at him deathly in the eyes. Her heart rate slowed, and her temper rose just as it always did before she killed, but she hurried to calm herself, hoping he didn't catch the change in her body. But that wasn't the case.

"You wanna fly, Gigi?" he asked while removing his S&W .45 automatic from his Amiri jeans and placing it on the counter.

"I'm going to bed," she tried moving past him, but he had her exit blocked off.

"You big and bad, aren't you? Bitch wanna stand up to me since you've been rocking with them other niggas. Okay, I feel that, so I'm gonna do you the honor you think you deserve and shoot you a fair one, killa," Rob stated with venom before delivering a dazzling two-piece to her jaw and midriff.

Caught off guard by his savage blows, Gigi stumbled and fell to one knee, blood boiling as death made its way back into her dark eyes. She swiftly launched a right uppercut that connected with his nuts before leaping from the floor with a knee intended for his chin. Rob was in excruciating pain with water flooding his vision, but he caught her movements just in time to sidestep her attack. Fighting through the pain, he grabbed her around the throat and lifted her off her feet before slamming her down hard against the cold marble floor. The assault knocked the wind from her body and dazed her pretty good.

"Bitch! If you didn't wanna have a nigga's lil' ones, you could have just said that shit," Rob antagonized her before punching her hard in the eye. She screamed out in pain while covering her eye with both hands and rolling around on the floor. "Get yo' slow ass up and take it to the room before I snuff yo silly ass." Rob knew that he was wrong for putting his hands on her, but his hatred for Young Mack and his crew had brought his wrath against Gigi, and he just couldn't find it within himself not to be mad at her.

He shook his head as he watched her cry out in pain. Hell, he figured that she was lucky he didn't kill her for the shit she pulled. Still clutching his aching nuts with one hand, he made his way into the living room. Once he entered the room, he was surprised to see both of Gianna's brothers staring at him with what he assumed was anger. They were both disgusted with how he'd been treating Gianna, not solely because she was a woman, but because they both knew how deadly she was. More importantly, she had sworn her love and loyalty to him, and he was dragging her through the mud. They both knew that she would only restrain herself for so long before she couldn't hold back anymore.

"Fuck you two niggas on?" Rob questioned, placing his gun on his right thigh. There were no words passed between them.

Chapter 10

"Yo, Young, how you feeling?" K-Dawg stepped up to his best friend, still feeling hollow himself. He wanted to crush everything in sight over their dead soldiers, as it felt like they were on the losing end now that Hogg and Ashton were gone.

The funerals for both of their fallen soldiers were paid in full by Young Mack, and he wouldn't accept any help from family or friends. He stood as still as a gargoyle as he watched family and friends crowd the joint service. His mind was on one thing: completely destroying Gurdo on sight. He was hoping the man would play grieving brother-in-law, so he wouldn't have to keep looking for him. But the chance wouldn't come that day. He watched Ambrea and her mother exit the stretched Cadillac limo, holding each other, followed by the elderly men of their family.

"Shit got me messed up with anything that looks like those mu'fuckas, bruh!" Young Mack expressed through clenched teeth.

"Yeah, same here. You think that nigga ballsy enough to show up here?" K-Dawg asked while observing the large turnout.

"We would hope so, but I'm sure he has eyes around somewhere. Have some of our men rotate around the cemetery and report anything that looks outta place. I gotta go holla at Ash's mom real quick."

"Say less, I'm on it," K-Dawg replied before bumping fists with him and heading out to do as he was ordered.

"Tree, shadow me and have Sham watch over the service," Young Mack ordered. It had been some time now that he had Tree and his brother Sham out in the field with him, but today was one of those days they would be needed.

He casually moved toward the approaching women with his hands inside his designer slacks. The women were both dressed in black with gold accessories, and the tears that wet both of their faces brought about a set of his own. He quickly wiped them away as he got closer to them.

"Afternoon, Ms. Clark," he greeted Ashton's mother. She reached out and pulled him close, crying continuously on his shoulder. Ambrea stood silently and watched, wishing it could be her tucked safely inside his arms.

"I-I just c-can't believe my baby is gone," Ms. Clark sobbed heavily.

"Me either. I wish I could've been there to protect him. Hell, I should've been there."

"Young man, you hush with that talk. You cannot be everywhere at once, so don't go blaming yourself for what happened to him. You are not at fault here because when the Lord comes calling for us, there is nothing and no one that can stop Him. Ashton loved you, and you were always like the older son I never had. I love you for being such a good and true friend to my son."

"I love you too, and if there's anything I can do for you, don't hesitate to call me."

"Oh, there is something," Ms. Clark said, pulling him close again. "I want you to find whoever is responsible for this and do them ten times worse than they did my son, your brother." Her words shocked him, but he didn't show it.

"You gotta know I'm already on it," he replied.

"Mmm hmm, you better know I do. Okay, now let me go entertain all this family we got out here while you two talk. And I mean really talk." Young Mack caught how she looked over her shoulder when she said that last part and saw Ambrea nodding in agreement. Ms. Clark kissed his cheek before releasing him and left to be with the family and friends.

"So," Ambrea spoke up, breaking the silence they'd settled into for the first thirty yards as they walked shoulder to shoulder. She had taken notice of all the Hispanic muscle, as well as the strong Black men Young Mack had shadowing them as they trekked through the burial grounds at Greenlawn Memorial Park.

Snapping out of his deep thoughts about life and the lives of those around him, he found her simple question—her request for conversation—much more complicated than it should have been. It was clear to her he was going through a lot of changes.

"Aw, yeah, um—it's been a minute, right?" Young Mack fumbled with his words, something she knew he never did. She thought she was making him uncomfortable.

"It's been more than a minute," she shot back, her own mind becoming heavy with thoughts of the past year.

"Yeah, it has. So, how have you been—"

"Pregnant," Ambrea cut him off, and he stopped walking.

"Wow," Young Mack sighed, taken aback by her revelation. He spoke as if he were in a trance and now noticed she'd picked up a few pounds in good places.

"Yeah, found out a week ago. There I was thinking I was eating too much and being unhealthy." She shook her head with a nervous smile as she watched her feet make contact with the ground once they started walking again.

"How far along are you?" he asked curiously, though he wanted to ask a different question. He wasn't sure why he felt a way about her being pregnant, because their relationship was nothing more than a strong friendship that used to have benefits.

"Sixteen weeks." Damn if it didn't feel like she'd lifted a boulder off her shoulders after telling him her truth, but she knew that wasn't the big news. She wondered how he'd feel after she told him.

"Sixteen weeks?" Young Mack whispered to himself, hating the fact that she was pregnant by the same mu'fucka he swore he'd kill at the first opportunity. Surely, she wasn't aware her husband had killed her brother, but that did nothing to numb his anger. "Where is your husband, Bre?"

"Huh?"

"Gurdo. Where can I find him?" Young Mack reiterated.

"You're mad that I'm pregnant, aren't you?" she naively asked.

"Why would I be mad at a married woman's pregnancy? Some shit just ain't my business," he lied.

"You hate me, don't you? I make you uncomfortable," she followed up once things got quiet again.

"Hate you? For what would I hate you, Bre?"

"You feel like I betrayed you by not going against my husband for those crazy mufuckas you're definitely rocking with now."

"First off, I knew you wouldn't go against him because it's not in your character to do some shit like that—"

"What about him trying to kill you at your parents' home?"

"You knew about that?" Young Mack was perplexed after that revelation.

"Ash told me," she said. He calmed himself after hearing that.

"Well, if you didn't know before it happened, you couldn't have warned me, so I can't be mad at you about something out of your control." He looked to his left and saw Tree, then to his right where Steven kept pace, nodding at both of them.

"I guess you're right, but I hated him doing that to you and your family."

"Good news, ma. You know I gotta find this nigga and crush him for all that he's done." Young Mack cursed himself for coming on too strong, especially now that she was pregnant with that sucka's seed. Her silence let him know he'd stomped out his golden opportunity for an easy conclusion. "Bre, he killed Ash and my lil' gunna. Look over there where those piles of dirt are and see how we have to leave them. Tell me you don't feel any kind of rage about that. He killed your twin brother, and I need to find him and do him ten times as dirty as he did them."

"What? Why would you say he killed Ashton? I know you don't expect me to believe that one!" She nearly became frantic after hearing his accusation.

"My people stumbled upon one of their warehouses and had a shootout with them. Gurdo and Daniel escaped, but they left the homie Hogg lifeless. That's where they found your brother, chained to the ceiling and the floor. They tortured Ash before they killed him, and for that, there is no way I can offer a pass or let anyone slide."

"If you didn't see it with your own eyes, Mack, I don't wanna hear it coming from someone else's mouth." There, she stood her ground and let him know where her stance was.

"I can't say I'm not disgusted, but it's cool. I know what it is, considering all that's going on around us, but make no mistake—I'm going to end that nigga sooner or later."

"Were you going to kill me too, that time at the house?" she asked, almost cutting him off.

"I honestly don't know, and I can't say, because I've never been that way before that day," he confessed.

"It's just—you had this look in your eyes. It screamed death, and I was afraid of you, even in that safe room."

"I gotta crush them, Bre."

"So I've heard. Look, Mack, I'm not about to beat around the bush. This child growing inside of me has as strong a possibility of being yours as it does being his."

His mouth hung open as he looked from her eyes down to her growing belly. "Damn, I would've never thought—"

"Ashton was on his way to tell you everything, but as we can see, things didn't go as we planned." Young Mack couldn't stop thinking about the violations to his crew and knew they had to pay for that, straight up.

"Does he know?"

"Of course not, but I—"

"Don't you dare tell him that!" Young Mack startled her a bit by grabbing her wrist tightly. "Bre, he killed Ash, and I am certain of that no matter what your thoughts are about it. If you tell him your child could be mine, I'm sure he'll try to use you as a pawn to get to me, and that shit ain't fair because you won't give me the edge on him. Don't be his edge on me, Bre!" He stared into her eyes to make sure she got what he was saying before letting go of her wrist. She nodded her understanding, and they continued walking in silence.

"Daniel," Young Mack shot his shot.

"What about him?" she questioned.

"I need a definite location on him."

"Well, that's a different story because I don't like him, and even though it will hurt Gurdo, I'll do whatever I can on that, but nothing's promised because they are very private now since you've joined their enemy—and they know about our past."

"Just do what you can and stay safe while doing it," Young Mack kissed her cheek before taking her phone from her hand, placing his secured number in her recent calls, then wishing her well. "Keep me informed as much as possible," he said, pointing to her slightly bulging stomach.

***

"How do you suppose we get off all this merch?" Monsta asked as he, Rob, Gigi, and his big brother Pop stared at the pyramid of gold bars stacked on top of Rob's pool table in the entertainment room of his new home.

"I'm not exactly sure, but for shit sure, Ken will know what to do with 'em," Rob stated matter-of-factly.

"Yeah, Ken be with the shits," Pop agreed.

"Yeah, but I think you should holla at your mom," Gigi threw in for the women.

"What will my ol' lady know about moving gold bricks?" Rob looked at her side-eyed.

"Well, she was your father's wife most of her life, and she's the one who introduced you to KenKen in the first place. That, and she went to college to understand business and finances, so I think she would have a safe way to make some moves. And she won't try to tap your pocket, which we can't say about KenKen," Gigi made her point.

"I'm sure they don't hold classes on gold, Gigi. You trippin', ma," Monsta laughed before taking a big pull from the blunt of exotic smoke he'd taken to selling.

"And I'm sure yo' big dumb ass ain't ever been in nobody's college either," Gigi rebutted, hating the fact that he always went against anything she threw in.

"How dumb you sound, girl? I'm always at the colleges. Shit, I got more hours in than most professors."

"Hell nawl, doing what?" That was Pop.

"Fuckin' bitches, nigga. That's straight-up physical education right there!" Monsta laughed, and Rob joined him, high as hell off Monsta's stash.

"Get a life," Gigi shot him the bird. "Seriously, your mom knows money and she's business savvy. I'm just saying you can get at dude first, but just make sure you don't sleep on your mom."

Rob definitely took in what she put out, even though he wouldn't admit it out loud. He was certainly gonna pull up on his mother to see what she could come up with or at least advise him on. In the meantime, he knew he had to prepare for war with Young Mack's crew after the stunt he pulled on them, but fuck it. He still couldn't believe how Gigi could go around pulling moves with anyone other than him and their crew.

"Pop, have you been on top of that situation we spoke on a few weeks ago?" Rob asked, hoping like hell that he had.

"Absolutely, and so far we got us a team of about twenty hittas. Some certified head bustas, hustlers, and murder-for-hire, real street niggas," Pop smiled before pulling on the blunt he'd gotten from his brother.

Rob's nostrils flared as the thought of becoming so powerful as to have over twenty killas under his reign. Smoke slowly came from his nose, and with his eyes so red, it made him look evil in a demonic kind of way.

"Here, take this and get y'all right," Rob picked up, then tossed Pop a duffle bag with three hundred thousand inside. "Let them niggas know they rockin' with us now, and for them to drop any affiliations they had before us. They're Bag Boys now, and it's gonna be work for everybody." Pop just smiled as he looked inside the bag at all the bundles of dead faces.

"In case you're wondering, that's three honey buns in that bag. Fifty a piece for you two, and ten a piece for the hittas."

"Damn, nice looking!" Monsta rubbed his hands together. "Y'all definitely deserve it, and there will be more for you two once we fence this gold."

"That's what's up," Pop said, closing the duffle and holding it over his shoulder.

"Alright now, y'all get to it while I holla at Gianna for a minute," Rob stated.

"Yeah, no doubt," Monsta replied dryly.

"I'll get everything right and have everyone ready to meet with you as soon as you make that call," Pop said as he exited the room.

"I like the sound of that!" Rob replied, keeping his eyes trained on Gigi in her form-fitting Dior dress and matching monogram slippers.

"You know I should kick yo' ass some more for that stunt you pulled," Rob smiled as he eased his way into her face. Gigi remained silent while studying his face. "That was some crazy shit you did, but all is forgiven because of this." Rob picked up one of the gold bars and waved it in her face.

"It wasn't about that. We went there to kill Daniel and hoped to get Gurdo at the same time, as I figured we were both working together to do. I really don't see the big deal." Her face frowned because she felt he was being overdramatic. She was a trained and skilled killer, not some certified housewife who needed to follow around in his shadow.

"Bitch! Did you forget that Young killed my pops?" Rob yelled at her.

"You never said he did that, you only mentioned that his name came up in some video you saw."

"Same shit! Guilty by association and circumstances, just like the courts do a mufucka." Rob chuckled a little before becoming serious again. "Don't make me crush you, Gigi. You belong to me. Fuck everything and everyone else, even yo' brother."

Gianna wasn't moved by his claim on her, because she had never met a nigga that could tame her. Niggas were too emotional and way too jealous to keep her attention solely on them, and Rob was no different. Sure, she had some strong feelings for him, but that killer shit didn't live inside of him. He only killed when provoked in life-or-death situations. Gianna, on the other hand, killed because she was damn good at it and loved the thrill in the kills, so his idle threats did nothing to move her.

"Bag that shit up while I make a few contacts. We got a busy day ahead of us." He kissed her lips before smacking her juicy, protruding booty.

Gianna did as she was told, with a murderous rage building up inside of her. Rob was really beginning to push her buttons more and more often. Yet she found herself thinking more about K-Dawg and if the slug Rob delivered took his life. She knew he was vested, but she didn't actually see where he was hit at; she only saw his body drop.

"Damn, I hope he's okay."

"What? Who are you talkin' to?" Rob popped his head back into view.

"Just thinking about my brother," she lied.

"Fuck yo' brother. Think about me and only me," he stated before slamming the door shut.

Pussy, straight pussy, she thought to herself, wishing she could hit him with a few of her favorite throwing knives.

Chapter 11

Gurdo sat inside his home office, fuming in frustration with everything that had taken place over the last several months. Never had he dealt with anything like the recent events when his father was in total control of their family businesses. Doubt very seldom entered his mind about being in charge, but thinking about the way things had been going lately made him wonder if things would be better if his dad were still running operations. He hadn't been in the field for years and had grown to love his boss position, where he got to sit back and spend quality time with his wife and parents while his men handled everything—from trafficking to distribution, muscling to murdering, collecting to depositing. All operations ran smoothly without him ever having to be on the scene. That was, until one person joined his long list of enemies. Young Mack's alliance with those Valdez idiots had changed everything.

Their joint forces elevated the Valdez's reach and resources in the streets, something they never had on this side of the U.S. and Mexico borders. The evidence of all his misfortunes told a story of how much it was affecting him and his family's operations.

He pinched the bridge of his nose and sighed in frustration just as his phone vibrated on his desk. Looking down at the screen, he saw the all-too-familiar number and questioned whether he should answer, his mind foggy. He watched as the phone vibrated until it stopped. Then, it started up again. Only then did he decide to answer—because it could be important.

"Yes," he answered, his voice low and solemn.

"Is everything alright? You sound out of it."

"You're the one in the field, brother. You tell me if everything is alright. Have you found anything on those roaches that stole our money and other properties?"

"We still haven't found anything yet. This motherfucker is a lot smarter than we gave him credit for. He doesn't do anything in his name or the names of any of his family."

"Give it a little more time, and I'm sure he'll slip up and land himself right in our hands. I know he has to be pissed after finding two of his men dead at our hands, so maybe we won't have to find him. He'll be too busy trying to find us, and that's when we'll—"

Gurdo paused as his wife entered the office.

"Hello, Gee, you there?" Daniel asked once he went silent.

"Yeah, umm—just keep an eye out for those bars. They'll need to make a fence because nobody in their right mind will try to bank with those things," Gurdo informed Daniel before telling him he had to go and hanging up.

"Morning, love. You're looking good. So, how are you?" He stood and moved around his massive marble desk to meet her.

"Nights are the worst with the sickness, but overall I'm good. The baby is healthy, so I'm happy. How are you?" Ambrea smiled and allowed him to kiss her lips softly at first, but more aggressively as their tongues found each other. Reluctantly, she pulled back even though their session was making her panties soak. She had other things on her mind after speaking with Young Mack, and she needed answers. It took her weeks to muster the courage to speak with Gurdo, and now that she had, she couldn't let her hormones get the best of her and miss the opportunity.

"That's what I love to hear," he replied, feeling guilty for their lack of time and intimacy together.

"Yeah, well . . . I came to ask you, when was the last time you spoke with or saw my brother before he was murdered?" There, she did it, and now she felt her confidence returning as she stared and waited for him to respond.

Her question really took him by surprise, and a pang of guilt nearly surfaced as she searched his eyes for any sign of his truth.

"The same night he died," Gurdo replied truthfully. He could see the hurt that immediately showed on her face. It puzzled him, since she already knew he saw her brother the same night he died, as he had come to their home to see her. "Which I'm sure you already knew. So, I'm curious as to why you should ask when you already know he came over to speak with you about your pregnancy news." He finished and crossed his arms over his chest, sitting back in his seat behind his desk.

Squinting, Ambrea thought she saw something in his demeanor change when she asked him about her brother. But just as quickly, it was gone, and he was back to himself. Was there really something there, or was she searching because of what Young Mack had revealed to her about what his people told him about her brother's murder?

"It just doesn't make any sense. One minute he was here with me, happy as ever, basking in our joy." She paused, reflecting on what she had just heard. That's it, she thought. Why would he say 'my pregnancy news' instead of 'our pregnancy news'? Did he already know there could be a possibility that he wouldn't be the child's father? Did Ash say something to him out of frustration before leaving the house? No, that couldn't be it. He was gone before Ashton left her to go after Young Mack. Plus, Gurdo would be pissed and raising all kinds of hell behind it. "Then the next minute, he's no longer alive."

"You know just as well as anyone how this game goes, love. Tomorrow isn't promised to any of us," Gurdo stated as he smoothed out his Brioni-tailored suit, now confident that she had no clue about his secrets.

"But why him? He wasn't out there like that, not like the average street guy," Ambrea whined, still trying to get a feel for her husband.

"Oh, he was out there, my love. He even killed some of my men in the war between us and them. I still have it on footage if you'd like to see him in action. He was pretty crafty with it."

Gurdo mentally blew her off, knowing damn well that Ashton was no saint. Plus, to make matters worse, Ashton played for the wrong team, and he felt no remorse for killing him.

"I don't want to see anything like that," she said, fanning him off before taking a seat in front of his desk. He eyed her juicy legs as her dress rose above her knees. His desire swelled at the thought of sexing her down—it had been weeks since he'd been able to play inside of her. He had taken to getting his rocks off with the many girls Daniel would prepare for him whenever he was in the mood for sex and didn't want to bother his grieving wife.

"Did you or your men kill my brother?" she finally asked straight out, watching him closely.

"No," he replied, now irritated and not even bothering to look her in the eyes.

She dropped her head in defeat, still not exactly sure what role he played in her brother's murder, but she was sure of one thing: Young Mack had brought her the truth. Gurdo had never been able to lie to her in all their years together, and now was no different. He prided himself on being a man and always looked her in the eyes when addressing her, and his failure to do so now gave her the proof she needed to confirm her suspicions. Anger quickly arose inside her, and if he had only taken the time to look into her eyes, he would have definitely seen it.

***

Mackmillions smiled as he watched the three figures approach his home from about half a football field away. Max stood stoically beside him, mentally preparing himself to meet Rastanya and Queeny after being apart for so long. He would never forget the last time he saw the sexy female assassins. After discussing business and explaining their role, the night had ended with hot and steamy sex between the three of them. He smiled inside, knowing the girls well, and certain that things between them and the former agent were still along those lines.

Mackmillions stepped away from his front door with Max close on his heels to meet the trio.

"How is everyone?" Mackmillions asked as he shook their hands.

"We're fine, Uncle Mack," Queeny spoke first, smiling gracefully. The girls had taken to calling him Uncle, and he did nothing to deter them. He felt like their guardian after their parents tragically died in a faulty plane crash on their way to America. Even while incarcerated, he made sure Max kept in contact with the girls and took care of any bills or money they would ever need.

"We are glad to see you and happy to be on this side of the world for a while," Rastanya followed up with a tight hug to his tall frame.

"Good, good. And how about you, Cedrick?" Mackmillions noticed the humble man standing back, silently observing his interactions with the women.

"Everything is everything, I guess. I'm sure we'll have our chance to talk and catch up soon," Cedrick stated.

"Most certainly we will. But for now, I want you all to kick your feet up and relax. Max will show you around the house while I have a word with these two beauties." Mackmillions smiled at the ebony duo.

They shook hands and shared a half embrace before Max, who didn't like the close contact between the former agent and his mentor, beckoned Cedrick to follow. Cedrick found himself lost in the beauty and grandeur of Mackmillions' new estate. To say it was huge would be an understatement, as the main house was enormous. Walking half a step behind Max, he admired the exquisite black art collection that he was sure had cost a fortune, as it lined the hallways and walls throughout the massive home.

"Come," Max directed as he held open a door that led down a pathway to what seemed like a different part of the estate. The walls held light fixtures that illuminated the path to a reinforced steel door with a touchpad secured above the handle. Max entered the security code, swiped upward, and the sound of locks unlatching followed by a low hiss as the heavy door clicked open.

Max stepped in before pushing the steel door wide enough for them to walk through. Cedrick's heart rate increased as his eyes adjusted to the dim lighting and the security monitors lining the far wall. It wasn't the opulence of the high-tech room that caused his pulse to slow; rather, it was the confusion over why Max was bringing him there.

His sight fell upon a female strapped to a metal chair with duct tape over her mouth. It puzzled him why a man of Mackmillions' stature would have a kidnap victim in his new home.

Her muffled grunts and groans snapped him out of his trance. His feet carried him closer to her as he began to remove the tape from her mouth, still wondering what she was doing there.

"Cedrick! Oh God, please tell these people to release me!" He immediately felt sorry for her predicament but knew he couldn't help her until he knew for sure what Mackmillions needed her for.

"I see Max has shown you to your gift," a deep baritone voice sounded behind him.

"Gift? I'm not even sure how she fits into all this," Cedrick responded. He had never been one to duck a fade but he loved fading worthy opponents, unless piles of blue faces were involved, and with Mackmillions they almost always were.

"You haven't put it all together yet, so let me give you a quick briefing to make the long story short," Mackmillions said before pulling a Cuban cigar from his suit's breast pocket. He carefully clipped the tip and lit it, emitting thick clouds of expensive smoke.

Cedrick watched him closely without a word. Mackmillions finally broke the suspense, nodding for Max to retrieve something from his pocket. Max pressed a button, and Cedrick turned to face the opposite wall.

His eyes focused on the objects posted on the screen that traveled down the wall. Pictures of faces, cars, houses, and sticky notes were connected by yards of different colored strings. Chandler left the woman's side and cautiously stepped closer to what seemed like a puzzle or riddle being solved. He quickly noticed the faces of the intended targets, some of which he'd terminated alongside Queeny and Rastanya. Others adorned the stringy web of targets and potential targets, but he didn't know any of them besides two. Upon seeing their faces, his jaw muscles tightened, and his teeth started grinding together.

"Okay, I see all that's here before me, but it still doesn't explain why she's here. Hell, she may not even be Drexler's real wife," Chandler said, turning back to face them.

"Oh, she's definitely not his wife. Isn't that right, Ms. Gaines?" Mackmillions smiled after releasing a big cloud of smoke from his mouth.

"No," the woman answered, then lowered her head towards the floor.

"Then who are you?" Cedrick Chandler asked the woman who had purposely perpetrated being his ex-partner's wife.

"Nothing to you, Cedrick," she stated, finally through with her damsel-in-distress act. "You are certainly just a pawn in all of this. A soldier of war being used by two rival tribes. So who I am is nothing to you but everything to him," the woman who was addressed as Ms. Gaines stated with a slight grin.

"She's the daughter of the man responsible for crashing my life. Her father, who is a very important man, just so happens to be the puppet master for those who are responsible for crashing yours. Just so that I am being clear here, I just wanted to prove to you that you were being used to take the fall for all of what they hoped to make happen since my release. But as you can already tell, it's not going exactly in their favor," Mackmillions explained.

"He's right about that, but damn, you are effortlessly good," Ms. Gaines chuckled.

"Excuse me?" Mackmillions eyed her.

"You're good at manipulating others with twisted truths and exposing their deepest pain and hurt, then exploiting it with your intended relations to their problems, in which you conjure up a solution to better help and assist both you and them," she further explained her examination of the person he was observing before her.

"Tape," Mackmillions ordered, and Max grabbed the roll for a fresh strip to do the honors.

"Wait, hear me out—"

"Why should I? What could you possibly have to say that I need to hear?"

"See, there it is again," she said as she moved her legs close together and bit into her bottom lip seductively.

Mackmillions moved in front of her, looking down with a grimacing scowl on his face and his hands tucked into his pants pockets.

"Clearly, you underestimate my father. But he's never underestimated you—not then, and not now." As if on cue, Mackmillions' phone buzzed in his pocket.

"You definitely want to get that," she smiled, sensing his annoyance.

Mackmillions reluctantly pulled out the phone, staring at the unknown number on the screen. "Speak," he answered, already knowing who it would be.

"At last, we get to the good stuff. How's my girl?"

The voice on the other end confirmed his suspicions.

"Fine, for now. But I'm not sure how long I can keep my hands off this one."

"I'm sure she'll love it. Hell, she's more obsessed with your legend than all the government agencies combined. Not to mention Sylvia and that young child of yours who's making quite a stir for some familiar friends of mine." Amir Castropella laughed.

"Fuck is you laughing at, Castro? Do you take me for a joke, you frail piece of shit!" Mackmillions could feel his blood beginning to churn, but he reminded himself that he could not give the man anything to use against him.

"Oh no, Mackentosh, don't confuse my humor as mockery, especially after you've just upped the ante by including my family in your charades." Amir Castropella was a powerful man through and through, and Mackmillions knew that as a fact. He needed him dead more than anything; he was the last remaining threat to his plans for the future.

"War is war, Castro. You know how I play just as much as anyone else."

"Yes, that I do, so I took the liberty to protect—how should I say this?—you know, certain assets with measures I believe you would recognize as pure genius. Yes, I do believe you'll see it that way, and who knows, you might even see that you and I could survive this world side by side instead of pitted against each other. Surely you're not the only one with pull around the globe, you know.

And as much as I would love to continue this conversation with you, business is calling, so tell my dear daughter to inform you on all that she knows. Then after that, I expect her to be placed back in her home no later than ten p.m. your time." The line beeped once, and Mackmillions knew things had just taken a complicated turn.

"I'll tell you whatever you want to know once I explain what he meant by protecting his assets," Ms. Gaines said after the call ended.

"I must admit that he has me intrigued, but he knows he will not be able to elude me forever. Our paths will cross one way or another," Mackmillions stated as he leaned up against the marble countertop of the mini bar and watched his captive closely.

"You know, after everything I've grown to love and admire about you, I would never have taken you for one to so drastically underestimate your opponents," Ms. Gaines replied.

"Love? Woman—you only think you know about me, but you have no idea who I really am."

"I believe that I know enough about the real you to hold on to, thanks to our lovely Sylvia, that is. But that's neither here nor there."

"Can somebody bring me up to speed on what's really going on here?" Chandler interrupted them.

"Just study the wall, Agent. I'm sure you're clever enough to put it all in order," Ms. Gaines stated as if she were the one calling the shots. "Where was I? Yeah, okay...long story short, Mackentosh, my father wanted to destroy you and all you held dear to you. But I somehow became so attracted to your legend that I couldn't allow for him to harm Sylvia or your son, who, oh my God, took after you in the bedroom because I swear I felt some of everything that your wife described about her feelings when you make passionate love to her—"

"Get to your point, please," Mackmillions ordered, not the least bit surprised that Young Mack could bag such a woman.

"Sorry, got a little lost there," she smiled as she rubbed her thighs together before snapping them shut. "Well, let's stray even shorter. You can't kill me because it will kill your wife too," she finalized her explanation.

"That's the craziest shit I've ever heard!" Mackmillions laughed until he had tears in his eyes. "You can't possibly expect me to believe that!" The look on her face told him that there were no games being played.

"Believe it or not, that's your choice, but I'm sure you are not willing to chance her life on it." Even she knew that much.

"Okay, let's say for a second I want to take you seriously. How could something like that even be possible if I put a bullet through this pretty face right here, right now?" Mackmillions removed a .45 ACP from his waist as he walked over to where she sat, bound, and pressed the barrel to her temple.

"Wait, wait, don't do that! It's nanotechnology, that's it!" she said as she squeezed her eyes shut tight.

"Keep going."

"Your wife and I had a joint surgery where the surgeon placed millions of nanobites inside of her brain. I'm sure she's expressed to you about the late-night migraines, am I right? Okay, has she spoken to you about never having the urge to use anymore or drink alcoholic beverages whatsoever? It's because the nanobites are specialized software that suppress those urges. And to answer your curiosity about my surgery and how we're linked as one: My heart carries the batteries, or should I say the power cells, that keep those nanobites active and at work. The moment they stop, so do her brain activities." There it was, all laid out for him, and it explained the cockiness of Castro's call.

He lowered his weapon, then looked to Max, who always kept his eyes trained on him. Even though Max hardly ever showed any emotions, Mackmillions could clearly see the concern in him. "Bring me my queen," Mackmillions ordered, and Max removed himself.

"He's the last piece!" Chandler exclaimed as he finished studying the string-clad screen board. "Then you'll be able to recreate what you started—and no one would be able to stop you."

"Bingo," Ms. Gaines mumbled.

"Hey!" Mackmillions said as he held up the roll of duct tape, which quieted her immediately.

"Sorry," she whispered.

"You gotta know this isn't gonna be easy," Chandler stated but was more than ready to aid and assist, for his reward waited near the end of this story plot.

Just then, Sylvia entered the room. "Yes, my love, you needed to—Molly?" Sylvia was stunned, to say the least, as she stopped and stared in disbelief.

"Hi, Sylvia!" Molly Gaines smiled as if she wasn't tied to a metal chair in their home, clearly having been abducted.

"Honey, why is my chemical dependency counselor strapped to a chair in our home?" Sylvia studied her husband while she waited for an answer to this craziness.

"Tell me about it," Mackmillions said to Chandler before turning to address his wife. "It's a long story, but I'm sure she can give you the short version."

Chapter 12

Young Mack couldn't keep his eyes closed for any longer than five minutes without dreaming of laughing and crying babies. He knew that it was pathetic, but hell, he couldn't do anything about it, so he chose to lay awake, staring up at the ceiling. The news Ambrea broke to him was surprising to say the least, considering he hadn't thought of her in what seemed like forever. So much had happened since the last time they slept together that it felt like an eternity had passed them by. The crazy thing about it was that he didn't even know how he really felt about possibly becoming a father. At times, it excited him; at others, it terrified him—especially being engaged to the love of his life and yet to be able to tell her the news.

Feeling Aeriella's body shift beside him snapped him from his parental thoughts and brought him back to their five-star suite at the Hotel Matilda in San Miguel de Allende, Mexico. The luxurious suite was a gift courtesy of Stephanie Valdez, as they met with clientele from all over the USA.

He watched as his cellphone vibrated, the screen lighting up on the nightstand right next to where he lay in bed. He picked it up with his right hand, being careful not to disturb Aeriella, who was snuggled up tight to his left side.

"Damn, can she read minds too?" Young Mack smiled as he read the late-night text from Stephanie congratulating him on his newfound position and clientele.

"Tell Stephanie it's past her bedtime," he heard Aeriella's voice before turning to see her smiling face.

"I love you," Young Mack said, kissing her sexy lips and doing as she requested after thanking Stephanie.

"I love you too," Aeriella replied before sliding out of bed and stretching her toned body. He loved how much her gym days paid off.

"She says she can't sleep," he read Stephanie's reply back to Aeriella.

"And neither can you! Tell her the door is unlocked, and we will be in the shower. It's time to see what all this tension between you two can reward me," Aeriella said as she removed the shoulder straps of her Dolce & Gabbana sheer monogram slip.

Young Mack's mouth dropped open as he watched the silky slip fall down her toned back, over her plump cheeks, and pool around her feet on the floor. Aeriella stepped over the material and walked her way to the master bathroom, smiling over her shoulder the whole time. Filled with excitement, Young Mack quickly texted Stephanie, then jumped out of bed, shedding his Dolce & Gabbana boxer briefs. He unlocked the door for Stephanie to enter on her own, then beelined into the bathroom behind Aeriella, his thoughts of fatherhood now at the back of his mind.

Stephanie's mouth fell agape after reading the last message from Young Mack. Could he be serious? No, he had to be joking, but why would he? Her mind boggled with indecisiveness until she decided to throw caution to the wind, calling for her driver to meet her in the lobby.

The five-minute ride to Hotel Matilda seemed to take forever, and Stephanie's excitement continued to rise once they finally got there. The young Mexican guy at the receptionist desk was well aware of who she was the moment she stepped through the door and offered her a wide smile and an easy nod. Stephanie acknowledged her nephew behind the desk and looked both ways, spotting her men posted at both ends of the lobby. She gave them a nod at each end while she waited for the elevator to arrive.

Stephanie smiled politely as she watched the elderly couple holding hands exiting the cart as she stepped on, the elderly man's eyes staying locked on her. She smiled and opened the sash on her mini blazer, exposing her perfect breasts and hard nipples, white Gucci lace panties, with matching garter and hose. The look on the elderly man's face was priceless. Her nephew laughed at her antics just as the doors closed and the cart began to climb.

She laughed her way to the suite she had situated for Young Mack and his fiancée, Aeriella. After approaching the door, she tried the handle, and sure enough, it was open, washing away any doubt she had. Being careful not to make much noise, she entered the suite and locked the door behind her, then called out to the couple but got no response. She moved past the spacious living room, then around the huge kitchen, and could hear their passion escaping the walls of the master bedroom. She was quite nervous, but that didn't stop moisture from finding a home between her thighs on her way past the doorway and into the bedroom. The bathroom door was wide open, and she watched steam rise from the high point in the doorway and into the bedroom. The erotic sounds of passion emitting from the shower propelled her feet to keep moving forward.

This was the moment she'd dreamed of for a long time, and to be so close had her panties soaked. To finally have Young Mack was blockbuster for her, and yet the added sensation of him pleasing his woman heightened her senses tenfold.

"Come on in, Stephanie; we can already smell you!" Stephanie entered the bathroom, where the couple was tangled together in the walk-in shower. Young Mack took a break from munching on his fiancée's juicy cunt lips and hardened clit to lock eyes with her as she stood with her blazer open and her sexy tits on full display. "I knew you'd come," Aeriella said as she rubbed her breasts together while taking a hard nipple in her hungry mouth before motioning with her tongue for Stephanie to come in and join them.

Young Mack went right back to work on Aeriella's center with her right leg thrown over his shoulder while she sat on the bench protruding from the tiled shower wall. It excited him to hear his woman opening up sexually, and the presence of Stephanie made him harder than he'd ever been. Stephanie wasted no time before shedding her threads and following the directions of the younger seductress. She hadn't said a word, just walked right into Aeriella's embrace. Young Mack stood and watched as the women's tongues fought each other in an aggressive manner that aroused him further.

Their hands roamed expertly over each other's bodies as they continued their heated kiss. After a few more minutes, the older seductress found a dominant role and was the first to manipulate the clitoris of the other. Aeriella moaned loudly as Stephanie slipped her other hand behind her and penetrated her slickened back door with her middle finger while keeping a steady circular motion on her clit. "Ooooh shiiit—I'm cum—cumming!" Aeriella sounded as she felt a monstrous climax quickly approaching.

"Is this what you wanted, mommy?" Stephanie whispered into her ear while speeding up her ministrations.

"Ahhhh—yes!" Aeriella huffed and puffed throughout the orgasm that rocked her body from its core.

"Come on, because we're just warming up. The both of you are mine for the rest of your stay here in Mexico." Stephanie kissed both of her stiff nipples before sucking them in one at a time, teasing them with her teeth and tongue until they were standing out at least an inch long.

"We'll see about all that tough talk you're putting out," Young Mack stated as he moved up behind her, wrapping his arms around her waist, pulling her plump bottom against his hard dick.

"I've needed you for so long!" Stephanie purred as he sucked on a thick vein on the side of her neck while his dick moved back and forth between her legs.

"You deserve this, ma." His voice alone caused her juices to escape her hungry pussy and run down her thighs.

"Make her cum hard for how she just treated your queen." Aeriella had calmed down a bit since her climax and now sat on the shower bench with her feet in the seat and her bald lips spread open, her fingers slowly going in and out of her pink.

"Yeah, I'ma make her cum alright," he said as he moved their bodies beneath the water falling from the shower wall, then smoothly entered her from behind.

"Finally—fill me with your big dick, baby! Ahhh, yes, you are finally inside of me!" Young Mack smiled inside, but a look of pure pleasure registered on his face.

"This pussy's so tight. Steph, have you been saving this for me? Fuck—tell me—why is this shit so tight?"

"Yes, I've been saving—ahhh—saving it—ahhh—yeah!" Stephanie moaned, weakened from his strong, deep strokes to her needy pussy.

"For what, huh? Tell me for what!" Young Mack demanded while quickening his thrusts in and out of her wetness.

"That's right, daddy, you show her ass the power of that big ass dick!" Aeriella's face contorted as she furiously fingered herself at the sight of them.

Stephanie bit into her bottom lip in an attempt to be defiant after hearing Aeriella praising her man for taming her.

"Oh, so you wanna be tough, huh?" Young Mack gripped her hips tightly with both hands and forcefully pulled her body into his while he slammed forward relentlessly.

"Ooooo-fuuuuck! You're killing meeeee!" Stephanie cried out. "Bae, get over here and wait for my signal!" Young Mack ordered, and Aeriella got down to her knees in front of

Stephanie, locking lust-filled eyes. Young Mack reached around and pinched Stephanie's nipples as he slowed his tempo to long, deep strokes.

"Suck her clit, baby. Get your lick back."

"Damn right I am!" Aeriella attacked Stephanie's swollen button, and just like that, Stephanie's body exploded. Her vaginal muscles squeezed his girth, trapping him in place while her secretions soaked Aeriella's lips and tongue.

Not to be deterred, Young Mack used his strength to overpower Stephanie's vise-like grip around his pole. The tightness of her walls caused him to feel all the ridges deep inside of her wetness. It didn't take long before she was cumming again, setting him off deep inside her womb. "Correction: you belong to us now, forever." Aeriella smiled before tonguing her down, allowing her to taste her own juices. She did the same to her man before spanking him on the ass. "Good job, baby!" she said before dropping down and delivering a kiss on his wet muscle, then took all of him down her throat, which had him hard in less than a minute.

"Damn," Stephanie gasped.

"You're gonna love this thing; it can never get enough."

Aeriella laughed before taking care of her man with her mouth.

***

"Look at these big dumb asses!" Rolla said to himself while trying to suppress his laughter to remain undetected as he watched his targets from a closer vantage point than intended. He was crouched low on the rooftop of a popular corner store just off the feeder road in Fifth Ward, watching his targets meet up with a few familiar faces. He just knew he had to make a call to his big homey.

"This better be good, blood, you know I'm on detail watching this punk mufucka," K-Dawg whispered as he too stayed out of sight from his targets.

"Yeah-yeah, I know," Rolla whispered before adding, "But I had to call and put you up on the play. These fuck niggas trying to run."

"What's poppin', nigga? Spit it out," K-Dawg demanded.

"These mu'fuckas just poured themselves out. They trying to build a team by dropping big cash—our cash—into the hands of some of our Fifth Ward homies."

"Fuck outta here," K-Dawg said, unable to ignore how grimy niggas could be, so he made sure to tell Rolla to watch himself.

"Without a doubt, but I need a green light to step to the homies. I'm talkin' twenty or better out here right now," Rolla stated.

"Fall back on that idea and just follow them clowns like planned. We'll address the homies later once big brudda's back in town."

"Say less, twelve! 'Twelve!'"

Rolla had a good feeling about this shit. He knew at least fifteen of the guys from Fifth Ward and had recently partied with them last week. They also planned to put in work together after the death of two of their big homies. The Fifth Ward homies were also in dire need of a steady supplier, and Rolla promised he'd get at Young Mack about that once they shared blood on their glocks together. He knew they'd be able to win these guys over; he just needed to catch them at the right moment. With that in mind, he texted Deuce and told him he needed to meet him at the spot after his detail was completed for the day. Deuce replied, hitting him with the thumbs-up emoji. Rolla smiled because he knew Deuce would know how to approach the situation.

Meanwhile, on the East side of town, K-Dawg watched as his marks unloaded designer carry-on luggage from the trunk of a Bentley and into a modest two-story brick home. It took a lot of self-restraint, most of which he knew he lacked, but he summoned the love and respect he held for

Young Mack, who gave them strict no-interaction orders, not to jump out and smack a mufucka.

It was hard watching snakes slither around loosely without setting a trap to dispose of them, but he realized that in due time it would be time to collect, and fuck the money and the gold; he wanted souls.

He was so deep into his revengeful and murderous thoughts that he didn't even notice one of his marks was standing outside, staring hard in his direction. He wanted badly to slide down into his seat, but he knew he was already spotted and could not find it in his heart to cower. Plus, he'd been thinking about this moment since the night everything went wrong. He watched as the mark made its way back inside of the brick house, and at that moment, he wanted to drive away, but something made him stay. He'd never been so hesitant—nawl, that just wasn't him. As soon as he pressed the button to start his rented I-Pace Jaguar SUV, the mark was back outside and climbing inside of the Bentley alone. He smiled at the thought of what this meant and watched as the smooth luxury vehicle glided down the residential street in front of him.

He quickly put the Jag in drive and followed closely behind it.

Moments later, he found himself parked in a crowded Walmart parking lot, watching as one of his marks exited their vehicle and headed his way. He grabbed the Colt M1911 .45 ACP and held it to his side as he too exited his vehicle, never taking his eyes away from the figure approaching him.

"Thought you were dead," Gianna smiled as she got closer.

Her smiling face was disarming, and K-Dawg tucked his weapon.

"Thought you set us up," he shot back without letting his guard all the way down. He needed to be sure that wasn't the case, but until he heard her say it, he would continue to think it because he trusted nobody besides his crew.

"And why would I do that?" Her smile disappeared after hearing those words.

"I could name a few million good reasons why," K-Dawg didn't let up.

"Are you serious right now?" She was becoming agitated, and the look on his face didn't make it any better. He leaned back against his whip, arms folded over his big chest, and gave no reply. "I can't believe I was worried about yo' ass in the first fuckin' place. Fuck you!" she spat heatedly before attempting to walk away.

"Hold up, okay? I'm trippin'," K-Dawg grabbed her by the wrist. She quickly spun with her back facing him in a desperate attempt at a backhand, but he caught her other wrist before pulling her body into his with so much force he nearly knocked her breath away. "Was you really checking for ya boy?" K-Dawg teased before biting into her neck, forcing a moan to escape her lips.

"Stop it, let me go," she said but put up no effort to stop him.

"Tell me you were checking for me and what made you bring me here," K-Dawg ordered.

"Maybe I was worried about you after you know—he shot you and all. I could only see you fall before he jumped in and sped away."

"And you brought me here and away from there, why?"

"I just needed to know it was really you because I couldn't tell from that distance. But I felt that if it were you, then you would follow me if I were alone."

"Is that right?" He bit into her neck again, causing her to grind herself into his hardening muscle.

"Yes. Do you want me, or do you just want to fuck me?" He respected her bluntness as being real as she turned herself in his arms to look him in the eyes.

"I wanted to fuck you ever since the day I laid eyes on you at that gas station, and I'd be lying now if I didn't say just looking at you makes my dick hard because it does. Then add that to the fact that you're a cold-hearted killer like me, yeah, we'd be a force together. So my question to you is, do you want me, or do you just want me to fuck the shit outta you?"

She didn't need to answer that question because she was sure that her body was giving her away. She wanted him in every way she knew she shouldn't and couldn't stop herself from jumping into his arms. She wrapped her legs around his waist before tonguing him down and grinding into him.

"Take me with you," Gigi's words broke their embracing tongues apart before she rested her forehead against his.

"What about your crew and ol' boy?"

"Fuck 'em! They'll just think somebody kidnapped me," she blew out hot air, knowing that wouldn't be a good idea.

"You do know I'm killing that pussy, right?" K-Dawg promised

"Are you speaking to my soul, or are you referring to him?"

Gigi snickered, bringing a diamond-toothed smile from him. Crazy because she'd never seen him genuinely smile before that moment.

"Both, now get yo ass down before I take you up on that offer." She reluctantly allowed him to unwrap her legs from his waist and then placed her on her feet.

"He's building a team of killers," Gigi said, putting him up on game.

"Yeah, we know all about it, but what he don't know will definitely hurt him. What's up with the gold bars? Was that in those bags y'all took into that house?"

"Yeah, but they'll be gone tomorrow. His mother found a buyer at sixty-five percent," she informed him.

"I'll definitely be around for that," he assured her.

"His whole beef with y'all is because he blames Young Mack for his dad's death, and he barely even knew the guy. Hell, he tried to kill the man his damn self."

"And who was his dad supposed to be?" he asked, puzzled.

"Phatts was his father . . ."

Chapter 13

Gurdo took a sip from his glass of Henny as he sat behind the massive marble desk in his home's study. The peace and tranquility he felt in the confines of his estate was nothing like the chaos going on out in the streets. Business was jumping like usual, but he and his organization could still feel the burn from the hijacked shipment and the takeover of the tunnel in Mexico. That tunnel was a true pipeline that had only been operational by his family for five years, one of fifteen that was considered their property by them and the larger cartel families. It was only one of three with a true Texas destination. Members of his family who didn't approve of his promotion blamed him for the shortcomings because of the never-ending war between him and the viciously stupid Valdez family. Stupid indeed, he thought to himself before a chuckle left his lips. He had to give it to the pesky family; they really came up this time. It was a blow, though not devastating; a shocking one all the same. Just thinking about losses brought him back to the thoughts of losing the money and gold from the warehouse. Young Mack was more than a thorn in his finger now; he was becoming a very bold, blistering patch of skin beneath his feet. He couldn't wait to put an end to him and those little corner hustlers, but with the backing of the Valdez family, he knew Young Mack was now really his worst threat. The chime of his phone stole his attention, and he sipped his drink again before answering.

"What's the word?" he answered, already knowing who the caller was.

"Got a hit on someone trying to fence," Daniel stated while taking a deep pull from his blunt.

"Handle it."

"Will do."

"And brother?" Gurdo paused before continuing, "Do 'em as dirty as possible this time. We need to make a statement that nobody fucks with our shit without crucifying themselves!"

Daniel didn't need to respond because the stage had just been set, and there was no question as to if he'd get it done. He was known as one of the most gruesome young killers since he was a kid, earning stripes back in his homeland of Mexico.

***

"Phatts!" Young Mack exclaimed much louder than he intended. He couldn't believe the news K-Dawg had just delivered. How could Phatts be Rob's old man? Damn, that meant Rob must have been in on the play, hell, he was the only one whose bread wasn't taken. The enigma of even the possibility of Rob being in the foul shit that dismantled their moves in the take game was almost more unforgivable than him actually doing it.

"It's what his bitch tellin' me," K-Dawg added after a brief silence.

"Go at Lil' Clay, bring him up on game and have him bring me that simple motherfucker. I'll have Stephanie send the jet out." Young Mack was pissed, his whole mood changed with the news of Rob's betrayal. Time and time again shit was just too much of like father like son, he thought to himself as he poured up a double shot of white Benny. He turned and noticed Stephanie watching his every move while his fiance slept soundly beside her.

"I'll have Rolla pull up on them niggas while I watch this transaction with the bars," K-Dawg stated.

"Sounds good, keep me posted."

"Overstood."

"Be careful, bro."

"You telling that to the wrong side," K-Dawg laughed.

Young Mack joined him before ending their call. He knew that his little homie was a force and didn't have to worry about him much at all.

"Trouble back home?" Stephanie's soft voice brought his eyes back over to her.

"Something like that. What are you doing up, did I wake you?"

"Would've been nice if you did because I love how you wake us up," Stephanie smiled. She had been more than satisfied with the way he made both her and Aeriella feel together, it was almost superhuman of him. Both women could take ultimate amounts of pleasure and returned it all the same. "I got a text from another buyer and things are still taking a turn in your favor."

"Care to share?"

"With you, I'm willing to."

"Hey, watch it," Aeriella spoke up as she rolled over to face Stephanie.

"You too, mamicita. I could definitely spend the rest of my life with you two just like this and I would leave this earth a very happy and satisfied woman."

"You are very sweet, Steph," Aeriella smiled while moving a stray strand of hair out of Stephanie's face before kissing her softly on the lips.

"What do you say to us three tying the knot and holding on to this forever?" Stephanie pitched while staring deep into her eyes. Aeriella looked to her man for answers, but he was once again lost in conversation on his phone.

"What if it's not as easy as it sounds, Steph? Because I can certainly envision it,"

"Nothing could ever be hard for a trio as selfless as us. We would all give our best without doubt of the love shared between us."

"Love? Are you sure you love us as a whole? I mean, I know you've pretty much had feelings for him for a time now, but what about me, do you feel a way about me like you feel about him? I'd hope so, but I'd say let's just take this thing for a walk for a while. We haven't really been around each other outside of these expensive hotel suites which hide all of our secrets. I think it's a beautiful idea and I believe he'd pretty much fall out at just the thought of having two beautiful and sexy queens as his wives." They both laughed at the thought of Young Mack's excitement. As if he could feel them, he looked back into their smiling faces and returned their smile.

"Let's shower and spend the rest of the day together. I say we pamper ourselves and make a dinner date for the three of us."

"Sounds like a plan to me," Aeriella gleefully agreed before rolling out of bed with her sexy athletic figure on full display.

"Amazing!" Stephanie sighed as she admired her body.

"Come on, I wanna play before we go!" Aeriella grabbed her hand and pulled her into the bathroom together, leaving the door wide open in case their man wanted to join them.

Young Mack looked over his shoulder and saw the women disappear into the bathroom together. He then decided to end his first call to make a much-needed one. Once he was sure steam was coming from the shower, he made his call. The line rang twice before he heard her voice.

"I got your message, what's good with you?" Young Mack asked, his voice barely above a whisper.

"I think you're right about him," Young Mack knew she was referring to her husband, Gurdo. "He's talking a bit differently and—I don't know—maybe I'm just in my feelings about my brother." He could hear fatigue in her voice, like she hadn't found sleep in days.

"My team was there right after it happened, 'Bre. I know I'm right about him and I'm gonna get him for all that he's put me through, and that other one too. Shit's just hard because I have to always think about you when we're stepping!" Young Mack blew out a frustrated breath.

"Why would you still care about what happens to me? It's my fault that all of this is happening. I betrayed him and I let you down. None of this would be going on if it weren't for me!" Ambrea cried.

"It's our fault, not just yours. You can't sit there and own all the blame like I had nothing to do with this. You can't take all the blame like he didn't betray your trust by coming after me and nearly killing my mother and fiance. Fuck that, this is all of us balled up into one big problem, and I care about what happens to you because—well, I'm supposed to care. You're Ash's sister and you're pregnant, 'Bre, and I could damn well be the father so I care now more than ever before." Young Mack wasn't certain that he was supposed to have feelings for her because he wasn't on it like that. Sex was amazing and all, but so was sex with his fiancée, and he knew for sure he loved her without limits. And now the added curveball of the sexy Stephanie Valdez—shit couldn't get any greater. Ambrea was pregnant and that definitely complicated things. Though he wasn't in love with her, he'd always love her through the history they both shared, and now with the possibility of him being her child's father— yeah, shit was complicated for real.

"Damn, you're always rocking me, Mack! How are you always so . . . damn . . . you?" Ambrea chuckled as she wiped away the tears from her swollen red eyes. She had been crying for hours over her life's situations and over the loss of her twin brother. Now, leave it up to Young Mack to make her feel wanted—not in a fantasy type of way, but just to be wanted as a person by people who cared to care about her.

"You know me, I'm just all I can be and you'll never have to question shit if I am the father, ma. You won't even need Beavis and Butthead in your life anymore, I'm all you'll need and I stand on that." He really got a good laugh out of her with his sense of humor.

"Beavis and Butthead, huh? You're silly, you know that! I shouldn't even be able to laugh with the way that everything in my life is right now." Ambrea hated sounding so weak, but Young Mack knew her inside and out, and she knew he would never judge her and would always protect her feelings.

"You should laugh though, 'Bre. You're alive and breathing and you're healthy. You're beautiful and strong, a little chunky now but that ass is still fat as fuck!" He laughed and she immediately joined him on the other end.

"See, you're just so silly all the time!" Ambrea really appreciated him more than she could express at that moment.

"Just wanna make sure that you're smiling because you deserve that and much more."

"Thank you, Mackentosh. I mean that more than you'll ever know."

"Maybe one day we could sit around and you can tell me about it," she smiled hearing those words.

"Can we meet—maybe not now but like later sometime soon? I'm sure you'd like to feel the baby kicking my ass and who knows, maybe we could take turns reading to it if you're up for that?" Ambrea was hopeful, but his silence made her nervous, and she hoped she hadn't run him off. "Mack, are you still there?"

"Yeah, I'm here and I would like that a lot—just allow me to make time for it. You know with everything going on, I don't want any distraction whenever that time comes. It'll just be us three for a whole day, how does that sound?"

"Perfect," she blushed and turned a bright shade of red just from the thought alone.

"That's what it is then. I'll text you when I'm free and we will decide on a location then, cool?"

"Cool."

"Be safe, gorgeous, and hit me if you need anything. Oh, and especially if you're ready for me to pull up and cancel that old show," Ambrea laughed slightly; the reference to the Beavis and Butthead show was hilarious, but she knew he was dead serious.

"Not my place to do that and I'm not sure if you'd respect me much if I ever did, but I'll hit you when I need you. I could definitely use you now, but I know I have to . . . respect . . . uh, what's her name again?" She chuckled.

"We ain't doing that shit!" he laughed with her. "Be easy, 'Bre. I gotta go now."

"Bye," Ambrea spoke through her smile before ending their call. Her eyes immediately fell to her lap where a fully loaded .45 ACP rested. A quiet evil that definitely wouldn't be necessary at all now because of Young Mack, always the gentleman. She smiled as she put her gun away inside of her Valentino handbag. She then started her car and peacefully drove out of the gates of her and Gurdo's estate, listening to H.E.R. while headed for her mom's house.

Young Mack smiled as the call with him and Ambrea ended, but that smile vanished quickly once he turned to see his fiancée standing on the opposite side of the king-sized bed, wrapped in a thick white towel with tears soaking her beautiful face. Stephanie stood next to her with her arms folded over her chest, also wrapped in a white towel with wet hair.

"So, you're about to be a father now?" Aeriella questioned, and he could see that the words alone crushed her to spit them out of her mouth. He silently thought about his situation and whether he should try to soften the blow for her, but decided to be truthful because either way he knew he'd be hurting her no matter how soft the blow landed. He hated the fact that she had to find out this way and that he hadn't found the right time to tell her earlier.

"Strong possibility," were his only words.

"And when did you plan to crush me with this news?"

"I've been trying to figure out the best time to tell you, but it never came up. I'm sorry you had to find out like this; you know I would never intentionally hurt you."

"Too late for that," Aeriella cried harder still.

"Ba—"

"Stop! Stop, because I don't like you much at all right now and I don't wanna hear any of your excuses; don't wanna hear shit besides one of y'all arranging transportation to get me home!" Aeriella shouted before storming back inside the bathroom.

"I'll get her, you make some calls," Stephanie said before whispering, "What the fuck!" then taking off to be with Aeriella.

"Fuckkk!" Young Mack punched the wall in frustration, knocking down the expensive television that once hung there and destroying it.

***

K-Dawg couldn't believe his eyes as he sat behind the wheel of his tinted-out Dodge Demon, stalking Rob and Gianna through professional-grade field binoculars. It seemed as if all was going well with the transaction, and he was planning the right time to zoom in and initiate his own takedown once the transaction was completed. His thoughts were deterred when he spotted two black SUVs speeding in their direction with long barrels hanging outside of their windows. Gigi was the first to notice the speeding vehicles, and she reacted as a true killer would by removing her twin .40 caliber handguns with the extended clips and spraying the guy they were there to meet. K-Dawg smiled as the huge mist of blood and brain fogged the air. Gianna quickly jumped across the hood of the dead guy's Range Rover, grabbing the duffle bags and tossing them inside before jumping behind the wheel.

Automatic gunfire lit the side of the expensive four-wheel drive as she maneuvered it to block the shots aimed to kill Rob, who was squatting low behind heavy metal cargo cases. Once he realized it was her there to extract him, he quickly leaped over the cases and grabbed a hold of the open back passenger door, but his movements were too late. Their attackers rammed their front end into the Range Rover and knocked him far away, up and over those same cargo cases.

Gianna shook her head in an attempt to clear her blurred vision. She banged her head pretty hard against the steering wheel from the powerful impact of the collision. Everything was hazy, but her ears worked fine as she listened to the echoing sounds of fully automatic succession. It puzzled her to hear what sounded like return fire, as she knew that Rob wasn't heavily armed. Looking up through the driver's side window, she noticed that the glass was still intact, with heavy scratches evident on the surface.

"Bullet-proof, how 'bout that!" She laughed, then quickly went in search of her dropped weapons. Once she had those in her hands, she looked to the back seat and noticed that Rob was not there with her. The killer inside her screamed, "Fuck him!" but the part of her that held love for him—outside of him putting his hands on her—wouldn't allow her to abandon him on the battlefield.

She slowly struggled to pull herself from the front seat and into the back, an aching burn and tightness in her rib area signaling that something was definitely badly bruised or broken, but she didn't let that deter her. After she made it into the back seat, she popped open the back passenger door on the opposite side of the damage and cautiously crept around the rear of the truck, clutching both weapons in her hands. Stealthily, she stole a quick glance around the driver's side and saw three gunmen firing over the hood and around the tail end of one of the attackers' SUVs. There were four men in total, with the last guy crouching down on one knee to reload his weapon, all with their backs to her.

Skillfully and in pain, she took a deep breath, calmed herself, then rounded the rear of the wrecked vehicle and delivered headshots to the closest two attackers before filling her third target with hot lead all over his body as he attempted to turn and fire in her direction, sending rounds into the hangar's high ceiling. With three targets down, her fourth target had the odds in his favor, but she was quick on her feet as she ran and dove back behind the Range Rover, then scrambled for cover inside. She made it inside and slammed the door shut just in the nick of time as fire leaped from her attacker's rifle and pelted against the reinforced glass and metal, causing her to duck and cover herself reflexively.

Minutes later, there was absolute quietness, and Gianna wondered what was going on. She hadn't realized it, but fatigue had caused her a momentary blackout, and it wasn't until the sound of something tapping on the driver's side window woke her. She raised her head and slowly turned to see who or what was there, and that's when she noticed her knight in shining armor. Throughout all the chaos, she had forgotten that he promised to be there to watch over the exchange, leaving out his plans to take from them what they had taken from his crew. She hurried out of the back door of the vehicle and jumped into his arms without a care that her ribs were killing her.

"They took your boyfriend and grabbed the gold right after they ran into the truck," he explained as he escorted her back to the truck.

"I tried saving him, but they came in too hot and too fast! The idiot tried to double-cross us and have his men rob us blind!"

"Let's get the money and get outta here. We'll talk on the way to the crib. I know this is a private location, but after all of those gunshots, I'm sure the police will eventually show up here." Gigi agreed, and as she reached inside to grab the bags of money, a sharp pain halted her movement and vibrated all through her body.

"Arrggh—shit!" she grimaced, her hand quickly clutching her left side.

"What's wrong? Are you alright?" K-Dawg asked, concerned as he watched her remove her hand and saw that it was immersed in blood right before she grew weak and passed out into his arms.

Chapter 14

Mackmillions sat discordantly and discontent as he stared at the MRI images of his wife and Molly. He'd called in a big favor and had to pay handsomely for it, but after seeing the results with his own eyes, he knew they were worth every penny. Neither he nor his wife could believe what Amir had done in his twisted plot to go after Mackmillions before he ever had a chance to confront him. The lengths Amir had gone to were unlike anything Mackmillions had ever witnessed before. These circumstances changed everything for him drastically, as his wife's safety and the safety of their son came before anything else in his life. Thinking of his son's safety, he realized they hadn't talked in a while. He checked his phone and saw no recent texts or calls, so he decided to send a message letting him know to contact him as soon as he got it.

"I can't believe you let him do this to us, Molly!" Sylvia expressed her distaste for their situation.

"Honestly, Sylvia, I know this seems harsh and you feel as if I betrayed your trust, but it was either this or your life, and I refused to let him kill you," Molly confessed, feeling unappreciated for saving Sylvia's life. The shock and horror on Sylvia's face nearly brought tears to her own eyes.

"My question is, can we reverse it—you know—"

"Without killing her?" Molly finished Mackmillions' stressful question.

"Without killing either of you," he corrected her.

Even though he didn't know the woman well, he felt obligated to see to her well-being. He understood the severity of her sacrifices in the deadly game he and her father had embarked on. Even though he knew her reasoning was self-centered, he still felt the need to show her gratitude.

"Yes, it is reversible. I'm not crazy at all, Mackentosh. My father doesn't know that it is because the surgeon and I—well, we had a rather nice long discussion away from my father's eyes and ears." Molly smiled at the memory of her conversation with the surgeon and for being able to deliver such good news.

"So is it safe to say you still have direct contacts with this guy?" Sylvia needed to know.

"Of course I do, but I kind of like being attached to you in this way." Sylvia shot Molly a look that needed no deciphering.

"Until we can get this all cleared up, Molly, you're not leaving our sight. I have some very important calls to make while you do whatever you need to do to contact that surgeon." Mackmillions was not in the mood for games, and Molly could sense his frustration. Being around him made her uncomfortable, but she remained calm.

Molly sat deep in thought as she reviewed everything that had taken place in her memory. Things were not going as well as she had planned. The fact that Sylvia really seemed annoyed with her after she had literally saved her life and gone against her own father made her feel unappreciated, and that angered her immensely. Mackmillions' understandable frustrations were directed at her, and he actually seemed pleased and thankful for her extreme sacrifices to protect his son and wife. But why was Sylvia so displeased with her? Why couldn't she appreciate Molly's sacrifices as her husband did?

After going back and forth with her thoughts for over an hour, with her phone glued to her hands, she stared at the number for Dr. M. L. Valenskova. Her mind pushed her to do what she knew was right, yet her heart pulled her in a different, more selfish direction that seemed so right to her and aligned with her desires. Why couldn't she pursue the outcome she wanted while everyone else unapologetically chased their own goals? Molly Gaines, daddy's little girl, had never been denied—not even by her selfish father, who could not resist the wishes and parental approval of his only child.

Molly smiled as her heart won the morality battle against her sane mind. She was a woman who wanted what she wanted, and just like her father, she didn't care what lines had to be crossed to accomplish her goal.

Backing her phone screen up to view all contacts, she quickly scrolled until she found the familiar number for her young gay secretary, then touched the green phone symbol on her screen and listened as the line went live.

"Hello, Ms. Gaines, is everything okay?" he asked over loud, boisterous music.

"Could be a lot better. How's *Matthew*?" Molly asked, initiating his code for operation.

"Ooh, he's perfectly fine." She smiled at the immediate change in his voice; she knew from experience what a machine he was in person.

"Time to go see the doctor, Matthew. I'll have the jet gassed up and ready for you to leave tonight."

"You won't be disappointed," Matthew replied.

"And, Matthew—make it clean," Molly ordered, then ended their call and tossed her phone on the king-sized bed before removing her clothes and walking into the bathroom for a much-needed hot shower.

***

It was certainly an active night out on the northside of Houston, and things were in full swing over on Market Street in the Bloody Nickel. Deuce and Rolla took in the scene from the cabin of his arctic-gray Porsche 718 Cayman GT4 RS. Deuce loved the sleek, near-500-horsepower, flat-six speed demon, and he turned plenty of heads with it, sitting on 22-inch Forgiato race rims with rubber band tires. He sat patiently with Rolla, puffing on some of the most exotic smoke they could find, as they waited for Clay and his crew to show up. They had arrived early, wanting to catch him before Rob's goons could drop those bands off on them. After close to an hour of waiting, their patience paid off.

"Ain't that Lil' Clay right there in the Hellcat?" Deuce could hear the Scat Pack screaming as the hood-famous machine pulled into the corner store's parking lot.

"Yeah, that's fam . . . fa sho," Rolla confirmed with a burst of excitement. He was tired of waiting on Clay, and had he been in his own ride, he would have left half an hour ago.

"Let's see what he got on his mind," Deuce said as he checked for the round in his FN before starting the Porsche and pulling into the parking lot along with the other hustlers.

All eyes were on the duo as they cruised to a stop in the $200,000 Porsche. Deuce revved the engine a couple of times just to show off the car's power, then shut it down. Both men stepped out of the whip looking like money. Rolla had convinced Deuce to turn up his drip for the pop-up in Fifth Ward, knowing that the fellas there had their own way of gauging a man's character by his style and sense of dress. Rolla knew that with these guys, and their women, every day was like a fashion show.

Rolla wasn't about to get caught looking crazy, so he wasn't slacking. He came dressed down in all-white Prada, with a leather Prada bucket hat and matching white Prada lows with the red signature stripe down the tongue. His jewelry was always on point, and tonight he was sporting three chunky, iced-out Cuban link chains of different lengths around his neck, with a pair of honeycomb, hand-set diamond earrings. He was rocking two bust-down APs, one on each wrist, with diamond Cartier bracelets to complement each timepiece. He was dripping, no doubt about it, and he knew it, but he wanted to impress these guys and didn't mind stepping out like that.

Deuce made sure Rolla didn't outshine him too much, knowing his young homie could fit in circles meant for the top-notch artists and ballplayers in the city. Deuce mobbed in an all-black monogram-printed Fendi set with brown-and-black Fendi running shoes and a black leather Fendi bucket hat. He sported two two-toned diamond Cuban links, one with a white diamond money bag spilling green diamonds and the other with his name in bold drip letters. His wrist boasted an iced-out, skeleton-faced Cartier timepiece, along with two gold-and-diamond bracelets.

Even though Deuce was comfortable in any ghetto in and around the city, there was one thing he always made sure of—it could mean life or death. He never left home without a cannon or two. The bulge on his hip made that clear, and the one on Rolla's hip let onlookers know they meant business.

"What it is, gents?" One of the bold young Blood members, clearly on security duty, stepped up into their path. The tattoos and heavy use of red ink on his face confirmed his affiliation, and the hammer in his grip made it clear he wasn't playing.

"Twenty-eight twelve, this way, and we here to speak with the homie, Clay," Rolla spoke up for the duo.

"You look familiar, but you don't. And since neither of y'all speak Trees, you might as well have come dressed in ills, ya feel me?"

"Fuck no, we don't feel you, nigga! But we'll spill you, though, for that slick, disrespectful shit you just let roll off your tongue," Rolla snapped, reaching for his hammer. But the young dude was quicker—already holding his weapon. He made the mistake of paying attention to the wrong one, though, and that gave Deuce all the time he needed to press his FN to the young man's temple.

"Oops, too slow!" Rolla laughed, moving the guy's weapon away from his face.

"Fuck all this playing around. Clay! We here on business, lil bruh!" Deuce shouted as more men began approaching the spectacle.

"Who that?" Clay squinted toward the scene, locking eyes with the pair and his hemmed-up man.

"Rolla and the homie Deuce! Young Mack's people!" Rolla yelled out, raising his voice over the blasting music coming from nearby cars in the spacious parking lot.

"Oooh shit, why y'all got Gonnie all hemmed up and shit?" Clay chuckled as he approached, flanked by three of his men.

"Lil' nigga was on goofy, and I don't feel like laughing. I'm Deuce." The men shared a signature handshake representing their culture.

"Rolla, what's goody!" Clay extended his hand, already familiar with him. "Damn, I ain't heard from Young in a sec, so what brings y'all by the Bloody Nickel?" he asked, eyeing their drip.

"Young sent us out this way to get at you about business that's now close to you and us," Deuce said as they walked side by side toward the Porsche.

"Well, if that's the case, I don't have to question if there's a bag involved. So whatever it is, through the loyalty for the homie, I want in," Clay said, getting straight to the point.

"We never said what it is," Deuce replied, impressed by Clay's bold loyalty to Young Mack.

"We'll discuss that later. Let the big homie know we steppin'—however he needs us, as long as that bag right, which I already know it will be." That was music to their ears, and the bright, diamond-toothed smile spreading across Rolla's face said as much.

***

Rob couldn't believe his bad luck. How the hell did he allow himself to get caught slipping at a time like this? His mind scrambled, running through countless scenarios, none of which changed the fact that he was now caught up, tied to a metal chair with a dark cloak over his head. Perspiration drenched his face and body as he sat quiet and still in the hot, humid space where he was being held. The heat was aggravating, and the cloak over his head only made it worse. But despite the discomfort, it wasn't life-threatening, and the fresh air in the confined area eased his nerves a bit.

After trying unsuccessfully to loosen the binds around his wrists and ankles, he realized things were stickier than he thought. There would be no escape. His thoughts of fleeing quickly faded just before he heard the sound of keys, followed by metal clanging as the large door rolled open, letting fresh air into the humid space.

Though he couldn't see through the cloth, Rob's hearing worked fine. He listened as four sets of feet approached. Seconds passed in silence until one of the Spanish-speaking men switched to English, addressing him while the others grew deathly quiet.

"Do you know who I am?" The unfamiliar voice asked, but Rob remained silent. A full minute passed, and just as Rob began to feel uneasy, a sudden torrent of ice-cold water rained down on him, soaking him and making him gasp in shock.

"Ooooh shit!"

"Okay, now that I know you're awake—though I'm almost sure you already were, and just chose to ignore me— let me ask you again. Do you know who I am?"

"How the fuck am I supposed to know who you are when I can't even see shit?" Rob growled through chattering teeth.

A few words were exchanged in Spanish before the cloak was finally removed. Rob's vision was blurred at first, but as he focused on the men before him, he realized he didn't recognize any of them. But Gianna's continuous warnings about how dangerous cartel men were echoed in his mind. Back then, he had dismissed her threats, his attention elsewhere. Now, though, he wished he had listened. As thoughts of her filled his mind, he hoped she had escaped their attackers. But if she had, didn't that mean she had abandoned him? The idea of such a betrayal made his blood boil.

"I'm guessing you already know I don't know who you are since we've never met," Rob half-lied, though he knew exactly who these men were.

"Well, let me put it to you this way. I'm someone you really don't wanna fuck with," the man, Gurdo, chuckled, lighting a perfectly rolled Kush blunt. "So here's the question of the day—where the fuck is Young Mack, and where are you punks hiding?" Smoke escaped Gurdo's flaring nostrils and his eyes bore into his captive.

"What the fuck!" Rob thought to himself, not understanding how this shit was playing out. This was all happening because of Young Mack? He thought back to how he almost lost his life to a man he later learned was his father—a father he had never known because of Young Mack, and would never know because of him, too. Yet here he was again, caught in the middle of Young Mack's beef. Disgusted, he shook his head. "Seriously, bruh, fuck Young Mack! Ain't no love this way for that nigga. He killed my pops and my brother. But I guess you big boys don't know much about what goes on in the ghetto because y'all too far up in the clouds for us normal folk. You wanna find Young Mack and where he's hiding? So do I, so good luck with that shit." Rob laid it on thick, hoping to give himself a fighting chance at getting outta this.

Rob's statements shocked both Gurdo and Daniel. Daniel, who was always in the field battling Young Mack, had to admit he'd never seen this unfamiliar guy with the deadly crew. So why did this unfamiliar guy seem so familiar if he wasn't with Young Mack's crew?

Gurdo chuckled as he observed the man before him. His initial plan was to interrogate Rob about his enemy's whereabouts and then put a bullet between his eyes—whether he was useful or not. But this revelation certainly changed things.

"Fuck the guy, huh? Is that what you said, or is that what you mean?"

"Both!"

"Sounds good, but that leaves me with one more question—and I'm sure you'll have the answer to this one." Gurdo extended his hand, palm up, and Daniel immediately placed a weapon in it. "How did you get my gold? Because we're certain that Young Mack's flunkies were the ones who raided our warehouse."

"Shit, that's easy to explain," Rob answered with confidence.

"I'm listening. And the moment I smell bullshit, that's curtains for you," Gurdo promised.

"Well, my bitch found a way to run around the city with these clowns once before, and the shit was a success," Rob said, leaving himself out of the picture, knowing they raided Gurdo's traps and killed his men and women workers. "Then I'm guessing on the night you mentioned, I followed her with two of my men in tow to a warehouse—which I'm guessing was your property—"

"Wait a minute . . . Gianna is your girl?" Daniel interrupted.

"Yeah, you know her or something?" Rob faked an attitude.

"Finish your story," Gurdo cut in, aware of the love-hate relationship Daniel had with his cousin.

"I followed them to that warehouse, saw a lot of flashes, heard a lot of gunfire, and watched as a Mercedes Benz truck sped away. Minutes later, I saw them exit the warehouse with what looked like two dead bodies. From where we were parked, I couldn't tell if it was my girl or not, so I dropped in on them as two of them went back inside. Once we pulled up, I saw my girl standing there, so we hopped out with weapons drawn, catching one of Young Mack's men off guard. I popped the dick-sucka upside the head, knocked him out, then grabbed my girl just as the other two came outta the warehouse with big bags in their hands. Me, I'm a jackboy by trade, so seeing them with those bags and me and my guys already having the upper hand—we took that shit. I shot the biggest one in the chest, and we split." Rob concluded.

He sat nervously as Daniel and Gurdo talked in their native tongue without sparing him a glance. Then, Gurdo asked the question that made Rob's chest swell with excitement.

"Do you wanna live?"

"Fuck kinda question is that, nigga? Of course I wanna live!" Rob exclaimed, grinning.

"Your life for Gianna," Daniel stated sternly. "Then you join us in killing Young Mack and all of his men. You'll not only keep your life, but I'll make you a very rich man," Gurdo added, releasing a thick cloud of potent smoke.

Rob needed no time to think it through, but he still played into the suspense. Without a shadow of a doubt, he decided to trade Gianna's life for his own.

"Should I put a bullet in her head, or will you be doing the honors?" he smiled up at Daniel.

"Bullet to the head? Fuck outta here. I'll decide how she dies," Daniel responded with a devilish grin. "But know this—it won't be as fast as a bullet to the head."

***

Soft groans echoed in a large room inside Young Mack's new secluded Sugarland mansion. K-Dawg stared intently as a private doctor worked his magic on Gianna's wounds, with the help of an assistant and Chloe, Young Mack's live-in maid. Gianna had suffered a bullet wound, which the doctor said was a through-and-through. But the pain she was in made it seem like the bullet had lodged itself in one of her ribs.

K-Dawg felt her pain as he watched the doctor clean her wound, inside and out, then stitch her up. He was grateful Young Mack had returned to the city and was nearby when Gianna was shot. She had lost her boyfriend and the gold bars in the process, but managed to secure nearly $675,000 in cash. K-Dawg didn't give two shits about Rob because he had sworn on the gang that he was going to rock him to sleep himself. If someone else helped with that, so be it, as long as the pussy stopped breathing.

The doctor and his assistants worked on Gianna for a little over an hour before they had her cleaned up as best as they could for the moment. She was hooked up to two IV drips, and the beeping monitors echoed inside the quiet, spacious bedroom. K-Dawg smiled at the somber look on her face as she lay back, looking over at him standing in the doorway.

"You should've taken that shot he offered you," K-Dawg broke the silence. Gianna shook her head, too tired and in too much pain to take any medication for her injuries.

"I almost came to a brazy conclusion while they were working on you," K-Dawg said as he pushed away from the wall and made his way over to her bed.

"Yeah? And what was that?" Her throat was dry and scratchy.

"I wanted to shoot the doc for how much he was hurting you." Gianna started to laugh but winced in pain from her side, so she calmed herself and settled for a smile.

"Sorry, I shouldn't be trying to make you laugh, but I was seriously thinking about doing it."

"Thanks for helping me. I think you saved my life out there, you know."

"You think I saved your life? Is that right?"

"Yeah, I think so." Gigi groaned as she tried to sit up, and K-Dawg hurried to help her. Once she was upright, they stared into each other's eyes before Gigi reached out and held one of his big hands in hers. "Thank you."

"You don't gotta thank me," he replied.

"I need a bath," she said, frowning as if she could smell the funk coming from her body.

"No baths, but a shower sounds like a good idea."

"Ooh, you got jokes, huh?"

"You started it."

"I think it's crazy how much you smile when we're alone," she pointed out, proud of the effect she had on him.

"I noticed that too," he agreed, their eyes locking again, silence falling over them.

"Okay, well, are you gonna help me or not?" she teased, pretending to get up on her own, which made him jump into action, helping her up through her pain.

Once inside the bathroom, with the IV drips still attached to her arm and hand, she looked up into his big brown eyes, and he stared back into hers. The sexual tension between them was so thick it could be cut with a knife. Gianna reached back and unclasped her bra, removing it and revealing her tattooed breasts, both with pierced nipples. He stared in amazement, and she smiled, shrugging her shoulders before asking him to help her out of the rest of her blood-soaked clothes.

Careful of her injuries, he moved with finesse, taking his time to admire her feminine structure as he unbuttoned her tight jeans and slid them over her shapely hips and down her toned legs. He smiled at the sight—every inch of her skin was covered in tattoos. Her natural scent, mixed with sweat and the antibacterial soap the doctor had used, had his pole rock hard. She balanced herself by holding his shoulder with one hand and the IV pole with the other, stepping out of her jeans. Now, she stood before him wearing nothing but a pair of black lace panties, a seductive smile on her face as if daring him to keep going. He smiled back, staying eye-level with the incredible puffiness tucked inside her panty front. Just the sight of how meaty her mound was excited him, and his dick ached to be released.

"You wanna know why I didn't wanna numb any of this pain?" she asked, looking down at him with a smile.

"Why's that?" K-Dawg asked.

Gianna took his hand and placed it on her soaked crotch. "That's not sweat either," Gigi laughed, unable to contain herself after seeing the look on his face. "The pain excites me, and you watching me the entire time only heightened my arousal."

"Damn," K-Dawg sighed, using his fingers to caress her meaty center through her soaked panty front.

"Take them off and shower with me," she requested. He quickly followed through, removing her underwear before stripping himself.

Both of their bodies were stunning, like works of art. They shamelessly admired each other's tattoos. K-Dawg marveled at how even her ass was inked, while his was bare—the only place he didn't have any ink besides his face. Their infatuation with each other's tattoos soon led Gianna to remove both IVs from her body before pulling him into the shower by his thug muscle. He smiled, unable to believe how gone he was over her. No chick before her had ever come close to possessing all the attributes of a woman who could lock him down, but the more time he spent with Gianna, the more he realized she just might be the one.

"Wait—do you think you can handle it?" he asked, eyeing her blood and water-soaked bandages.

"Only one way to find out," she replied, turning to face the wall with her hands pressed against it and her feet spread.

"Fuuuck," he hissed, and they both moaned as he entered her, slowly settling in so she could adjust to his size. He was only about three inches in, with a whole seven more to go.

Her wetness, combined with the water, helped him slide deeper into her.

She moaned loudly, pushing back to meet him halfway, taking him all the way deep inside her body. He was deeper than any man had ever been, once fully inside. Her side wound ached terribly, the pain mixing with the tightness in her stomach as she leaked a thick white secretion all over his pole from climaxing the moment he filled her completely. He pulled back, admiring how her lips pouted and gripped his thickness before slowly thrusting forward again, tapping her G-spot in the process.

"Aaahhh, that feels so damn good, now go harder!" Gigi moaned, and he picked up speed at her command. "Yeeesss—please fuck meee and stop teasing meee—aaaahhh, I'm cumming again!"

After hearing those words, he kicked up his drill game, crashing into her and pulling out in quick succession. She was sticky and wet, her insides feeling like pure velvet as he felt every inch of her vaginal anatomy while hitting every wall of her pussy at once. His thickness and length filled her up to capacity, the snugness of her tunnel hastening his own release. The closer he came to climaxing, the harder he stroked, until he found himself buried as deep as he could go, releasing his load deep inside her womb. Her eyes rolled back as another orgasm wrecked her body, causing her to shiver uncontrollably. It was her fourth one.

"Four for one," she smiled, as his erection softened enough to slip out of her. She turned around and captured his lips with her own, loving the feel of her tongue tracing over his expensive diamond teeth.

"Don't be so nice about it next time," Gigi said between kisses, and he promised not to.

Chapter 15

Weeks after things had gone bad in Mexico, Stephanie remained in Sugarland, TX, right by Aeriella's side, supporting her and Young Mack. Things hadn't changed much between Aeriella and Young Mack, no matter the gifts and apologies. He'd tried explaining himself to his fiancée many times, often through Stephanie, but nothing worked. Aeriella refused to talk to him and wouldn't even let Stephanie relay his excuses. Her reasoning was simple: he had made her look like a complete fool by keeping her in the dark, and she had to find out the way she did. Hearing her man—her fiancé—comfort another woman, a pregnant woman possibly carrying his child, while Stephanie stood beside her and witnessed it all was devastating. It was going to take time for her to heal from that blow, not the gifts he tried to shower her with.

Stephanie understood Aeriella as a woman, and though she wanted them to mend their differences, she knew she had to remain neutral, standing between them to avoid overstepping her boundaries.

Now, Stephanie stood wide-eyed, admiring Aeriella's honey-brown sculpted body, unable to deny the wetness forming between her legs. They had just finished their daily workout before hitting the shower together and drying each other off. It had been weeks since the incident, and neither of them had shared much intimacy—if any at all. Stephanie's eyes followed Aeriella's sexy body as she moved around the master bedroom of the luxurious new home. Stephanie had silently helped Young Mack purchase the house for them. With ten bedrooms and just as many bathrooms, the home was more suited for a large family, but she saw no reason why it wouldn't work for the three of them.

Aeriella moved about the room in a sexy red lace bra and panty set by Julien Macdonald while she took call after call, speaking lawyer talk with several people. Stephanie eyed her with lust the entire time.

"One hundred thousand dollars, and I'll be expecting half upfront within the next forty-eight hours, or you can settle for a more price-efficient civil lawyer trying to play ball in the big leagues. My price is my price, and I'm more than sure I'll win your state case, as well as your federal trial. If we go to trial, my price doubles for state and triples for federal. My prices are suited to fit everyone's needs, and you won't find anyone better than me. Okay, then let's do business. I'll meet with you within the next two days—just make sure my funds are delivered before then." Aeriella ended the call with a deep sigh before tossing her iPhone on the king-sized bed and playfully flopping down face-first onto the soft mattress.

Stephanie eyed her without saying a word, her need for pleasure rising by the second.

"You don't have to stand there staring, Steph. You can always touch me in any special way you feel the need to," Aeriella said, her face buried in the bed linens before she rolled to her side, facing Stephanie, who stood by the door in a sexy white Gucci bra and lace shorts set. Her words, combined with the reality of their truths, and Stephanie's dire need for sexual relief, brought one foot in front of the other until the older seductress crawled across the bed to meet her lover.

Both women moaned into each other's mouths as their tongues danced in an eager bout, chasing the other's submission. Hands roamed, touching places with just the right amount of pressure, providing maximum pleasure to their heated bodies. Stephanie moaned when Aeriella's teeth bit into the thick vein on the side of her neck, causing her to pull back from Aeriella's embrace.

"We shouldn't," Stephanie said, catching her breath.

"Yeah, I figured you'd feel that way . . . not without him, right? That's why I haven't tried anything with you since the hotel," Aeriella chuckled, her voice tinged with disappointment. She had been keeping things neutral with Stephanie ever since they left Mexico. She wanted to return to Houston alone, but neither Stephanie nor her fiancé would allow it. Now, Stephanie had worked her way back into her bed, only to arouse her and leave her hanging—wet pussy and all.

"Do you think I'm not as aroused as you are? Do you think I don't want to feel your tongue caressing me while mine does the same for you? I know you don't think that, so please understand that it just doesn't feel right for me, being stuck between you two. I'm doing my best to stay neutral in all of this," Stephanie explained, staring deep into Aeriella's eyes.

"It's part of what you signed up for, and you were talking about marriage. You do realize that you would be marrying two people, not one, right? Shit happens, fights happen, but we don't get to choose sides between us. Your commitment should be to both of us, Steph, not just the one you work with."

"You think I'm choosing sides in all this? How is that even possible when I'm with you nearly twenty-four hours a day, week in and week out? I'm not some young woman lost in a whirlwind relationship with two beautiful people, Aeriella. I've loved Young Mack for a while now, and I cherish you both. Through him, and now through being with you, I've grown to love you too. When I talked about marriage, I meant every word. I would devote my life, my love, and my loyalty to both of you. It was never about one, and I'm sorry if I made you feel that way. But I will never apologize for missing him. I need him, and so do you!" Steph spoke her truth before rising from the bed, looking down at Aeriella with her arms folded across her chest.

"Damn, I'm sorry, Steph. I know where you stand, and I should've never said those things to you. I know that's not who you are, and I mean that from my heart." Aeriella stood from the bed and closed the distance between them, wrapping herself in Stephanie's embrace. "I guess I miss him more than I admit, and my anger got pointed at you instead."

"We're good as long as you know where I stand in this union. Hell, I'm sure he's just as sexually frustrated as both of us." They both laughed at that, but a knock on the door stole their attention.

"Yeah?" Aeriella called out.

"It's me," Young Mack's voice sounded from the other side of the door. Aeriella was tempted to tell him to go away, even though she didn't want him to. Add to that the pleading look in Stephanie's eyes, along with the feelings from her own heart, and she was no match for them.

Slipping from Stephanie's arms, Aeriella went and sat at the foot of their king-sized bed, then nodded for Stephanie to let him in.

"Hi," Stephanie said before kissing his lips and stepping aside to allow him entrance. His Burberry cologne was intoxicating as it filled the room once he stepped inside.

"Hey," he greeted Stephanie before his eyes found Aeriella sitting on the bed, looking scrumptious as fuck in her bra and panties. His dick twitched, gaining strength at the sight of both women in their underwear, their body fragrances mingling in the air. "Do you plan to be away from me forever? I mean, I don't mind waiting because I'd wait until forever comes and goes if I have to." He spoke from his heart, seeing her with her head down.

She stayed silent, looking up to meet his stress-filled eyes boring into hers. She hadn't seen him in days, and seeing him so down, not his usual confident self, hurt her heart. But she didn't blame herself for his hurt feelings—he deserved her anger.

Still, her resolve quickly dissolved when he told her he loved her. A lone tear escaped her eyes as she brought her hand up to caress his now-bearded face. She had never seen him with even a shadow of facial hair before, and that alone showed her how much their distance was affecting him.

"I love you too," she whispered, standing and kissing his lips lovingly as tears soaked her face. Stephanie smiled with teary eyes from her place in the doorway before moving over to join them.

"I'll go help Chloe with dinner while you two talk," Stephanie said, kissing both of them on the cheek before leaving them to it.

"I'm sorry about everything, love. I couldn't stand hurting you with that news, but now I'd take that over going through what we've experienced these last few weeks. Being without you was killing me, you know that."

"I know, and I'm sorry for how I reacted, making us go through being apart for so long."

"I love you more than anything, and I'm willing to explain it all to you again if you need me to," Young Mack offered.

"I love you too, and that won't be necessary. I'm more focused on getting the test results when the baby comes."

"Same here," he agreed.

"There's something I need you to know, and I hope you don't take this as me needing attention," she said, looking him in the eyes.

"Talk to me," he replied, a hint of his smooth self showing up. She bit her bottom lip after watching him lick his perfect lips—yes, she was definitely in need of some sexual healing.

"My period is two weeks late, but before you think too much into it, I haven't taken a pregnancy test yet. I've been so mad at you that I didn't even tell Stephanie."

"Well, unlike you, I'm not waiting to see what's up. I need to know now!" Young Mack grinned big before rushing into the walk-in closet. He came back out carrying a Balenciaga jogging suit for her, with matching designer shoes, then quickly helped her get dressed. He even sat her down on the bed and tied both of her shoes before standing her up and kissing her lips.

"I love you," she said, joyfully, after weeks of being without him.

"I love you, and I love you too, junior!" he said to her, then spoke to her flat stomach. She couldn't contain her laughter, the sound coming from deep within her soul, as he whisked her down the hall and they took the stairs of their beautiful home.

"Hey! Where are you two rushing off to?" Stephanie yelled joyfully after seeing them happily running off hand in hand.

"Drug store! We'll be right back!" Aeriella shouted over her shoulder in rushed excitement.

"Drug store?" Stephanie questioned curiously, and Chloe shrugged with a knowing look that told Stephanie everything.

"Drug store!" Aeriella repeated, then Stephanie and Chloe laughed together.

***

On the other side of the huge home, the excitement wasn't building, which was unfortunate for K-Dawg and Gianna. Over the past few weeks, they had spent every day together, and their bond and sexual chemistry had shot off the charts. He was everything she'd always wanted in a man, blowing those expectations out of the water on every level. He never once shied away from anything when it came to her needs, and pleasuring her came naturally to him. Over the weeks, she had given him every part of her body to explore, and he accepted her completely, handling her with both care and aggression, always with perfect timing. She had lived most of her life as a stone-cold killer, but she was still a woman with needs and craved unwavering love. The way he was with her kept her mind and heart open to the possibility of them as a serious couple in the near future.

After weeks of unbridled joy and passion, things had suddenly come to a standstill for the lovebirds. Gianna couldn't take her eyes off the iPhone K-Dawg had bought her a few days ago so she could communicate with her other two crew members and with him while he was out handling business. She stayed at Young Mack's new home while K-Dawg was in the trenches. She had to reach out to Monsta and Pop because the three of them had been close ever since Phatts brought them together, pulling them off the streets to groom them as protectors of his son—before Rob was even in the picture. After checking in with them and letting them know what happened with the exchange, she assured them she was alright and just needed some time to herself. What she wasn't prepared for was the response she got back.

"I don't like it," K-Dawg said, leaning back against the wall, his large arms folded across his chest.

"How is it even possible after what you saw?" Gigi asked, her eyes still glued to the phone. "That pussy nigga's gotta be running a scam. How else could he have gotten away from those clown-ass niggas that snatched him up?"

"The more I think about it, the more I know you're right. He's gotta be sliming," Gigi agreed, still deep in thought.

"What are you thinking?" K-Dawg asked as he sat down next to her, kissing her neck and shoulder while his big hand squeezed her naked thigh.

"I'm thinking that if he's sliming, then I have to kill him. And after experiencing you, I know I'll pull through on it. Hell, just thinking about it is making me wetter than your touches." Gianna purred as K-Dawg pulled her hair, causing her neck to arch, giving him better access. "Ummmm, that feels good. I think I have a plan that could kill three birds with one stone." She sighed as he moved down her body, stretching her boy shorts to one side before capturing her lower lips with his lips and tongue.

"I'm listening," he mumbled, not breaking contact with her delicate flesh.

"You're making me cum!"

"Hurry up and tell me, or I'll decide how we'll handle it," he said, sitting back on his haunches, staring at her with her juices glistening on his lips and chin.

"I'll show up willingly, already knowing what his plans are," she said, pausing as she watched his brows tighten, though he remained silent, listening intently. "That way, we can lure them all to one location. I'm almost positive that if Daniel has bargained for me, he won't allow them to kill me. He'd die before he let anyone else take me out, especially by someone else's hands. Once we have them all in one spot, we can kill them there and finish this war."

K-Dawg didn't say a word once she finished, as she had hoped he would. She really needed his approval of her plan. Instead, his face was back between her legs, his tongue and lips continuing their work while he gave her plan some careful thought, adding a few ideas of his own for extra security. He didn't stop, even when he felt her body tremble with that now-familiar sensation. Pushing two of his thick fingers inside her wetness, he pumped them at full speed until she screamed out in pleasure as her orgasm rocked her world.

"We'll have to run things by Young Mack after we put in some of my own ideas to make your plan foolproof," K-Dawg said, sucking her juices from his fingers, thighs, and her shorts.

"I'm ready," she replied, one of her breasts exposed, her fingers pinching and pulling her nipple. She bit down on her lip before leaning in to suck his lips into her mouth.

"You talking about the plan, or are you asking for this?" he asked with a devilish grin before pulling himself out of his briefs and plunging deep into her tightness.

***

"Jefe, it's been ages! How have you been?" Mackmillions greeted the graying Mexican drug lord with a firm handshake.

"Good, good. And how are you today?" Jefe Juanita graciously replied, offering Mackmillions a warm welcome.

Seeing all the armed men patrolling the perimeter of the prestigious Mexican-American restaurant made Mackmillions miss Max in a major way. But more pressing issues needed to be handled, so he had sent Max away to protect his queen on their mission to undo what his enemy had done. Just thinking about it made his temples throb, and his jaw flexed with the realization that Castro was one step ahead of him—a near-impossible target to terminate.

Sensing the disturbed demeanor of the usually composed man before him, Jefe Juanita decided not to keep him longer than necessary.

"Anything to drink?" Jefe Juanita offered, gesturing to the extensive drink menu on the table.

"Hennessey, double, two cubes of ice," Mackmillions ordered as they sat across from each other.

"Life can really be stressful at times, no?"

"Tell me about it," Mackmillions chuckled, and the old man smiled in response.

Mackmillions couldn't tell if it was chance or destiny that brought Jefe Juanita to request his presence without warning. He had definitely planned to reach out to the old man once everything with Castro was settled, aiming to creatively and successfully align the seats at the Realm's round table of bosses. He smiled inwardly at the thought of restarting what he had once built and led in the earlier chapters of his legendary life.

"As one of my oldest living associates, Mack, you know that it's imperative for me to have knowledge of all things going on in and around this kingdom of ours. I know you've been a very busy man since your release, and I, my friend, know where your plot for revenge stops." Jefe Juanita paused to ensure Mackmillions understood that he, too, was aware of and respected his code. "You need help, Mack. And as sure as I am that you do, I'm just as sure that I need your help as well."

"I see some people never change, huh, old friend?" Mackmillions shook his head with a slight grin.

"Likewise," Jefe Juanita smiled, revealing his platinum-trimmed teeth.

"Okay, now that I'm interested, enlighten me on how you can help me. Then, I'll need you to explain what it is you want from me in return for your help." Mackmillions leaned forward, resting his arms on the table.

Jefe Juanita waited until the waitress delivered their drinks and quietly departed before explaining his connection to Castro's little shadow and his comrades. Jonathan Dickerson could be delivered to Mackmillions, gift-wrapped, if he was willing to help.

After hearing the details, Mackmillions wasn't surprised at all by Dickerson's extreme sexual fetishes. He knew there were all types of disgusting individuals in the world, especially after serving over fifteen years in federal prison. The thought of getting his hands on Dickerson, and possibly gaining a lead on Castro, made him smile graciously.

"You know I can't and won't turn down such an opportunity. Now I'm curious to know what this prize will cost me," Mackmillions said, leaning back and sipping his dark liquor.

"Your son," Jefe Juanita said.

Before Mackmillions even realized what he was doing, he was on his feet, the business end of his M9 pressed hard against the drug lord's forehead.

Jefe Juanita's men hurried to take aim at Mackmillions, but the drug lord raised his fist, halting their movements.

"Mack, please excuse my delivery of words in the English language and allow me to explain my sincere intentions," Jefe Juanita said calmly.

Mackmillions' nostrils flared as he stared into the old man's eyes. He wasn't one to let emotions drive his actions, but the mention of his only child hit him deep. Though he had been busy handling his own situations, he knew his son was at war with a rival in his drug trade, a war that had cost him a home and nearly claimed his family's lives. Hearing his son's name roll off Jefe Juanita's tongue made him question whether letting the old man live was worth the risk. Should he eliminate the threat altogether, even if it meant dying by the hands of the armed guards, to ensure his son's rise to power?

"I assure you, I mean no harm to your family. If you will just hear me out, everything will become much clearer," Jefe Juanita expressed honestly. Mackmillions was a powerful man who killed for entertainment, but Jefe Juanita was no one's bitch—he was just as dangerous and as lethal as any cartel boss before him.

"You have sixty seconds to make me understand," Mackmillions growled.

"Put your weapon away, and please, take a seat," Jefe Juanita gestured toward Mackmillions' chair. After a moment of thought, Mackmillions reluctantly complied but left his gun on the table instead of putting it back in his waistband.

"I'm not at all surprised that you aren't aware of the intense war happening between our sons. It pains me to see our only children, now grown and capable men, going at each other without mercy," Jefe Juanita explained as

168

Mackmillions slowly holstered his gun and listened. "A hundred thousand kilos?"

"Yes, and the bigger issue is control of that passage tunnel," Jefe Juanita continued. "I am willing to let it all lie, as well as assist your cause—"

"Cut the shit, Juanita. What's the cost?" Mackmillions interrupted.

"A seat at the Realm's table of bosses," Jefe Juanita said firmly, yet with hope.

"Even with the contribution you're offering, it doesn't seem worth all your troubles and sacrifices. What's really going through that wise mind of yours, old friend?" Mackmillions asked, knowing full well the drug lord had more up his sleeve.

"You mistake my request," Jefe Juanita smiled.

"I'm pretty sure I got it head-on. So, go ahead and tell me what it is you're really asking."

"The seat isn't for me; it's for my son."

Mackmillions took a moment to absorb the request before responding. "He's not old enough, and he's already an enemy of my own flesh and blood. How could we possibly make that work?"

"Come on, Mack. We'll both compromise and make it worth everyone's while. I'll do my part in whatever's needed, but you have to help me save our sons from themselves. Because, sure as day, one or both of them will die in this ridiculous war between them."

As much as Mackmillions hated to admit it, he knew the old man was right. He trusted his son to stand tall in the face of opposition, and he trusted his son's judgment. But what he didn't trust was how unpredictable life could be. The tables could turn in any direction, like the roll of a dice, and that was a chance he didn't want to take.

"How fast can you deliver Dickerson?" Mackmillions asked, ready for the next phase of his master plan.

Jefe Juanita smiled, snapping his fingers to signify his swift delivery.

"Well, let's get to it. We've got a war to smother out," Mackmillions said with a smile, and the men shook hands.

Chapter 16

Young Mack stood silently, water threatening to escape his teary eyes as he stared up at the massive still shots he had developed and framed to hang on both sides of his living area fireplace. The still shots were of Ashton and Hogg in their own solitary moments of joy. Both men wore bright smiles that highlighted their happiness in those good moments of life, and it pained Young Mack that both of his youngins were now gone and never coming back.

He closed his eyes tight, and a tear braved its way down past his cheek before he caught it with his index finger, then wiped it away along with the wet stream it left in its wake. He hated the way it felt, but the solemnity of the moment only deepened the pain he felt. He knew it would never go away with time, and he wouldn't stop until their enemies were six feet deep.

After paying his homies a silent moment of respect along with the rest of his crew, he slowly turned around with a mask of anger and looked over every person that had been summoned to attend the mandatory meeting. He knew his team was official in every facet of the game—his killers killed relentlessly, and his hustlers flipped through dope like sports fans flipped through cable channels on NFL Sunday. Even those who hustled were always ready to body shit. As he looked over the mugs on all their faces, he saw that everyone at least felt some, if not all, of the pain resonating throughout his entire being.

"Ummph-hummm. I'm glad all of y'all were able to get free to join this meeting, but most importantly, I'm glad that all of you are still alive and breathing here with me right now." He paused, and a deep scowl formed on his face as he concentrated to control the tears that once again were threatening to escape his eyes. He couldn't control his emotions while seeing everyone there together, but Ash and Hogg couldn't be there after losing their lives to Gurdo's hands.

"Take yo' time, Young. We ain't in no hurry, bruh, we right here with you!" Pooh spoke up. Pooh was a young and determined hustler who had been by Young Mack's side in the drug game ever since he bought his first wholesale pack and needed someone to flip it for him. Pooh felt his pain even more since he and Hogg had grown really close through transactions for the operation. Hogg was the one who always came through and delivered him his assigned package, being that he had taken over handling the same route Young Mack himself used to handle.

"I appreciate y'all being patient with me. This shit harder than a mu'fucka—being back now and can't kick the shit with them. But I gotta brave this shit like a champ in a twelve-round bout tryna defend his title, same as I need for all of y'all to do no matter how tight shit gets. We clutchin' on anything that don't resemble this family. We are these streets, and these streets are us, and when a mufucka touches anyone in this family, that shit is un-fuckin-forgivable! From here on out, this city is now inoperable to any other drug faction outside of our allies and those that are outside of our product trade. Mu'fuckas done fucked around and pissed me off, and the head of every mu'fucka that bucks our takeover is urgently needed to mount that bitch up on our mantle." Young Mack was so heated that his eyes burned and sweat lightly coated his skin.

"Excuse me, big bruh!" A voice spoke up from the rear before the guy stood, and everyone saw that it was Lil' Jay.

Lil' Jay was a certified hustler who was on the rise after being bumped up from corner boy to weight holder for his section in the hood.

"Better be good, Jay. What's on yo' mind?" Young Mack asked with a raised brow.

"First, I'd like to offer my sincerest condolences." Young Mack nodded before he continued. "This takeover shit sounds good, and I'm definitely with it, but my concern lies in the fact that in order to make it work, we'll either have to rob every single mu'fucka that ain't our allies holding weight, or we're gonna need one helluva plug because some of these niggas are holding enough work to supply some small countries out here." Once again, Young Mack nodded without a word. "I'm not at all ungrateful for every opportunity that being a part of this crew has provided me with, but to emphasize my point . . . I've been requesting to get our usual bumped up a few books for as long as I've been holding shit down for my section, and Allah knows we really need it." Lil' Jay concluded and prayed that Young Mack didn't feel slighted by his open honesty.

"Well, I am aware of your many requests as well as what's gonna be needed for a takeover of this magnitude, but timing and position is everything out here in these streets. One can't go from being rock-boy to being the plug in one night and not expect to lose everything he worked so hard to get. It's all about the whole of transitioning, and while in transition, you cannot put all of your eggs in one basket and then rely on hope to keep shit up to par. Hope is a busy bitch, just as well as I am a busy man, so I don't have time to deal with all that comes with making time for her. And now, with that being said, I need to know how much work your section in the Brickz can handle."

"On the bust down tip, I'd say two books easy a week, and that's not counting wholesale orders mu'fuckas be putting in because they only wanna do business with us, so I'd say four—"

"Ten it is," Young Mack cut him off, and the young hustler's eyes grew to the size of saucers in surprise. "And we will not be robbing shit from the ops if it ain't cash, weapons, or jewelry. Burn that trashy-ass shit." Gasps and murmurs erupted throughout the room. Young Mack knew that the fellas would have differences of opinion on how he chose for them to conduct themselves while dealing with the ops, but he was judge, juror, and decision-maker. "Drugs will not be a problem anymore for a long time to come, which brings me to my next order of business," he added before reaching up and taking a glass of 1942 from the shelf above the fireplace. "As of this moment in our operation in drug supplying, everyone is to report to Pooh for direct orders, and that goes for money pick-up too."

"Wait, what?" Pooh asked, more surprised than anyone in the room.

"You've just been promoted, my G. What you gon' do?" Deuce smiled and raised his glass of 1942 high in the air, and everyone else followed in salutations. He was proud of Pooh, and Young Mack had definitely made a good choice in appointing him, knowing it would be both profitable and structured for their team.

"Shit, you already know it's on and poppin', family!" Pooh replied, as excited as anyone in his position could ever be to receive such a promotion. The small crowd applauded and whistled in excitement for their hood brother.

"Pooh, you will now in turn report straight to Deuce for any needs for yourself, and you are the voice of them," Young Mack made a show of swinging a pointed finger at all around them. "You will be the only link between the weight and our suppliers for distribution, and you will no longer sell or construct sales of any products. Welcome to the big table, my nigga. Loyalty!"

"Loyalty!" All others shouted in unison.

"K-Dawg, you and young Rolla are now assigned to hammer duty for this takeover, effective immediately," Young Mack informed them, and they nodded in agreement.

"Deuce, my mu'fuckin' guy. You will now be the only link between Pooh and me. It will be your job to load and secure any and all shipments from my choice destinations, and without you, our crew will dry out and be forcefully condemned. It's now your show, big bruh, and for now, I have arranged for fifty thousand bricks of the purest Columbian cocaine to be brought to us here from Mexico, and that should arrive any hour, so be ready to make it shake." Young Mack spoke and raised his glass high, followed by everyone else. Deuce was now receiving the same applause and whistles as the others had.

"You niggas listen to me closely. This product that we are now dealing with is as pure as the big heads get it once it enters Mexico from Columbia, so the shit is so strong it could easily be hit twice and still out-smoke the comp around the city. We will not be stretching this shit but once in order to leave action for our allies to produce more profit, and in turn, that's a profit they will certainly be spending back with us. And since we will not be tolerating the comp, there will be no challenges to if we have the best shit in Houston or not—because we most definitely will. This is only the beginning of our climb to the top in our own city, so leave the big-headed shit on the shelf and don't underestimate anyone, ever! Any problems or signs of the comp in our areas, K-Dawg and Rolla should be you niggas' first call, not your weapons. We are now in transition to being one of the biggest and baddest black movements the streets of Houston have ever seen, even bigger than Meechie and them from back in the day. This is our day, and from this day forward we will be acknowledged as Guap!" Young Mack hyped his team.

"This that type of shit I been waiting for!" Lil' Jay popped off in a rush of excitement, mixed with his second round of 1942.

"Nawl, for real!" someone else added, and then everyone in the room shouted and whistled in excitement for their new status.

"It's time to stop playing out here. We got shit to do," Young Mack spoke to K-Dawg and Rolla, while Deuce and Pooh shared a moment to themselves. Everyone else crowded around the scantily clad, model-fine women that were catering to them during the meeting. Young Mack had hired a professional chef for their meeting as well and smiled with joy as he watched everyone trying the new exquisite dishes he was sure none of them had ever been able to enjoy before now.

This was definitely a great time for him, and he gave thanks to Stephanie Valdez and her brothers for paving the way for him to make it all happen for himself and his crew. And with everything being as it may, he knew there was only one thing standing in the way of his true happiness, and he was now more determined to destroy them than he had ever been before.

***

"You mean to tell me that y'all got ambushed at the gold transaction and Gigi left you for dead?" Monsta asked skeptically, still not believing that bullshit. He knew Gianna wasn't capable of no slimy shit like that when it came to the well-being of her own people.

"Yeah, that's exactly what I'm sayin', nigga. Is you deaf? I guess the bitch got tired of me tagging her ass for doing stupid shit and said 'fuck me.' I don't know why she did it, but the fact is she did, and now I gotta crush the stupid bitch," Rob lied his ass off.

"Shit ain't addin' up, big bruh!" Monsta stated, looking to his big brother for verification. His lack of response pissed Monsta off more than Rob's lying words, and he didn't hide his ill feelings from either of them. "Lame-ass niggas, I can't believe this shit! How the fuck is we really here talkin' about steppin' on Gigi, of all the people in the world we could be fuckin' over!"

"Fuck is you callin' lame, bitch nigga!" Rob stood and immediately drew his weapon, with Monsta only seconds quicker than him.

"Both of you cornball as—" Monsta yelled out before his body took a nose dive into the thick carpet of Rob's dining room floor from the impact of his brother's big fist crashing into his temple.

"Talk too fuckin' much, bruh. I can't even think, damn!" Pop said, as if his brother could hear him in his unconscious state.

Pop was both angered and confused at the moment, and his brother wasn't making matters any better with his temper tantrum. He delivered the knockout blow not because of his brother's mouth but because he didn't want Rob to have a chance to kill him for the blatant disrespect, then he'd be forced to kill Rob, and he didn't want that either.

The sound of keys entering the locks drew their attention before the front door opened, then closed. Rob and Pop sat quietly, waiting for Gianna to come into the big dining room where they sat, now passing a thick blunt between them.

"Whoa! What the fuck happened to big mouth?" Gigi chuckled, looking both shocked and amused once she stepped into view and saw him laid out on the floor.

"Pissed me off," Pop stated flatly.

Gigi shook her head, not wanting to speak on their family dysfunctions. She tossed the duffle bag filled with rubber-banded bundles of money onto the pool table, with both Rob and Pop's eyes following the black bag until it hit the tabletop.

177

"How you?" she asked, remembering that he did get hit with the ass end of a Range Rover and tossed across a hangar before getting snatched up by their attackers.

"I'm Gucci, and you?" Rob replied while ice-grilling her.

"Got hit twice, but the shots went through and through, nothing major I guess," Gianna spoke sarcastically, then lifted her shirt to prove her words.

"Cute, but where have you been?" Rob asked, his voice full of suspicion.

"Hospital, then I shacked up in a hotel room while I healed. Didn't wanna be around anyone while not knowing what happened to you or who hit us. What about you?" Her question surprised him because he hadn't let on that he'd been missing in action since the attack. He knew then that she had been keeping contact with Monsta and Pop while he was in the hands of Gurdo and his men.

"What's in the bag?" he asked, completely ignoring her last question.

"Loot from the transaction. You didn't think I'd leave without it, did you?" She raised a brow while studying his reaction.

"Chose the money over me, huh? Classic. That just makes my decision that much easier," Rob stated before snapping his fingers.

"What are—" Gianna ducked once she spotted movement at her right side, sending Pop's big fist swooshing over her head like an angry torpedo. His charge both shocked and hyped her as she dodged his right knee, which was intended to connect with her chin.

"Pop, what the fuck!" Gianna yelled as she took a stance to defend herself while Rob sat back in his chair, arms folded over his chest with a shit-eating grin on his face. This was definitely something she hadn't pictured happening.

Pop didn't say a word as he steadily approached her, ready to get it over with. He'd rather trade her life for the life of his brother any day. Unbeknownst to Monsta, Rob had told him the whole story, also explaining the promises from the drug lord, which were all too good to pass up.

"I don't wanna hurt you, Pop, please stop!" Gigi pleaded.

"Yeah, right!" Pop laughed mockingly, which only angered her.

"So, no more love and loyalty? Is that how it is?" Gigi had tears streaming down her cheeks from the way Pop was turning on her for Rob's snake ass. The shit was truly breaking her heart to see him choosing the wrong side.

"I'm not him," Pop nudged his head toward his still unconscious brother.

"Stop talkin' to the bitch and put her down so we can get on with this shit," Rob ordered from his seat at the dining table.

Pop lurched at her with both hands, and she made his ass regret it by using his size and momentum against him. She swiftly sidestepped out of his reach before hammering down with her right fist on his right wrist, then delivering a bone-crushing left uppercut to his right elbow. Pop yelled out in agonizing pain, grabbing at his broken arm with his left hand. Feeling no remorse for his pain, Gigi used all the strength she could muster to kick his right knee past its breaking point. Another scream bellowed from his throat as he went down for the count.

She couldn't believe Rob was able to convince Pop to go against her, knowing that her advanced skill set would be way too much for him to handle. There was no time for games now that she understood it was her life being traded over theirs.

Stepping forward, she slightly paused as Pop's left hand swung out in an attempt to halt her. She swatted his weak attempt with ease before rotating behind him, wrapping her arms around his neck, ready to end his treacherous ass. But before she could, she felt that all-too-familiar feeling of hard steel pressed into the back of her neck.

"Let 'em go, then back up slowly with your hands behind your back," Rob growled in frustration.

Though he was extremely disappointed in Pop's failed attempt, he was even more surprised by Gianna's masterful takedown of such a big opponent. Seeing her move with so much ease made him think back on all the times he put his hands on her—she could've easily taken him out with her bare hands if she'd chosen to. The reality of it made him feel a pang of remorse, but it quickly evaporated as his choice to live overshadowed his guilt trip.

"Just couldn't stand the pressure of being a real nigga, huh, Rob?" she asked as she did what he said.

"Real niggas take their lives serious, and that's exactly what I'm doin'. The ops want you alive in order to secure my wealth and my life, so who am I to deny them their just due?" Rob didn't give a shit about how she felt about his decision to live—hell, she'd be too dead to argue in a minute.

"A real nigga woulda died with honor before trading the only mufucka willing to die for his bitch ass. Pussy!" Monsta growled as he stood behind Rob with his .50 cal Desert Eagle parked against Rob's cranium.

"Fuuuck!" Rob sighed.

"Let her go, drop the gun, and let's get my brother to a hospital. We'll figure the rest out afterwards. I really don't wanna crush you to make that happen, my nigga—I mean, I kinda do, but I won't unless you buck this G-shit that runs through my veins. Unlike you, this murder shit makes my dick hard," Monsta stated, even calmer than his usually hyped self.

"A'ight, fuck it." Rob caved and reluctantly lowered his weapon, then turned around to find Monsta there, but he wasn't standing there alone. "Wh—" Gianna took full advantage of his shocked state, punching the gun from his grip, then delivering a massive roundhouse kick to his face that dazed him and dropped him to his knees as he braced himself up with both hands.

"Pussy! I oughta kill you! I was loyal to you when I knew I deserved better, and you were about to hand me over to those crazy-ass people! I would've gone to war with them over you against all odds, Rob, what the fuck! They let you go to hand me over . . . we could've gone against them!" Gianna continued to slap the shit out of him before turning away, tears drenching her face.

K-Dawg stood with his back against the wall, left foot propped up and his arms folded over his big chest as he watched Gigi become undone behind Rob's betrayal. He shook his head and sneered at the pathetic mu'fucka before him. He knew such a weak-ass nigga could never fully understand what he had in Gianna because he was nothing like her. That killer shit was driving deep inside them; it was part of their genetic makeup, whereas Rob was a true thief and a cowardly mu'fucka.

"Guess you're here to finish me off?" Rob chuckled, trying his best to lift himself up and seem unnerved, but deep down he was a nervous wreck.

"Nope," was K-Dawg's only reply before he pushed off the wall and made his way over to Gianna. "I'm here for her, and now that it's clear you can't handle her, I'll handle her for you."

Rob frowned with a deep scowl on his face as he watched Gianna step into the arms of another nigga right before his eyes. He even had to laugh to himself at his raging jealousy. He felt pathetic and knew he looked the part as well, and all he could do was think about what was next to come for him.

"Good look, Clay," K-Dawg saluted Young Mack's Fifth Ward goon.

"Over easy, bruh. Monsta is a good young nigga, and with the right guidance, I know he'll develop into his own boss one day instead of hiding out under pussy mufuckas all day," Clay said with his hand on Monsta's shoulder.

"What's up with my brother?" Monsta knew his big bro had crossed the line. Hell, his head was still aching from the blow his brother had delivered earlier.

"That's between you and her," K-Dawg said, pulling Gigi into his arms and looking into her honey-colored eyes.

"Because of you, I would never hurt him more than what's necessary to keep his big ass up off of me," Gigi replied, and they both laughed at the thought.

"Well, that's that. And now for you," K-Dawg moved until he was standing only inches from Rob. "Grab your phone and let them mu'fuckas know you got what they want and to get here pronto," he ordered.

Rob was hesitant to move, but the sound of guns being cocked all around him, then aimed at him, hastened his movements. He snatched up his iPhone—the one they had given him to call from—and quickly dialed. The line rang a few times while K-Dawg busied himself with a mock tie-up of Gianna to a chair and placed a gag prop in her mouth.

"Yeah," Daniel's voice sounded throughout the room, as K-Dawg had set it to call on speaker.

"Gift-wrapped that package you ordered, like promised," Rob stated, sounding very convincing.

"Damn, I love the sound of that. Put the phone to her ear for me," Daniel ordered.

"Umph, hummmph mmmmph ummmphuh!" Gigi pretended to yell out obscenities through the fake gag.

"Gianna, long time little cousin," Daniel spoke in Spanish. "You've betrayed your own blood time and time again, and now you must pay for your sins. I hate that this will hurt cousin Raul, but it's a necessary evil—"

"Alright, my man, I'm here where you left me. I'm tired of being on edge around this bitch, so get here and take this bitch, kill the bitch, or whatever—makes me no damn difference, but I gotta get my guy to a hospital, she almost killed the nigga," Rob added theatrics to sound even more convincing.

"I'm already ten minutes out," Daniel said before the call
ended.

Chapter 17

Max couldn't bring himself to get even a minute of shut-eye on the private jet taxiing from Texas to Florida. He felt guilty about not being there beside his best friend and mentor, silently worrying about how the meeting had turned out. Looking down at his aching hands, he thought about his own situation with his health that he had yet to explain to his best and only friend. Things would be difficult for him moving forward, and he couldn't help but wonder how his mentoring friend would take the news of his weathering health.

"We're here!" Molly's excited voice brought him out of his mental state of worry as the Uber driver pulled up to a nice high-rise building with a perfectly manicured lawn and overly expensive cars in the driveway.

Max wasn't a man of many words—hell, he hardly ever said anything at all unless it was to Mackmillions or those sex-crazed Jamaican beauties. He smoothly went into his linen dress pants pocket and peeled the driver a crispy hundred from a large wad of cash. The driver nodded his appreciation for Max's generosity.

After exiting the Uber ride, the trio walked together up to the front door of the multi-leveled dwelling before Max stepped ahead of the two women to position himself as their shield in case any danger popped out at them. He kept both of his hands tucked inside his Yves Saint Laurent pockets as he approached the door, but after a closer look, he could see that the door was slightly ajar, and that sent him into security mode quick. Holding a hand back to halt the women in their steps, Max removed the 93R 9mm Beretta from his back as he slowly came closer to the opened door before silently stepping inside.

The home was clean and quiet, and nothing seemed to be wrong or outta place, but Max knew never to assume anything when it came to security. He always analyzed everything thoroughly before making any decisions that could cost more than he was willing to lose. He slowly crept up the stairs after clearing the first floor of any potential threats, with the business end of his weapon leading the way. After making it to the top of the stairs, he had an option to go left or right, but the choice was made for him once he noticed a pair of bare legs lying out in the hallway to his left. Keeping his weapon trained ahead of him, he took a quick glance behind him and shook his head at the sight of both women peeking their heads up from the stairs, watching his every move. He refocused his attention on the legs out in the hallway as he stealthily made his way over until he had a clear view of the rest of the man lying out on the bathroom floor.

He didn't see a need to search the man's body for a pulse because he could smell the familiar smell of death rising up from the corpse. The huge puddle of congealed blood beneath the guy's head and upper body also expressed how dead he really was. A clean cut across the man's throat gaped open, the skin still a bit swollen from the pressure applied to inflict such a wound. It told Max that he'd been dead since last night. Max looked to the stairs and waved for Molly to come to him, and she did.

Max nodded in the direction of the corpse laid out on the bathroom floor between the doorway and the hallway once she had a complete view of what lay there. Molly secretly smiled inside at the flawless job her Matthew had done once she spotted the dead surgeon. She pulled her phone out and pulled up a picture of the late doctor before handing it to Max.

"We leave now!" Max said and grabbed both women by their hands before racing down the stairs. Beside the door, he spotted two key fobs and immediately snatched one up, using his shirt to open the front door while ushering the women out and staying close on their heels.

***

"Ummmm, you smell so good," Stephanie inhaled Young Mack's scent while wrapping her arms around his waist as he looked himself over in the mirror. His father had summoned him via text message and had set up a meeting for them this evening, and though he really wanted to be other places and doing other things to avenge his homies, he knew better than to miss out on a meeting with his father. Plus, K-Dawg and Rolla assured him that they had everything under control and that Lil' Clay and his men would be accompanying them on their mission. So with everything as it was, he was excited about being able to sit down with his father and see what was on his mind.

He chose a three-piece tailored Armani suit that caressed his athletic figure like a glove and paired it with matching Armani loafers. The color was ash with a white undertone. He took a glance at his diamond-encrusted Cartier timepiece before making sure the rest of his jewelry was in order. He smiled at the exotic wonders of the queenpin that was Stephanie Valdez. Since the first time he saw her on his chance trip to Mexico, he knew that he wanted her—a want that he never really thought would materialize. And now, after all that they'd been through and shared as friends, she was now the best complement to a relationship between him, her, and his childhood love. He was grateful, knowing there was really nothing more as a man that he could ask for. God had shown him over and over again just how blessed he was, and he wasn't taking any of it for granted, especially now with the surprising confirmation that Aeriella, his fiancée, was indeed with child.

"Thank you," he turned and kissed her forehead, then her perfect nose before moving down to capture her soft lips. Their tongues effortlessly found one another as the heat rose between them. His dick bricked as he held her firmly against his body with both hands cuffing her ample cheeks.

"Mmmmm," Stephanie moaned, then reached between them to cuff his pipe.

"Wish I had enough time to bless my queens once more, but you know how I get when Pops come calling," Young Mack said, prying himself away from his sexual desires and separating them in the process.

"It's okay, last night and early this morning was more than enough to keep us satisfied until you return."

"You shouldn't worry there, because I'm sure we could find lots of ways to take care of each other," Aeriella stated, looking up over the rim of her Fendi reading glasses and smiling at the two of them. He loved the way she looked when she was busying herself with the lawyer side of her. The slicked baby hairs laid down against her forehead and the careful application of her makeup done by a professional stylist that she and Stephanie also found to be suitable for living in their spacious home made up a look that he could never grow tired of. He loved it, and he loved her—just as well as Stephanie, who was aggressively forging with his heart.

"Still working on that new case?" he asked, proud of his woman and her dominant stance in a male-dominated field as a highly achieved defense attorney.

"Walk in the park, love. Typical railroad of a so-called African-American male, same old same old."

He smiled as he silently walked over to where she sat and stared down into her beautiful eyes. Her smile made her eyes pop as they shared their connection through each other's portals before he leaned down and tasted her luscious lips, not caring at all that they were covered in light gloss. "You two be easy, security will be posted—"

"We know!" both women said in unison, then laughed at his embarrassment.

"Do you remember how I always used to make comments about Stephanie and how I felt she was overreacting with all the security around us all the time?" Aeriella asked.

"Yeah, what about it?" he answered curiously.

"Remind you of anyone?" she laughed, then kissed his lips one more time.

"Okay, you win, but you're gonna have to get used to having so much security around you. You're in love with an evolving king and a much more evolved queenpin." Young Mack smiled as he took Stephanie back into his arms, then placed kisses all over her face and neck. She laughed and playfully fought against him to be free from his wet kisses. "Okay, like I said, I wish I had more time, but I gotta get up outta here and meet with Pops."

"Love you," Stephanie whispered seductively in his ear before taking a step outta his embrace, then wiping his lips clean of the light sheen that covered them.

"Love y'all."

"Love you more," Aeriella said, then blew him an air kiss.

Young Mack felt confident as he stepped outside of his Sugar Land home, and after a quick survey around his property, he quickly spotted something outta place. A quaint sedan sat right outside his home's security fence. "Fuck is that car doing there?" he thought to himself as Josh, his head of security, held the back door to his armored Chevy Suburban open for him.

"Been there for the last twenty minutes or so," Josh said, already knowing that his boss had spotted the unwelcomed visitor.

Young Mack didn't say anything in return, and they went about their regular talks just like they did every time they got together. Their conversation halted once Young Mack spotted the man who stepped from the driver's seat of the vehicle outside his gate.

He shook his head as they made their way through the security gate en route to the private street that led out to the public streets from his private home, securely tucked away from the view of the public roads and highways. The crooked federal agent just stood, leaning back on the driver's side door of his work vehicle with his arms folded over his chest as if being there was making a loud enough statement that he didn't need any warrant or reason to be there.

The rear passenger window slowly lowered as the armored Chevy passed through the security gate—stopping only inches from the agent. Young Mack stared intently at the man, who was clearly doing his best to make a mockery of him by being there without cause. A crooked grin appeared in the corner of Young Mack's mouth before he broke the hard silence.

"I am not my father." Words that he was sure the crooked-ass agent could not understand at the moment, but he was sure he would find out sooner rather than later.

Young Mack made a call to inform the women of the agent's presence in case matters escalated before calling to inform his father as well. To his surprise, his father almost sounded excited by this news, then gave him the order to have the agent snatched up and held until he could deal with him.

"Pass me one of those Kush blunts, Tree." Young Mack grabbed the blunt after the passenger lit it and took a quick pull. His mind ran rapidly with possible things his father could have planned for their meeting as he inhaled the potent smoke from his Kush blunt.

***

Agent Alex Drexler smiled at the sudden discomfort in the young man's face after seeing him posted outside of his home. He slid back inside his work car, then pulled out his cell and phoned his Director to let him know that his orders had been followed. The Director immediately cleared him to leave the premises of the young boss's private property.

The thought of the disrespect that came from the piss-ant's mouth caused a bile taste to form in his own. He cockily stepped out of his service vehicle, spotting two women standing off in the far distance with four men in black suits, two on either side of them. He chuckled at the presence before stepping up to the security fence and unzipping himself. He smiled in their direction as he pulled his semi-hard penis out, then proceeded to piss on their property.

"That oughta teach him," he said to himself.

He laughed sinisterly as he shook his relieved penis, then righted himself back inside his pants. His smile nervously dissolved once he turned around and saw six Hispanic men in black suits surrounding him with grimacing looks on their faces. Using his best authoritative voice, he warned the men that he was a federal agent, but it did nothing to stop their approach, and he was roughly snatched up before he could get his hand on his service weapon.

Stephanie smiled from afar as she stood next to Aeriella and witnessed the man being thrown into a throwaway van.

Aeriella shook her head, then placed her phone to her ear. "It's done."

***

"Dead? Are you seriously telling me that the man is no longer amongst the living?" Mackmillions asked, puzzled and disturbed by the news Max had delivered to him about the special surgeon who had conducted the scientifically complex surgery that altered his wife's life—ordered by his enemy and paired with the alteration of his own daughter's life. Shit was really getting too thick for comfort, and he was growing even more propelled to eliminate Castro.

"Yes, King. We arrived there only to find the good doctor slaughtered in his own home with the front door left open."

Sylvia stood up and moved into her husband's strong embrace, then kissed his strong jawline. She could tell the news made his blood pressure rise as his anger mounted, and she didn't want him flying off the handle.

"Molly, what other options do we have to successfully handle a surgery this complicated?" Mackmillions asked, and Molly could see the hope in his eyes. His concern for his wife made her wet between the legs, and her infatuation with him grew even more. She hated to alter his heart, but she couldn't let her control of their awkward situation slip from between her fingers.

His heart slowed, and disappointment appeared in his manly features once she shook her head with terrified eyes.

"Baby, don't stress yourself out about me. Look at me, I am happy. I am good and healthy and in love with the most amazing man in the world. And most importantly, baby, I am clean." Sylvia smiled as her husband held her hand above her head, spinning her around in a slow circle while showcasing her new and improved healthy body.

Mackmillions eyed his beautiful queen with love. Joy radiated from her soul and traveled through him through the portals of her eyes and her bright smile. He loved his woman with his whole heart and couldn't imagine asking God for a better soulmate. As he watched his wife, the slight thought of Em came into the picture, and he saw a clear vision of her angelic features before shaking her from his mind. He made a mental note to check in with her before he retook his throne. Just as thoughts of Em fought to interrupt the moment with his wife, his phone came to life. He gently kissed his wife's lips and watched her playfully blush like a young schoolgirl that had kissed her high school crush. He smiled even more at the sight of his son video calling him once he removed his phone from his pocket.

"'Sup, Prince?" Mackmillions smiled big into the camera and pulled his wife close so both parents appeared in the video.

"Hey, son!" Sylvia smiled warmly, unaware of the piercing blue eyes transfixed on their family moment.

"Man! Y'all look so good together!" their son laughed, even through his anger.

"Correction, main man, we look great together," Sylvia smiled and kissed her husband's cheek after hearing his loving words.

"Big facts!" Young Mack laughed. "Hey, Pop, you remember that swine problem we used to have with the gardens?"

"The one we mentioned earlier, am I right?"

"Yeah, did as you asked, and now we're waiting on your word."

"Where is that wonderful daughter-in-law-to-be of mine?"

"At home with company, why do you ask?"

"And you left her with extra detail, yes?"

"Absolutely, more than a small army," Young Mack stated with pride.

"Assign some men to prepare him for a dinner fit for a king. I have a special guest that would love nothing more than to get a taste of him."

"I'm on it." Young Mack did as his father requested once their call ended—with love.

"What's going on?" Sylvia asked after kissing his smiling lips.

"Sunshine in a dark forest, love, that's all." Mackmillions kissed her lips again. "Max, let the girls and Cedrick know that they're needed."

***

Daniel nearly stepped outta his truck before his driver brought it to a complete stop in front of the same house they had just dropped Rob off at days prior. He was proud of their decision to let him go. To him, Rob was a nobody, and even nobodies wanted to live, so he figured his life for Gianna's would be more than a worthy trade. And to finally get his hands on her after all that she'd done to their family had him so hyped he was even considering allowing Rob to live and using him as a worker for Gurdo's distributions.

He damn near had the decision made until anger filled him behind Rob's cowardice ways. Here he was about to trade over the woman he loved, a skilled killer and loyal partner, in order to save his own ass. He spat on the ground for even having thoughts of not killing the rodent he saw Rob as. Sure, he wanted Gianna's head for her crimes against their direct family, but that didn't mean he didn't still love her. She was his little cousin, and he always felt that he failed her for some odd reason, but to know that she had fallen for such a coward as Rob made him wanna chastise her and knock Rob's head off at the same time.

He hurried and made his way inside Rob's home with three of his men right on his heels. "Where are you?" he called out throughout the spacious home.

"In here!" he heard Rob's voice, then followed the unseen path to where the sound had come from.

After entering the spacious room where they were, Daniel first took in the scene, then eyed Rob with approval, even though deep down all he felt for the guy was disgust. And now, seeing as though Rob was really ready to trade her life for his, he hated Rob even more than when the feeling first set in.

His eyes fell away from Rob to the injured giant laid out, still groaning in pain. He smiled from the corner of his mouth at how bad Gigi had laid it on the big fella and found it surprising that she hadn't killed him—he was sure Rob had stopped her.

He slowly turned away from the injured guy and made eye contact with a bound and gagged Gianna. Seeing her like that both excited and angered him all at once. He reached behind his back, then removed a shiny chrome .45 automatic while he made his way closer to where she sat, eyes of hatred glaring at him.

"You've been away a long time, Gianna, and the family has really missed you," he spoke, only inches from her face. He could easily see the distaste she had for him burning in her eyes, but it did nothing to him. "You made a grave mistake going against this family. You've shed the blood of your own family and therefore forfeited your own life," Daniel scowled while using the barrel of his weapon to move loose strands of hair from her face to behind her ear. "Don't you wanna say something? Perhaps beg for your life?" he smiled evilly while removing the scarf from her mouth.

"I know what you did to my parents, you dick! I hate you!"

Gianna spat in his shocked face. He slowly used the back of his weapon hand to wipe it away, and that proved to be a great mistake on his behalf.

Gianna took full advantage of his distracted state, and once his hand had blocked his vision, she used all the power and strength she could muster from her sitting position to kick his weapon hard into his face. He yelled out as blood spurted from an open gash above his eye. The impact from her attack stunned him, and he stumbled back in temporary blindness. Gigi quickly unraveled the mock restraints, then leaped from her seat and kicked his weapon from his hand with the precision of the trained and skilled assassin she was.

Dazed and feeling naked without his weapon, Daniel launched an attack—landing three of the six haymakers. He stood back with a look of surprise as he stared down at her defenseless state. His punches had rocked her, and she was now on her hands and knees with a bloodied mouth, trying to shake the cobwebs free. His eyes scanned the floor, and he quickly located his dropped weapon. He knew that hand-to-hand, he stood a very slim chance to win against her, and he wasn't about to play himself short, so he went for the weapon—but was stopped short when a thought popped into his mind like a gust of wind. His men.

Why hadn't they reacted to Gianna's attack on him? He took a quick glance around and noticed that none of them were there. He didn't even feel their presence at all—it was as if they had never entered the room behind him. Suddenly, his thoughts turned back to Rob, and he turned his head to scan the room, only to find him missing as well. Beside him, the giant lay staring up at him with eyes he couldn't read.

He then turned his attention back to Gianna as she climbed to her feet, still looking disoriented, before his eyes went back to his weapon—and he found the shock of his life. Standing there was a man he'd tried numerous times to kill. How the hell had he allowed himself to be caught up like this? He could see the hatred and need for blood—his blood—glowing like embers in those hardened eyes. His weapon lay only inches behind where his enemy now stood.

Unable to submit to the grave feeling of defeat, Daniel balled up his face in anger and launched a sudden attack with swift, hard swings of his fists. Though uncalculated and a bit uncoordinated, he swung with strength and fury, but had no luck this time connecting with his intended target.

K-Dawg easily blocked the blows intended for his head and face before delivering a devastating straight right that sounded like concrete slapping concrete when it connected with Daniel's chin.

Daniel felt his knees weaken tremendously. His legs no longer held strength enough to carry him, and he came crashing to the floor with a clumsy last attempt at a swing that went sailing up into the empty air. Laying there on the floor, blinking wildly, he couldn't believe he'd been caught slipping so bad. He blamed his eagerness to put Gianna down for all of her murderous sins against their family. To be horribly honest with himself, he didn't even know why he was going at her so hard when he too had sinned against their family. He was indeed responsible for the deaths of Gianna and Raul's parents—a hit ordered and orchestrated by Senior Juanita.

"Pick him up and tie him to that chair," K-Dawg ordered, and his men did as they were told.

K-Dawg stared into the eyes of the ruthless killer, now weakened without a weapon to hurt someone with, and knew he was gonna love watching him die by their hands. He pulled out his phone and made a call to his brother from another mother.

"Young, we got that big package and we're waiting for your orders. Hit me back ASAP. I'm posted," K-Dawg spoke into his phone before throwing his big arms around Gianna's shoulders and pulling her to him possessively. "You know I'm letting you rock this bitch nigga once that call gets made, huh?"

"It'll be my pleasure, baby," Gianna said while wiping leftover blood from her busted lip.

Chapter 18

Johnathan Dickerson smiled like a child in a candy store as he watched the scene unfold before him. He had been stressed out the past few weeks leading up to this moment, and now, with an ample amount of liquor in his system, about four grams of the purest Mexican cocaine on a mirror in his hand, and a rolled-up hundred-dollar bill, he couldn't contain his joy.

After sniffing down two thick lines in each nostril, he wiped his nose using his thumb before holding his head back and sniffing loudly, trying to swallow down any run-off. He then took a gulp of the brown liquid fire before settling back in the comfortable recliner and enjoying his circle of friends as they partook in all different variations of sexual pleasures with both sexes. His mind was in the clouds, and his heart thumped excitedly against his chest cavity. He felt like he'd died and gone to heaven, minus the pure devilment he and his circle of power players were unapologetically participating in.

He struggled to open his eyes, unaware that he'd even closed them after the familiar warmth of a skillful pair of lips wrapped themselves around the plum of his modest six inches. The skill with which those lips and tongue worked him made him draw in a deep breath, his toes curling up as he kept his eyes locked with the mystic blue eyes of his seducer. It didn't take long for him to pulse and erupt in spasms into the wonderful warmth of his friend's throat. It still amazed him that after working with Paul for more than five years, he'd finally come around to party with them.

Shortly after being sucked dry of his man juice, he decided to make his rounds around the very exclusive warehouse that his contact had designed and fitted to cater to the wealthy and powerful men and women members of this particular circle of clientele. His contact was a very rich and powerful man and had no problem supplying everything needed to keep their fantasies alive and happening.

The first floor was decorated and catered to the exotic pleasures of leather and bondage, something he had yet to experiment with but knew that he enjoyed watching. He looked around and smiled at all the wicked excitement going on around him. Nothing was off-limits for this group, no matter the age difference, color of skin, or status in the world. This crowd was all about pain and pleasure. His prick stirred and began to harden from all the action, so he quickly made his way to the elevator before he got himself involved in something he wouldn't soon get away from.

Once the elevator doors opened, he cocked his head to the side in surprise as he watched his boss of fifteen years positioned down on all fours, taking on two young boys who couldn't have been any closer to eighteen than the sky was to the ground. He chuckled at the beast she was as he stepped inside, then pressed the button for the second of five floors.

Cassandra Mims kept her eyes on him the entire ride up while keeping her slow rhythm going on her young stud's pole. All of his inches glistened as her lips pulled back and he went back inside, chasing the confines of her tight throat. She moaned with pleasure as she sucked him down and continued to hump back into the dark-skinned kid whose eyes were locked in on the spot where their sex parts intersected. The dark kid's tongue hung out to one side of his mouth as he continued to pound forward into her wetness, meeting her stroke for stroke.

Dickerson grabbed at his now fully erected six inches and thought about how hot and tight her pussy must have felt, but before he made the decision to join in, the elevator came to a stop, and the doors opened with a ding. He winked at his boss and gave the young boys a pat on their shoulders before stepping off to explore the second floor of their sex palace.

He laughed inside as his eyes adjusted to all of the soft and bright rainbow color patterns painted all over the place. Costumed men sat around in huge-backed furniture while costumed trannies pranced around in various stages of undress. He also smiled at the group of young mermaids skipping around in a line, holding onto each other's waists as they smiled and sang along to the lyrics playing over the sound system.

He joyously made his rounds, temporarily participating in the excitement of the transgender fetishes of his friends and their friends and associates alike. After making sure that all was running smoothly, he made his way back to the elevator. As he patiently waited, he silently hoped to catch Cassandra still there so maybe he could join their fun this time around.

As the doors opened, he saw that he would be having no such luck—the cabin was empty. He stepped inside and pressed the button for the next floor, then removed the thick ball of powder cocaine he had tucked away inside of his right sock, the only place he wasn't in the nude. He quickly stuck the open end of the plastic to his left nostril and sniffed hard, then did the same with his right. The powerful rush that consumed him made him lean back against the handrail inside the elevator cabin. He closed his eyes tight as the euphoric wave took him for a ride. After a quick moment, he slowly opened his eyes and noticed that the elevator was climbing past his point of clearance. The number on the digital screen above the door moved past four, then five, before reading "PENT." Immediately, he knew that his contact was summoning him.

Once the doors opened, he reached to his right just outside of the elevator and retrieved the cherry cloth robe that hung down past his ankles. He put it on, then tied the sash tightly.

"Johnathan, come in. I have a few important men here that would love to speak with you." He heard his contact's distinctive voice bellow out. Once he had himself decent enough, he hastened his steps and made his way around the elevator bay and into the office area, where he saw his contact standing behind a thick mahogany-gold framed desk.

He smiled at the boss of the Mexican cartel and nodded before turning to where the two men stood from the comforts of their seats once he came into view. Looking the men over from head to toe, his heart nearly dropped into the acidy pit of his stomach once he finally realized who was standing before him.

"So, you're Johnathan Dickerson, huh? Castro's little bitch boy?" He heard before his heart began pounding inside of his chest like a Congo drum. Sweat sheened his forehead and upper lip as he concentrated on not losing his bladder while staring death right in its eyes.

"M-Ma-Miller, how are you?" Dickerson fumbled with his words, then lost his battle with his bladder at the mention of that name before everything went black.

***

"Aargh," a muffled sound came from the awakening agent, and at that moment, Cedrick Chandler couldn't have been more excited.

Agent Alex Drexler was, once upon a time, the assigned partner of ex-special agent Cedrick Chandler; a young and prominent agent transferred to Houston, Texas, from his homeland back in New York. Originally from New Jersey, Chandler attended school, then later joined the force in New York. A street-savvy detective that worked exceptionally well undercover in the field, he climbed the ladder by dominating the department in arrests and solving crimes all over New York and Jersey.

Shortly after joining the Houston branch, the senior Director immediately paired him with the piece of shit sitting bound and gagged before him. He was not at all prepared for the dark and devious plots being orchestrated and executed around him—that was until Mackentosh "Mr. Mackmillions" Miller came into the direct fold of things.

"Glad you finally decided to wake yo' bitch ass up," Chandler spoke to his traitor of an ex-partner before snatching the black cloak from over his head. Drexler blinked repeatedly while trying desperately to bring his vision back into focus to see who was speaking to him as if he were nothing but chewed-up bubble gum spit out on the ground, waiting for someone to step on it.

The guy before him was a statue of fuzziness, but that voice—his voice—could never be mistaken. But how could that be when he had taken those fatal shots that snatched his soul from the land of the living? The very thought of him still breathing after supposedly being dead for so long made his pulse quicken. He cursed himself for not checking for a pulse that day in the bowels of one of the Realm's many warehouses. He silently cursed his senior Director even worse for summoning him back on the heels of the Miller family. Nothing good ever came from hounding them, and he swore that if he made it away from this alive, he would never answer the call to trail them or bother them again.

"You really should tighten up your looks. You look as if you have just seen a ghost or you just found one of the world's newest invented snack cakes, you fat fuck!" Chandler laughed even through his mounting anger.

"Hummmp-hooooo!" Drexler sounded, inaudible.

"Sorry about that, let's get this outta your way." Chandler removed the gag from his mouth, and before Drexler could even make an attempt to curse him like Chandler was sure he did while the gag was in place, Chandler slapped the shit outta him. Hard slaps—one on each side of the face—damn near caused Drexler to bite his tongue in two while simultaneously causing tears to escape his eyes.

"Shut the fuck up!" Chandler yelled, as his hunger for blood rode him like a cowboy on a stallion. "You don't get to say shit unless you're asked, or I'll make an executive decision and end you—just tell the big man you tried to escape."

Rastanya and Queeny both loved the sight of Cedrick taking charge, and it was making them both horny for him while he was in true form.

"I have questions for you, Drex, and I'm gonna need you to be as honest as you've ever been in your entire life, that is if you wanna make it outta here with your life at all." Chandler eyed him closely to make sure he understood who was in charge. "You almost killed me, you fat fuck!"

"You weren't supposed to try to play Dick Tracy, but only you could do some shit like that," Drexler scoffed with distaste.

"Dick Tracy? We're the FBI, muthafucka, we're supposed to be Dick Tracy times ten, you dick!" Chandler yelled.

"Wow! I never took you to be so damn naïve, Joe." Drexler shook his head in disgust. "You of all people should know how this show gets ran, especially coming from up top."

"Up top? Nawl, we don't shoot or try to murder our partners. How the fuck could you do me like that and live with yourself?"

"You were not supposed to be there following Gamble. Why did you follow him? Couldn't you just look the other way? You just had to be the self-righteous fake-ass hero you pride yourself on being. You brought it on yourself, fuck you blaming me for?"

"Why? Because I chose not to be a puppet in whatever evil bullshit you muthafuckas are involved in? Not to mention, illegal schemes to frame and murder supposed criminals like you and Gamble obviously wanted me to? Yeah right, you muthafuckas are sick! What is it about? Money? It has to be, why else would you and Director Gamble be into such illegal dealings?"

"You have no idea how deep this shit really goes," Drexler chuckled.

"Yeah, but I bet you do, and I'm gonna get it up outta you one way or another," Chandler said before unsheathing two custom-made machetes from the Jamaican beauties' arsenal of murder weapons.

"Wait-wait, what are you about to do with those?" Drexler instantly became nervous at the sight of the big knives.

"Who do you work for?" Chandler growled as he moved toward the obviously shaken crooked agent.

"I am an agent of the fed—" his words stopped short once he felt the sharp tip of the blade touch his knee, which caused his body to jerk hard. "Okay, listen—listen—I work for Gamble, okay, it's Gamble."

"And who does he work for? Be careful how you answer that because my tolerance for bullshit has already hit zero." Chandler stated truthfully. He wanted nothing more than to kill Drexler's slimy ass in the sickest of fashions.

"The Realm—he works for the Realm, or whatever is left of it anyway."

"Names, I need names!" Chandler said, digging the blade a tad bit deeper, careful not to break the skin through his jeans.

"Whooa, now that's above even my pay grade and knowledge. All I do is follow orders from Gamble, no one else. You'll have to get that from him."

"You idiots were really planning to set up Miller and then frame me for his murder. Just how stupid do you dicks think I am?"

"Under the right circumstances, you would have blown that son of a bitch to pieces, and I'd have been right there by your side to witness it all," Drexler smiled deviously.

"You're not smart enough."

"So says you, the silly muthafucka I almost killed with his own gun," Drexler taunted.

"Kirk!" Chandler called out.

"Kirk? Who the fuck is Kirk? Are you losing it?" Drexler asked, confused, but kept a shit-eating grin on his face.

"Uh—that would be me."

Chandler smiled once his best friend and old college roommate stepped into the room, carrying a USB chip between his outstretched fingers.

"Fuck are you?" Drexler asked, unfazed by the nerdy-looking mu'fucka talking all proper and shit.

"Special Agent, Kirk Drumfield. Internal Affairs." Drexler almost shit himself at the mention of Internal Affairs. Chandler had just tricked him into rolling on not just himself but on his senior director as well, and now all hell was about to break loose. He knew his life as a free man was now over. Oh, how he'd rather be killed instead!

"Fuck boy," Chandler taunted with a sinister grin after seeing the look on Drexler's face. "Full confession, smart guy!" Chandler laughed so hard he nearly lost his voice.

"Shit!" Drexler grumbled in defeat.

***

"Johnathan, my boy, we can do this the easy way or the hard way." Mackmillions cracked his knuckles after removing his dress shirt to reveal a muscular figure and a body full of tattoos. His muscle shirt looked as if it were painted on his sculpted figure.

"I-I don't want any trouble! I-I-I'm just a pawn in all of this," Dickerson cried out, near panicked.

"I'm glad you know that, so we can make this brief and you can get back to your drugs and liquor and your very, very pedophilic and sick evening." Hearing those words, though they stung a little, still gave him hope as he looked from one person to the next. Everyone did seem a lot more relaxed, and that also heightened his hope factor and nearly made his prick harden. Well, that was the drugs mixed with his new excitement.

"Sure, I'm willing to help in any way I can. All you gotta do is tell me what you need from me," Dickerson quickly submitted.

"I need a list of addresses, security codes, plate numbers, and anything else you have that can help me find Castro," Mackmillions stood directly in front of the weak man.

"Oh, that's easy." Dickerson didn't even break a sweat as he rattled off all the information needed for them to track down Castro.

The way Johnathan Dickerson saw it, once they destroyed Amir Castropella, there would be no way to attach him to anything in the criminal world outside of the agreement he held with the powerful drug lord. He wasn't worried at all about the partying, especially with everyone who's anyone in his world attending; that news would never break past any reporter's lips. He smiled as he stood against the handrail inside of the elevator headed down to rejoin the dirty, dark fantasies and fetish caterings with his colleagues. Not only was he free to go on with his life after divulging every piece of information he had on Castro, his contact even blessed him with a free kilo of his favorite candy dust, saving him a hefty thirty thousand dollars in the process.

After getting off the elevator on the third floor, he was happy to see his boss, Cassandra, sitting gap-legged on a sectional sofa while enjoying playing teacher to a studious group of barely teenaged boys who hung on to her every word and body part. He locked eyes with her and smiled while giving her a head nod to follow him, before showing her a glimpse of his free nose candy.

"Johnathan, I would have never taken this place to be this seriously amazing if I weren't experiencing it for myself," his boss spoke to him while rubbing her huge tits together, then tweaking and pulling on her hardened nipples.

"I told you it would be everything you ever dreamed of. I always knew you were a dirty, dirty witch of a woman," he said, then took one of her cum-dried nipples in his mouth. She moaned while caressing his head with one hand and driving two fingers deep into herself with the other.

"Wait-wait, let's get some of this candy on this nice piece of meat so I can suck it all down at once." Dickerson wasted no time ripping the package open to get to the good stuff.

He couldn't contain his excitement once he saw the crystals glistening from the purity of the potent cocaine. After dumping a copious amount of the powdery white substance on the glass tabletop, he separated four thick lines from the rest, then kneeled on the floor and vacuumed the lines—two in each nostril. Once he'd cleared his share, he jumped to his feet with a start, eyes bucked, mouth wide open.

"Johnathan, baby, calm down. Is it that damn good?" Casandra laughed while rubbing his naked cheeks.

Immediately after sniffing those lines, he knew something was seriously wrong. There was no immediate euphoric rush, his throat didn't drain the normal taste into his mouth, and the taste he did detect was very familiar. A coppery-tasting drainage cascaded down his throat, then suddenly he could no longer breathe without an agonizing feeling that his trachea was being ripped into shreds. Instinctively, his hands wrapped around his throat as blood oozed from his nose and eyes.

Casandra let out an ear-piercing scream as Dickerson coughed up thick globs of blood. Everyone rushed to his side, hoping to aid their dying friend and colleague, but it was all of no use. There would be no saving Johnathan Dickerson. The finely-ground glass was tearing through everything it came in contact with internally, destroying his lungs and intestines, causing him to release his bowels on his way outta this life. The internal bleeding could not be stopped, and his life was slipping away from him one painful second at a time.

He heard everyone around him as their voices became distorted, as well as their faces. He tossed his head from side to side, but the struggle to breathe was fruitless. Blood flooded his mouth and escaped through his nostrils without mercy. He could feel himself becoming weaker as his life continued to slowly escape his flesh while everyone continued to panic above him. He knew he'd lost his battle to live and finally accepted his fate. His head rolled to the side one last time, and that's when he saw them standing there—Senior Juanita, Miller, and his ever-silent assassin staring. This was their easy way that he had chosen. Clean and without any use of force. He tried to muster a smile to show them he now understood the irony of it all, but everything went black and he was finally gone.

Chapter 19

Young Mack stared at the massive mansion in awe as he and his men were being escorted through the immaculately manicured passageway leading up to the equally massive entryway into the main house. He noticed almost immediately that the burly, armed Hispanic men were not his father's style of security and silently wondered what exactly his father had planned for the evening. He had already received the message from K-Dawg letting him know that they had both Rob and Daniel in their possession, and that news brought a smile to his face. As bad as he wanted to kill both of them, he knew for sure Rob would have to wait because he wasn't quite sure if he wanted to cash in on their relationship—especially now that they had lost Ashton. He could already hear Ashton telling him that Rob was their guy and he should give him a chance. The thought of Rob being Phatts' son made him think back to all the pouting and complaining Rob did once the order came down from his father to fall back on the capers. If Rob knew that his father was the one that robbed them, he wasn't sure, but he was dead set on getting some answers before deciding Rob's future.

His reverie was broken by the sound of the beautiful Hispanic woman's voice as she stood before him in the doorway of the main house. The slight appearance of crow's feet just above her upper lip and setting into the corners of her honey-colored eyes gave away the wisdom of age in the beautiful woman.

"Welcome, young man," her angelic-like voice grabbed his full attention.

"Evening, ma'am," he greeted her with a handsome smile as he stood before the elegantly dressed woman. Her makeup was light, with dark eyeliner and bright blush applied to her cheeks. Her hair, he could tell, was long and silky, shining nicely with a straight part down the middle that caused it to hang down past both her shoulders and end somewhere behind her.

"It's nice to meet you. Your father and my husband have been awaiting your arrival. Please, come in and follow me, but your men will not be needed past this point. Come." The small woman turned and led the way, and he confirmed his thoughts after seeing that her hair was much longer than he had guessed. It dropped down over her back, past the hump of her cheeks, and stopped below her calves. He smiled as he followed the beauty, still captivated by her femininity. She led him through the big, expensive home until they came upon the dining room where his father and an older Hispanic man sat talking amongst themselves.

Both men stood once Young Mack and the woman entered the room. He nodded his appreciation to the kind, hospitable woman, then made his way over to his father's side. They shook hands and shared a warm, loving embrace before his father made the introductions. Young Mack was certainly intrigued by them being there to meet with the obviously rich man and his wife, but he couldn't help wondering what his father's plans were, especially how they involved him. He decided now wouldn't be the best time for questioning his father, so he remained silent and listened as they talked diligently about everything from stocks to the recent trends in the currency exchange market, to real estate, both residential and commercial. He listened closely, and even when he had questions, he still didn't interrupt them.

Young Mack's curiosity was beginning to get the best of him.

He had very urgent business to tend to, and he had yet to explain to Stephanie that they had captured Daniel, Gurdo's right-hand man. He subconsciously sought her approval and knew that she would be proud of him and would beg his favor to be the one to torture Daniel into revealing Gurdo's whereabouts.

Half an hour had passed before the older man, whom his father had introduced as Senior Juanita, stood and excused himself for a bathroom break. Young Mack found this to be the perfect time to speak with his father because his curiosity was torturing him.

"Pops, you gotta explain this meeting for me. Been sitting here for hours and it's like I'm not even here. Why did you need me here to discuss trends and relevancies?"

Mackmillions smiled as he silently studied his son's face and dapper appearance. He wasn't aware of all the things his son had going on in the game, but from the things that he did know, he already knew that his son, like him, was a busy man with a crew of loyal followers that depended on him. Self-made, independent, and the leader of his own organization—attributes that he deemed necessary and worthy of a seat at his roundtable of elites. Yes, he could definitely see his son not only as his successor but as a general chair holder of the Realm's revitalization.

"Son, this meeting is important for a number of reasons, and I know that you feel like you're in the blind, so let me fill you in on some vital information." Mackmillions gave his son a strong yet summarized version of the structure he had completely orchestrated with his own hands known as *The Realm*. He went on to explain why he was framed and taken away when Young Mack was only a small child. He explained it all to him, even down to his current thoughts and strategic moves to revamp the Realm's order and board members.

"Okay, I get everything that you're telling me, but I gotta ask, Pops—where do I fit into all of this, and what does it have to do with me?" He could only guess, but he needed to hear it come out of his father's mouth.

"Two reasons...First, I know this is kinda unceremonious, but we will have a time and a better place later. Son, I want to make you a general chair member of this new order I have set forth. I mean, you are already set by default to be my successor if you choose to accept a role as large as filling in your old man's shoes." Mackmillions sat back and threw his arm across his son's shoulder while maintaining direct eye contact, the way he'd taught him since he was a small kid. "What do you say? Would that be something you'd be interested in doing?"

Young Mack smiled a handsome smile while he took in all that his father had just offered. He didn't have to think twice or wonder what it would be like—his mind was already made up ever since his father began his journey home. He knew this day would come. He didn't exactly know the circumstances or what his path would be leading up to this moment, but he wanted nothing more than to become his own man and then join forces with his father and Max. Things had fallen directly in that order, and he was proud of himself and knew that he was beyond blessed—not just for himself but for his entire crew as well.

"Absolutely, Pops. You know I'm in!"

"There is only one condition though, and I need you to really consider how this move would change the lives of your entire crew and organization as a whole." Mackmillions stood to his feet while maintaining eye contact with his son, then looked up with a nod.

Young Mack followed his father's gaze until it fell upon Max, who was standing stoically by the entrance of the dining room like a trained sentry. Max locked eyes with his mentor, then Young Mack, and gave a slight nod as he adjusted the buttons on his tailored Armani suit.

"And for the second and most important reason..." Mackmillions offered up a smile as the young couple entered into the dining area, holding hands behind Senior Juanita and his wife, Estellia.

"What the fu—" Young Mack yelled and instinctively reached to his waist for his gun before realizing his hip was bare. Still fueled with a raging fire burning deep within, he attempted to rush over to the doorway where his enemy stood, wide-eyed and just as surprised as he was. He immediately felt his father's big hand grip his shoulder before he could even take a step in that direction.

Gurdo could not believe that his eyes were staring at the one person he wanted relieved of his life more than anyone in the world. How could he be standing there, looking into those eyes of disgust and hatred—the same as he was sure that his enemy saw in his soul portals after the initial shock wore off. His hatred for his enemy caused him to look at his father in anger as he dropped his wife's hand and reached for his waist where he knew his weapon was.

Before his fingers could get a good grip on the handle of his weapon, he felt an intense pain ripple through his body, totally stunning him. The pain was severe but only lasted a few seconds. The temporary paralysis allowed his weapon to be taken away. His eyes angrily landed on Max as he placed the gun on his hip and watched him with eyes of death. The death staring into his soul told him that this strange man would be the wrong one to try, but he didn't want to look like a pussy before his father's eyes.

"Son!" his father barked just as he began to take a step in Max's direction. Max nodded with a smile in the direction of Gurdo's father without breaking eye contact with him.

Reluctantly, Gurdo tore his eyes away from the killer and looked to his father, who stood next to his saddened mother. Just seeing the hurt and embarrassment in his mother's face and body language was enough to pull him in her direction.

"Take a seat, son," his father ordered with a show of his hand. He wanted to apologize to his mother. He wanted to kiss her cheeks and tell her that he loved her more than anything, but he wasn't about to disobey his father any further in order to do so.

He slowly turned to face his nemesis with a distasteful frown still decorating his face before pulling out a seat for his wife, then took one for himself after getting her situated and kissing the hairy top of her head, his eyes still trained on Young Mack. The tension in the air was so thick it could be cut with a knife. It was clear for everyone in the room to see that the two hated each other's guts. Young Mack was frustrated, and the flexing in his jaw muscles showed his father just how bothered his son really was. Mackmillions had never seen this side of his son. His usually light brown eyes were now dark brown, and his brows furrowed deeply as he stared unflinchingly across the table.

"Boys, excuse my choice of words," Senior Juanita started out with a struggle in his English. "Men, we are here to settle the deadly and disabling dispute between you two—"

"That'll never happen! If I had it my way, I'd blow his head and shoulders from his body right now!" Young Mack grilled Gurdo with hatred.

"Son, life is not always about the battles we've won or lost in the physical. It's more important to understand the knowledge that you gain mentally throughout the entire war. Mind over body. This thing we have set here before you will catapult you to the next level; it's about longevity in this game of life. You can either use your head and play for a lifetime, or you could not and crash and burn for using your heart in less than that lifetime." Mackmillions jeweled his son where only he could hear him.

"Pops, he killed Ashton, and he was his own brother-in-law, her brother." Young Mack spoke so that everyone could hear him.

Gurdo's eyes turned into slits at the mention of Ashton's murder, with his wife sitting only inches away from him. Young Mack wasn't playing fair, but he couldn't let him get away with it—not with an unborn heir to his throne hanging in the balance.

"Your lies and threats don't bother me," Gurdo spoke, then adjusted his crisp Italian suit.

"Lies? Pussy, I'm at your forehead behind mine, and nothing will ever change that." Young Mack flexed his fist as visions of beating Gurdo to death with his bare hands played out in his head.

"Get over yourself because you're clearly out of your head right now, and I'm sure your father expects more from you, as he seems to be a very prominent and important man," Gurdo stated before tearing his eyes away from his enemy to look at his father seated next to him. "I am willing to at least hear you out."

"You will do more than hear him out, Jaime. This meeting, this favor from this important man, is all being extended to your father in the sake of your life and the longevity of this family's organization. Whatever you have to do to settle this dispute with that young man, you will do it in the name of this family, without hesitation or second thought." Gurdo was surprised, to say the least. He loved and respected his father a great deal, admired everything about him, but his heart and soul were his mother. He loved his mother more than life itself. She never went against him, never undermined his potential to run their family's business. She had never once criticized him for his mistakes and always stood behind him, and now she had spoken. Even through his anger, he would never think to disobey his mother; she was his world.

"Yes, Mother, I will do all that's expected of me." He nodded in submission to his mother's will.

"And you, son?" Mackmillions eyed his son. He knew all too well the fire that raged in his veins because it was a fire created by his blood. A rage to eliminate any potential threats, enemies to his well-being and the lives of his loved ones. Death could be the only option, and he completely understood more than his son could know.

Young Mack stared into his father's eyes for what felt like an eternity before shifting his gaze over to Ambrea. She had sat quietly throughout this whole scene, and he wondered where her head was in all of this. Morally, he knew that she was sound, and the death of her brother would forever hurt her soul. He also knew that Gurdo would stop at nothing when coming for his head, and the feelings were super mutual, but he couldn't allow for a pregnant Ambrea to be a pawn in their war games—especially if the child turned out to be his and not Gurdo's. He had a hard decision to make, and all he could think about at that moment was his crew. They would surely be hurt by a decision to squash things with Gurdo, and he wondered just how many would question him or, worse, leave and potentially become his enemies.

Young Mack took out his phone and immediately started tapping away at its screen before setting it down on the table. The suspense of his decision held the room in a vise-like grip.

"Seeking permission?" Gurdo teased with a sarcastic grin. Young Mack grilled Gurdo still with a complete look of disgust and pure hatred and would have loved nothing more than to chop his head off. Minutes after he sent out his first message, his phone chimed, garnering everyone's attention. He never even peeked at the screen before forcefully shoving the device across the table, and Gurdo quickly stopped it with his palm.

Gurdo's curiosity wouldn't allow for him not to look at whatever it was that Young Mack wanted him to see. He lifted the device and touched the screen, seeing an alert for a new video message. His eyes slowly left the screen of the phone and landed on his enemy as crooked thoughts began to surface in his mind. Young Mack wore a sarcastic grin of his own, practically daring Gurdo to take a look at what he already knew the video would display. Gurdo mumbled a few words of hatred towards him before tapping the screen to activate the video, and his eyes shot open, his mouth stretching wide at the sight before him.

Ambrea's eyes bugged out as well as she looked at the video playing out in Gurdo's hands. Gurdo grew dizzy, his face flushed from his steaming temperature as he set the phone down in disbelief. Ambrea continued to watch as Daniel's head was grotesquely sawed from his neck while he was still alive. The sight nearly caused her to vomit.

"That's for almost killing my mother and fiancée, pussy. Those crimes were unforgivable. As for Ash and Hogg, I'll be seeing you about that, whether it be on earth or in hell. I'm at your shit," Young Mack stated before he stood and adjusted his expensive suit.

"Son, understand what you're doing here. If he's a member of my society, he will be protected, and it will allow him all that he needs to destroy you. There will be nothing you can do to protect yourself or your crew. Just think about the last decade and a half I spent behind those walls. One of the most powerful figures that ever graced the streets, yet I was stuck and had to rely on you." Mackmillions tried pleading with his stubborn son.

"Thanks for the offer, Pops, but you taught me to always honor my loyalty and to never choose greed over perseverance. So, I'll take my chances with any foe with my head up and chest out."

Mackmillions didn't like his son's decision, hated it really, but he understood him like no one else in the world would. He was a self-made boss now, and the characteristics were exuding loudly from his younger self. He proudly looked his son in the eyes and nodded without another word. Young Mack returned the respect and thanked Gurdo's parents for their genuine hospitality before his eyes landed on a teary-eyed Ambrea.

Her mind and heart were racing like those cars in the Indy 500. She couldn't believe her ears, and now the man standing before her was staring deep into her eyes. He was all man now. She had been with him most of her teenage life and even as an adult, and to now see the man he had become made her heart cry as well as her eyes. Oh, how she cursed herself for not allowing him to fall in love with her because she had certainly fallen in love with him years ago, and now she knew she could never have him for herself. His eyes bore into her soul portals, and she dared not to look away.

"Let's go." His words took her breath away, and she was sure that everyone heard her gasp. Damn, he couldn't have meant that, but if he didn't, why was his face balled up now? *Because you're still sitting there, silly*, Ambrea thought to herself.

"Young—"

"Save it, 'Brea! He killed Ashton, and I'm not about to allow you or that baby growing inside of you to be in harm's way. Divorce him or stand with him, but until you're sure what you're gonna do, you're not living close to him." She caught on to his true meaning, and before she could stop herself or mentally evaluate her thoughts, her legs were operating on their own. She stood from her seat, gasping from the immediate pressure of her husband squeezing her forearm.

"Jaime, let her!" Estellia shouted as she rose to her feet. Gurdo turned evil eyes from his wife to his mother, and for the very first time in his life, he actually thought about disobeying her.

TO BE CONTINUED...

COMING SOON
P.O.T.S. 4

Lock Down Publications and Ca$h Presents Assisted Publishing Packages

Due to an increase in the price of services we have increased our prices. The prices below reflect the price increase as of 11/1/24.

BASIC PACKAGE $699	UPGRADED PACKAGE $1000
Editing Cover Design Formatting	Typing Editing Cover Design Formatting Upload eBooks to Amazon Upload Paperback to Amazon
ADVANCE PACKAGE $1,400	**LDP SUPREME PACKAGE $1,700**
Typing Editing (line editing/content) Cover Design Formatting Copyright Registration Proofreading Upload eBooks to Amazon Upload Paperback to Amazon	Typing Editing (line editing/content) Cover Design Formatting Copyright Registration Proofreading Set up Amazon Account Upload eBooks to Amazon Upload Paperback to Amazon Advertise on LDP's Amazon and Facebook Page

***Other services available upon request.
Additional charges may apply

Lock Down Publications
P.O. Box 944
Stockbridge, GA 30281-9998
Phone: 470 303-9761
Email: lockdownpublications@gmail.com

Submission Guideline

Submit the first three chapters of your completed manuscript to ldpsubmissions@gmail.com. In the subject line add **Your Book's Title**. The manuscript must be in a Word Doc file and sent as an attachment. Document should be in Times New Roman, double spaced, and in size 12 font. Also, provide your synopsis and full contact information. If sending multiple submissions, they must each be in a separate email.

Have a story but no way to send it electronically? You can still submit to LDP/Ca$h Presents. Send in the first three chapters, written or typed, of your completed manuscript to:

LDP: Submissions Dept
P.O. Box 944
Stockbridge, GA 30281-9998

DO NOT send original manuscript. Must be a duplicate. Provide your synopsis and a cover letter containing your full contact information.

Thanks for considering LDP and Ca$h Presents.

NEW RELEASES

BLOODLINE OF A SAVAGE 1&2
THESE VICIOUS STREETS 1&2
RELENTLESS GOON
RELENTLESS GOON 2
BY PRINCE A. TAUHID

THE BUTTERFLY MAFIA 1-3
BY FUMIYA PAYNE

A THUG'S STREET PRINCESS 1&2
BY MEESHA

CITY OF SMOKE 2
BY MOLOTTI

STEPPERS 1,2&3
THE REAL BADDIES OF CHI-RAQ
BY KING RIO

THE LANE 1&2
BY KEN-KEN SPENCE

THUG OF SPADES 1&2
LOVE IN THE TRENCHES 2
CORNER BOYS
BY COREY ROBINSON

TIL DEATH 3
BY ARYANNA

THE BIRTH OF A GANGSTER 4
BY DELMONT PLAYER

PRODUCT OF THE STREETS 1&2
BY DEMOND "MONEY" ANDERSON

NO TIME FOR ERROR
BY KEESE

MONEY HUNGRY DEMONS
BY TRANAY ADAMS

Coming Soon from Lock Down Publications/Ca$h Presents

IF YOU CROSS ME ONCE 6
ANGEL V
By Anthony Fields

IMMA DIE BOUT MINE 5
By Aryanna

A THUGS STREET PRINCESS 3
By Meesha

PRODUCT OF THE STREETS 3
By Demond Money Anderson

CORNER BOYS 2
By Corey Robinson

THE MURDER QUEENS 6&7
By Michael Gallon

CITY OF SMOKE 3
By Molotti

CONFESSIONS OF A DOPE BOY
By Nicholas Lock

THA TAKEOVER
By Keith Chandler

BETRAYAL OF A G 2
By Ray Vinci

CRIME BOSS
By Playa Ray

Available Now

RESTRAINING ORDER 1 & 2
By **CA$H & Coffee**

LOVE KNOWS NO BOUNDARIES 1-3
By **Coffee**

RAISED AS A GOON I, II, III & IV
BRED BY THE SLUMS I, II, III
BLAST FOR ME I & II
ROTTEN TO THE CORE I II III
A BRONX TALE I, II, III
DUFFLE BAG CARTEL I II III IV V VI
HEARTLESS GOON I II III IV V
A SAVAGE DOPEBOY I II
DRUG LORDS I II III
CUTTHROAT MAFIA I II
KING OF THE TRENCHES
By **Ghost**

LAY IT DOWN I & II
LAST OF A DYING BREED I II
BLOOD STAINS OF A SHOTTA I & II III
By **Jamaica**

LOYAL TO THE GAME I II III
LIFE OF SIN I, II III
By **TJ & Jelissa**

IF LOVING HIM IS WRONG…I & II
LOVE ME EVEN WHEN IT HURTS I II III
By **Jelissa**

PUSH IT TO THE LIMIT
By **Bre' Hayes**

BLOODY COMMAS I & II
SKI MASK CARTEL I, II & III
KING OF NEW YORK I II, III IV V
RISE TO POWER I II III
COKE KINGS I II III IV V
BORN HEARTLESS I II III IV
KING OF THE TRAP I II
By **T.J. Edwards**

WHEN THE STREETS CLAP BACK I & II III
THE HEART OF A SAVAGE I II III IV
MONEY MAFIA I II
LOYAL TO THE SOIL I II III
By **Jibril Williams**

A DISTINGUISHED THUG STOLE MY HEART I II & III
LOVE SHOULDN'T HURT I II III IV
RENEGADE BOYS 1-4
PAID IN KARMA 1-3
SAVAGE STORMS 1-3
AN UNFORESEEN LOVE 1-3
BABY, I'M WINTERTIME COLD 1-3
A THUG'S STREET PRINCESS 1&2
By **Meesha**

A GANGSTER'S CODE 1-3
A GANGSTER'S SYN 1-3
THE SAVAGE LIFE 1-3
CHAINED TO THE STREETS 1-3
BLOOD ON THE MONEY 1-3
A GANGSTA'S PAIN 1-3
BEAUTIFUL LIES AND UGLY TRUTHS
CHURCH IN THESE STREETS
By **J-Blunt**

CUM FOR ME 1-8
An LDP Erotica Collaboration

BLOOD OF A BOSS 1-5
SHADOWS OF THE GAME
TRAP BASTARD
By **Askari**

THE STREETS BLEED MURDER 1-3
THE HEART OF A GANGSTA 1-3
By **Jerry Jackson**

WHEN A GOOD GIRL GOES BAD
By **Adrienne**

THE COST OF LOYALTY 1-3
By **Kweli**

BRIDE OF A HUSTLA 1-3
THE FETTI GIRLS 1-3
CORRUPTED BY A GANGSTA 1-4
BLINDED BY HIS LOVE
THE PRICE YOU PAY FOR LOVE 1-3
DOPE GIRL MAGIC 1-3
By **Destiny Skai**

A KINGPIN'S AMBITION
A KINGPIN'S AMBITION II
I MURDER FOR THE DOUGH
By **Ambitious**

TRUE SAVAGE 1-7
DOPE BOY MAGIC 1-3
MIDNIGHT CARTEL 1-3
CITY OF KINGZ 1&2
NIGHTMARE ON SILENT AVE
THE PLUG OF LIL MEXICO 1&2
CLASSIC CITY
By **Chris Green**

A GANGSTER'S REVENGE 1-4
THE BOSS MAN'S DAUGHTERS 1-5
A SAVAGE LOVE 1&2
BAE BELONGS TO ME 1&2
A HUSTLER'S DECEIT 1-3
WHAT BAD BITCHES DO 1-3
SOUL OF A MONSTER 1-3
KILL ZONE
A DOPE BOY'S QUEEN 1-3
TIL DEATH 1-3
IMMA DIE BOUT MINE 1-4
By **Aryanna**

A DOPEBOY'S PRAYER
By **Eddie "Wolf" Lee**

THE KING CARTEL 1-3
By **Frank Gresham**

THESE NIGGAS AIN'T LOYAL 1-3
By **Nikki Tee**

GANGSTA SHYT 1-3
By **CATO**

THE ULTIMATE BETRAYAL
By **Phoenix**

BOSS'N UP 1-3
By **Royal Nicole**

I LOVE YOU TO DEATH
By **Destiny J**

I RIDE FOR MY HITTA
I STILL RIDE FOR MY HITTA
By **Misty Holt**

LOVE & CHASIN' PAPER
By **Qay Crockett**

TO DIE IN VAIN
SINS OF A HUSTLA
By **ASAD**

BROOKLYN HUSTLAZ
By **Boogsy Morina**

BROOKLYN ON LOCK 1 & 2
By **Sonovia**

GANGSTA CITY
By **Teddy Duke**

A DRUG KING AND HIS DIAMOND 1-3
A DOPEMAN'S RICHES
HER MAN, MINE'S TOO 1&2
CASH MONEY HO'S
THE WIFEY I USED TO BE 1&2
PRETTY GIRLS DO NASTY THINGS
By **Nicole Goosby**

LIPSTICK KILLAH 1-3
CRIME OF PASSION 1-3
FRIEND OR FOE 1-3
By **Mimi**

TRAPHOUSE KING 1-3
KINGPIN KILLAZ 1-3
STREET KINGS 1&2
PAID IN BLOOD 1&2
CARTEL KILLAZ 1-3
DOPE GODS 1&2
By **Hood Rich**

THE STREETS ARE CALLING
By **Duquie Wilson**

STEADY MOBBN' 1-3
THE STREETS STAINED MY SOUL 1-3
By **Marcellus Allen**

WHO SHOT YA 1-3
SON OF A DOPE FIEND 1-4
HEAVEN GOT A GHETTO 1&2
SKI MASK MONEY 1&2
By **Renta**

GORILLAZ IN THE BAY 1-4
TEARS OF A GANGSTA 1/&2
3X KRAZY 1&2
STRAIGHT BEAST MODE 1&2
By **DE'KARI**

TRIGGADALE 1-3
MURDA WAS THE CASE 1-3
By **Elijah R. Freeman**

SLAUGHTER GANG 1-3
RUTHLESS HEART 1-3
By **Willie Slaughter**

GOD BLESS THE TRAPPERS 1-3
THESE SCANDALOUS STREETS 1-3
FEAR MY GANGSTA 1-5
THESE STREETS DON'T LOVE NOBODY 1-2
BURY ME A G 1-5
A GANGSTA'S EMPIRE 1-4
THE DOPEMAN'S BODYGAURD 1&2
THE REALEST KILLAZ 1-3
THE LAST OF THE OGS 1-3
By **Tranay Adams**

MARRIED TO A BOSS 1-3
By **Destiny Skai & Chris Green**

KINGZ OF THE GAME 1-7
CRIME BOSS 1-3
By **Playa Ray**

FUK SHYT
By **Blakk Diamond**

DON'T F#CK WITH MY HEART 1&2
By **Linnea**

ADDICTED TO THE DRAMA 1-3
IN THE ARM OF HIS BOSS
By **Jamila**

LOYALTY AIN'T PROMISED 1&2
By **Keith Williams**

YAYO 1-4
A SHOOTER'S AMBITION 1&2
BRED IN THE GAME
By **S. Allen**

TRAP GOD 1-3
RICH $AVAGE 1-3
MONEY IN THE GRAVE 1-3
CARTEL MONEY
By **Martell Troublesome Bolden**

FOREVER GANGSTA 1&2
GLOCKS ON SATIN SHEETS 1&2
By **Adrian Dulan**

TOE TAGZ 1-4
LEVELS TO THIS SHYT 1&2
IT'S JUST ME AND YOU
By **Ah'Million**

KINGPIN DREAMS 1-3
RAN OFF ON DA PLUG
By **Paper Boi Rari**

THE STREETS MADE ME 1-3
By **Larry D. Wright**

CONFESSIONS OF A GANGSTA 1-4
CONFESSIONS OF A JACKBOY 1-3
CONFESSIONS OF A HITMAN
By **Nicholas Lock**

I'M NOTHING WITHOUT HIS LOVE
SINS OF A THUG
TO THE THUG I LOVED BEFORE
A GANGSTA SAVED XMAS
IN A HUSTLER I TRUST
By **Monet Dragun**

QUIET MONEY 1-3
THUG LIFE 1-3
EXTENDED CLIP 1&2
A GANGSTA'S PARADISE
By **Trai'Quan**

CAUGHT UP IN THE LIFE 1-3
THE STREETS NEVER LET GO 1-3
By **Robert Baptiste**

NEW TO THE GAME 1-3
MONEY, MURDER & MEMORIES 1-3
By **Malik D. Rice**

CREAM 2-3
THE STREETS WILL TALK
By **Yolanda Moore**

THE STREETS WILL NEVER CLOSE 1-3
By **K'ajji**

LIFE OF A SAVAGE 1-4
A GANGSTA'S QUR'AN 1-4
MURDA SEASON 1-3
GANGLAND CARTEL 1-3
CHI'RAQ GANGSTAS 1-4
KILLERS ON ELM STREET 1-3
JACK BOYZ N DA BRONX 1-3
A DOPEBOY'S DREAM 1-3
JACK BOYS VS DOPE BOYS 1-3
COKE GIRLZ
COKE BOYS
SOSA GANG 1&2
BRONX SAVAGES
BODYMORE KINGPINS
BLOOD OF A GOON
By **Romell Tukes**

CONCRETE KILLA 1-3
VICIOUS LOYALTY 1-3
By **Kingpen**

THE ULTIMATE SACRIFICE 1-6
KHADIFI
IF YOU CROSS ME ONCE 1-3
ANGEL 1-4
IN THE BLINK OF AN EYE
By **Anthony Fields**

THE LIFE OF A HOOD STAR
By **Ca$h & Rashia Wilson**

NIGHTMARES OF A HUSTLA 1-3
BLOOD AND GAMES 1&2
By **King Dream**

GHOST MOB
By **Stilloan Robinson**

HARD AND RUTHLESS 1&2
MOB TOWN 251
THE BILLIONAIRE BENTLEYS 1-3
REAL G'S MOVE IN SILENCE
By **Von Diesel**

MOB TIES 1-7
SOUL OF A HUSTLER, HEART OF A KILLER 1-3
GORILLAZ IN THE TRENCHES
By **SayNoMore**

BODYMORE MURDERLAND 1-3
THE BIRTH OF A GANGSTER 1-4
By **Delmont Player**

FOR THE LOVE OF A BOSS 1&2
By **C. D. Blue**

KILLA KOUNTY 1-5
By **Khufu**

MOBBED UP 1-4
THE BRICK MAN 1-5
THE COCAINE PRINCESS 1-10
STEPPERS 1-3
SUPER GREMLIN 1-4
By **King Rio**

MONEY GAME 1&2
By **Smoove Dolla**

A GANGSTA'S KARMA 1-4
By **FLAME**

KING OF THE TRENCHES 1-3
By **GHOST & TRANAY ADAMS**

QUEEN OF THE ZOO 1&2
By **Black Migo**

GRIMEY WAYS 1-3
BETRAYAL OF A G
By **Ray Vinci**

XMAS WITH AN ATL SHOOTER
By **Ca$h & Destiny Skai**

KING KILLA 1&2
By **Vincent "Vitto" Holloway**

BETRAYAL OF A THUG 1&2
By **Fre$h**

THE MURDER QUEENS 1-5
By **Michael Gallon**

FOR THE LOVE OF BLOOD 1-4
By **Jamel Mitchell**

HOOD CONSIGLIERE 1&2
NO TIME FOR ERROR
By **Keese**

PROTÉGÉ OF A LEGEND 1&2
LOVE IN THE TRENCHES 1&2
By **Corey Robinson**

THE PLUG'S RUTHLESS DAUGHTER
By **Tony Daniels**

BORN IN THE GRAVE 1-3
CRIME PAYS
By **Self Made Tay**

MOAN IN MY MOUTH
By **XTASY**

TORN BETWEEN A GANGSTER AND A GENTLEMAN
By **J-BLUNT & Miss Kim**

LOYALTY IS EVERYTHING 1-3
CITY OF SMOKE 1&2
By **Molotti**

HERE TODAY GONE TOMORROW 1&2
By **Fly Rock**

WOMEN LIE MEN LIE 1-4
FIFTY SHADES OF SNOW 1-3
STACK BEFORE YOU SPLURGE
GIRLS FALL LIKE DOMINOES
NAÏVE TO THE STREETS
By **ROY MILLIGAN**

PILLOW PRINCESS
By **S. Hawkins**

THE BUTTERFLY MAFIA 1-3
SALUTE MY SAVAGERY 1&2
By **Fumiya Payne**

THE LANE 1&2
By Ken-Ken Spence

THE PUSSY TRAP 1-5
By **Nene Capri**

DIRTY DNA
By **Blaque**

SANCTIFIED AND HORNY
by **XTASY**

BOOKS BY LDP'S CEO, CA$H

TRUST IN NO MAN
TRUST IN NO MAN 2
TRUST IN NO MAN 3
BONDED BY BLOOD
SHORTY GOT A THUG
THUGS CRY
THUGS CRY 2
THUGS CRY 3
TRUST NO BITCH
TRUST NO BITCH 2
TRUST NO BITCH 3
TIL MY CASKET DROPS
RESTRAINING ORDER
RESTRAINING ORDER 2
IN LOVE WITH A CONVICT
LIFE OF A HOOD STAR
XMAS WITH AN ATL SHOOTER

www.ingramcontent.com/pod-product-compliance
Lightning Source LLC
Chambersburg PA
CBHW071149260626
47162CB00003B/977